Invincible Summer

Invincible Summer

a novel

Alice Adams

Little, Brown and Company

New York   Boston   London

Copyright © 2016 Alice Adams

Little, Brown and Company
Hachette Book Group
1290 Avenue of the Americas, New York, NY 10104
littlebrown.com

First North American edition: June 2016
Originally published in Great Britain by Picador, June 2016

Little, Brown and Company is a division of Hachette Book Group, Inc. The Little, Brown name and logo are trademarks of Hachette Book Group, Inc.

The publisher is not responsible for websites (or their content) that are not owned by the publisher.

The Hachette Speakers Bureau provides a wide range of authors for speaking events. To find out more, go to hachettespeakersbureau.com or call (866) 376-6591.

ISBN 978-0-316-39117-7
LCCN 2015953903

10 9 8 7 6 5 4 3 2 1

RRD-C

Printed in the United States of America

For my family, blood and otherwise

Au milieu de l'hiver, j'apprenais enfin qu'il y avait en moi un été invincible.

In the depths of winter, I finally learned that there lay within me an invincible summer.

Albert Camus, 'Retour à Tipasa', 1952

Invincible Summer

1

Bristol, Summer 1995

'Okay, here's one. If you could know the answer to any one single question, what would it be?'

Eva was lying on her back and looking up at the sky as she spoke. Summer had finally arrived, late that year, and the feeling of sun on skin combined with the wine and Lucien's shoulder beneath her head was intoxicating. She had sat the last of her first-year exams that morning and would be going home for the summer the next day, but in a couple of months she'd be right back here in a life that was as far removed from her old world as she'd dared to hope it would be when she'd set off for university the previous autumn.

The four friends were clustered on a blanket close to the top of Brandon Hill. They hadn't bothered to enter the stone tower perched at the hill's brow and climb the spiral staircase to the viewing platform, but in any case their vantage point afforded them an impressive view of the city, out across the treacly river and past the derelict warehouses towards the endless sprawl of streets and houses beyond. In the long grass by their feet were two open wine bottles, the first propped upright in one of a pair of battered lace-up boots, the other lying on the ground spilling its last drops onto the earth.

Sylvie rolled over onto her stomach and brushed a few strands of coppery hair from her eyes. 'Any question at all?'

'Yes,' said Eva. 'Foof.'

'Huh?'

'That was the sound of the genie disappearing after you wasted your question.'

Sylvie glared at her. 'That's not fair. I'm having another one. I want to know the meaning of life.'

'That's not actually a question.' Benedict elbowed her gently in the ribs. 'Anyway, the answer would probably turn out to be forty-two, and then you'd have wasted your question again.'

Sylvie tugged her index finger and thumb sharply along a stalk of sedge grass, strimming the seeds into her hand and then blowing them into his face. 'Okay, smarty-pants. What would you ask?'

Benedict blinked. 'I'd have to think about how to phrase it, but basically I would want to know the grand unifying theory for the universe.' He thought for a moment. 'Or else, what happens when we die.'

'How about next week's lottery numbers?' asked Eva lazily.

'You'd have to be insane to waste your question on something so banal,' said Benedict, prompting a scowl from Eva. It was all very well to think there was something trivial about money when you came from a family like Benedict's, but when you'd grown up in a small Sussex town short on glamour and long on stolid conformism the world was a different place. Benedict would never understand what it felt like to get up every weekend and trudge to work in a mindless supermarket job as Eva had for the four long years before she arrived in Bristol, where the same kids who regularly threw her bag over a hedge on the way to school would come in and pull things off the shelves just to get her into trouble. She couldn't win: if she ignored them she ran the risk of getting fired, but if she called security they'd make sure her bag landed in a puddle on Monday.

In a place like that almost anything could make you an outcast: wearing the wrong clothes, doing too well in exams, not being able to talk about the 'in' TV shows because your father didn't believe in having a TV. The only real glimpse of daylight had come in the form of Marcus, who was briefly her boyfriend, because no matter how unpopular you were there was always a teenage boy whose libido could propel him past that barrier. Marcus was himself quite popular and had taken a surprising interest in Eva, and for a few short months she had been his girlfriend and basked in a grudging acceptance.

The relationship led to the pleasing if rather undignified loss of her virginity in the woods behind the school after half a bottle of cider on a bench, which apparently constituted both date and foreplay. Marcus had eventually grown resentful and dumped her after a much-anticipated afternoon in bed while his parents were away ended prematurely before he'd even removed his trousers, and Eva had ill-advisedly tried to lighten the mood by cracking a few jokes. She'd read in *Cosmopolitan* that it was important for couples to be able to laugh together in bed, but then, the article had also said that slapping the male genitalia as if lightly volleying a tennis ball was a good idea and that hadn't gone down particularly well either. At least by that time she'd made it into the relative safety of the sixth form, but while her life had become bearable it was hardly the stuff that dreams were made of. The day before she finally left for university Eva had taken the polyester uniform she'd worn for four long years of Saturdays out onto the patio and set fire to it, making a vow into the smoke that she was never going back.

'What about you, Lucien?' Benedict nudged Sylvie's brother's leg with his own, his voice breaking through Eva's reverie. 'What's your question?'

'Christ, I don't know. A list of everyone who's ever got their jollies thinking about me?'

Eva closed her eyes to avoid involuntarily glancing at him and hoped her cheeks weren't visibly reddening. Nobody knows, she told herself. They can't read your mind to see the *Atlas of Lucien* mapped out there, from the messy dark hair to the freckle on the inside of his surprisingly delicate wrist.

Sylvie let out a long, low moan of disgust and Benedict laughed. 'I don't think I'd like that,' he mused. 'It would take all the mystique out of things.'

'The virginity is strong with this one,' taunted Lucien in his best Yoda voice.

'Hardly,' muttered Benedict. 'Anyway, there'd probably be some hideous people on there. Your sports master from school or someone like that.'

'Okay, women only. Under the age of thirty.' Lucien leant over to retrieve the almost empty wine bottle from Eva's boot, carelessly dislodging her head from his shoulder as he did so.

Eva sat up, trying to look as if the brush-off didn't bother her. Typical of Lucien, she thought, to pull her down onto his shoulder like that and then push her away. They'd been doing this dance for most of the year since she'd arrived in

Bristol and her new friend Sylvie had introduced her to her hard-living elder brother. Lucien wasn't a student; he described himself as an entrepreneur, though Eva was hazy on the detail of what that actually involved. Sylvie had chosen to study at Bristol only because Lucien was already living there, presumably doing whatever it was that he did in the little time that he didn't spend loitering around halls with the rest of them.

'Right,' said Sylvie, levering herself up from the ground and brushing the grass off her jeans. 'I can't listen to any more of this. I'm off to the library to pull an all-nighter, my last essay's due in tomorrow.'

Sylvie was known for her aversion to writing the essays that she always seemed slightly appalled were required by her History of Art course, and claimed to find it impossible to work without a deadline less than forty-eight hours away. The degree was merely intended to buy her some time on her trajectory to being a revered artist, which, it was generally accepted by the group, was inevitable. The ingredients were all there: a prodigious and obsessive talent for drawing and painting, a quirky, original eye, supplemented by striking good looks and a tough, irreverent attitude to life. She had a certain shine, a vividness about her; she was just one of those people who generated their own gravity, causing people to cluster around her and try to please her. It was impossible to imagine her being anything other than a great success.

'I've got to go too,' said Benedict reluctantly. 'I'm leaving first thing and I haven't packed yet.'

Eva and Lucien said goodbye to the others and lay back on the grass, watching them walk away down the hill. A tinge of purple was seeping into the late afternoon light announcing the onset of dusk, and Eva was feeling light-headed from the cheap, acidic wine. Lucien rolled over onto his side so that he was facing her.

'And then there were two,' he said, reaching into the plastic bag beside him. 'Looks like it's just you and me left to drink the last bottle, Eva.'

The way Lucien said her name made it sound dark and alluring. It was the most exotic thing about her and she had always liked it. Her socialist father sometimes joked that she was named after Eva Perón, but she knew her mother had chosen it just because she loved it. If it had been left to him she'd probably have been called something drab and unostentatious, like Jane or Susan.

'Eva,' he said again. 'It's a pretty name.'

'My mother chose it,' she told him.

'She's dead, isn't she?' he asked, not unkindly.

'Yes. She died of breast cancer when I was five. I don't remember her much.'

Lucien rolled over onto his back and turned his face up to the sky, closing his eyes.

'Sorry,' he said. 'That can't be great. Still, it can't be much worse than having an alkie for a mother.'

Eva's eyes widened. Sylvie had told her a bit about how tough it had been for them growing up, how their parents had split up and how their mother drank too much and how often they'd had to move, but Lucien had always seemed to have an impenetrable veneer of invulnerability. This was the first time she'd ever heard him mention their childhood.

'Sylvie told me your mum's a bit of a drinker,' she said cautiously.

'Yep. And I've got the scars to prove it.'

He opened his left hand, holding it out towards her. The last two fingers and part of the palm were swirled with satiny pink tissue, the scarring so extensive that the little finger was noticeably narrower than it ought to have been between the two lowest joints. Eva had asked Sylvie about it not long after they'd met, not wanting to risk offending Lucien, but she'd just shrugged and said something about an accidental burn when he was a kid. At the time Eva had sensed something unsaid but hadn't wanted to push; although Sylvie could sometimes be voluble and entertaining on the subject of their flaky home life – recounting stories about finding her mother asleep in the shrubbery or getting told off at school for taking in a family pack of KitKats for lunch because that was all there was in the house – Eva had quickly learned that it was something she only talked about on her own terms.

Now Eva reached out and ran her fingers across the taut, glossy flesh. 'Lucien. I'm so sorry. Your mother did that to you? I had no idea.'

He didn't look at her. 'Nah, not exactly. She was passed out drunk with one of those old-style bar heaters on in the room when I was little, three or four maybe, and I reached out and grabbed it. She never hurt me on purpose, though that's more than I can say for a couple of her boyfriends. She was just a bit of a shit mother when she was drinking, which was quite a lot of the time.'

'You and Sylvie are lucky to have had each other at least,' Eva said. 'No wonder you're so close.'

'Yeah. We've always looked out for each other.'

His eyes met hers for the first time since he'd held out his hand, and they both realized at the same moment that her fingers were still resting against the damaged tissue. For a fraction of a second she glimpsed something she'd never seen before behind his eyes, something at once more human and more animal than the usual sardonic, bullet-proof version of himself that was all he'd ever shown her. She had a searing feeling of seeing him for the first time, not just what he wanted her to see but the child he'd once been, and the life that had shaped what he'd since become. But even as these thoughts were running through Eva's mind his gaze was changing, retreating and flattening, and he closed the fingers over the scars and tucked the hand away so that they were no longer visible.

Unable to bear their new intimacy being snatched away, Eva did something she'd never have been bold enough to do before: she leant over and took his hand again, lacing her own fingers between his damaged ones. He was half beneath her on the ground now, her face above his, her hair grazing his cheek. When he lifted his eyes to hers something new passed between them, something electric, and this time he didn't take his hand away. Instead, he grinned a wolfish grin and raised his other hand and slid the fingers around the back of her neck, tangling them into her hair and tugging her down towards him.

*

More wine, more talk, and then a walk home in the fading light, drunkenly swaying towards each other as they walked, arms brushing, little fingers half entwined, swigging from the cans of beer they'd bought on the way in an attempt to neutralize the strangeness and embarrassment of what they were doing.

Any ambiguity had dissolved the minute they'd got inside her room and closed the door. He'd shoved her up against the wall and kissed her hard and started to unbutton her shirt, and she hadn't had time to think, only to get lost in the urgency of the moment.

In bed, though, the urgency had dissolved into comedy. There had been clashing teeth and rumbling stomachs, and her jeans had got wedged around her ankles so that she'd nearly fallen over trying to wriggle out of them. There was the first condom that had pinged across the room, and the second one that had fallen into the ashtray. An eventual five minutes of panting and thrusting was rapidly followed by Lucien's snoring. When she woke furry-mouthed and queasy beside him, with the morning sunlight trickling in around the edges of her curtains, she'd reached out and taken his hand to try to recapture something of the closeness of the night before but he'd pulled it away, kissing her quickly and passionlessly before rolling out of bed to pull on his jeans.

'Best be off then,' he said once he'd found his T-shirt. 'We don't want Sylvie finding out about this, she hates it when I shag her mates.'

He grinned and made a run for the door, leaving Eva to lie back swathed in her clammy, rumpled sheets and a palpable sense of rejection.

2

Bristol, Summer 1997

'Hard to believe it's finally over, isn't it?' said Sylvie. 'No more lectures, no more exams, no more diabolical vending-machine coffee.'

The friends were back in their spot on Brandon Hill, which over the last few years had been the scene of many a boozy afternoon. The day felt dreamy and momentous all at once. Was it possible to feel nostalgic about something before it was even over? Eva shook her head gently to dislodge the thought that the afternoon, their last all together in Bristol, was slipping away from them minute by minute. She was sharply aware that after today it could be any amount of time before she saw Lucien again. He and Sylvie were leaving to go travelling, and while Sylvie was definitely planning to join her in London afterwards, she knew from bitter experience that Lucien was altogether more unpredictable.

'It's not over for *all* of us, don't forget,' grumbled Benedict. 'Think of me, won't you, when you're off swanning around the world and I'm right back here after the summer.'

'If you're mad enough to stay on for a PhD you deserve everything you get,' Sylvie said. 'I couldn't be more ready to get out of here.'

He shrugged. 'Well, a change of scene would be nice but at least the work's going to start getting interesting. We barely touched on proper particle physics in the undergrad years, so I'll finally get a chance to get stuck into the really exciting stuff.'

Sylvie raised a sceptical eyebrow. 'Yes, well. I'm going to stick my neck out here and say that travelling in India is going to be quite a lot more exciting than being stuck in a lab in the basement of the physics department.'

'In some ways it's very similar,' Benedict said, and then laughed at her incredulous expression. 'No, really. We're all looking for answers to the big questions in life. Maybe you'll find enlightenment in an ashram and I'll find it in a particle accelerator, but the questions are the same.'

Lucien let out a snort. 'We're not all looking for the meaning of life, mate. I'm not, and nor's Eva for that matter.'

Eva glanced across at the reclining figures of her friends, trying to gauge their reaction to Lucien's comment. Normally she would have been pleased at his allying himself with her, but had she imagined it or had they been a bit sniffy when she recently announced that she'd made it through the fiercely competitive selection process to land a traineeship in derivatives trading at one of the top investment banks? During their undergraduate years she'd constantly struggled to keep pace with Benedict and lived in burning envy of the minimal hours that Sylvie's course seemed to require, but now, exams finally over, she could at least allow herself a certain amount of satisfaction that her hard work was about to translate into something more tangible than another three years of study. Someone like Benedict might go on to discover the secrets of cold fusion but Eva was reasonably confident that the world of physics wasn't going to be shaken to the core by her decision to pursue Mammon instead of elusive particles.

Besides, there was an intoxicating buzz around the City these days. The guys manning the Morton Brothers desk at the recruitment fair had only been a few years older than her but they were so effortlessly confident, smart and worldly that they might as well have been a different species. She'd tried for a moment to imagine *them* scrabbling about for a school bag in a bush in front of a jeering crowd and when she found she couldn't, had accepted an application form for their graduate programme.

'Oh, yes.' Sylvie's face spread into a smirk. 'Thanks for reminding me that my best friend's selling out to The Man.'

'Are you calling me a sell-out, Comrade?' Eva paused to search for a suitable comeback but eventually gave up. 'Okay, fine, I'm selling out, but at least it's to a high bidder. And do you know what, I have lived the alternative to selling out, and it's towns full of shit buildings with nothing to do, where everyone dresses the same and has the same views on everything and woe betide you if you're different in any way.'

Unmoved, Sylvie twirled an imaginary moustache. 'Capitalist running dog.'

Everyone was smiling now, but each of the smiles contained a glint of steel, the flinty protrusion of a serious undertone which had been the subject of a thousand drink-fuelled arguments over the last few years. Simultaneously aware of the futility of the endeavour yet unable to resist making her case one last time, Eva launched into her spiel.

'All you have to do is open your eyes and look around at the world: capitalism is the system that's produced the greatest wealth and freedom. It may not be terribly equal but then, nothing is more equal, and no equality easier to arrange, than ensuring that everyone is equally fucked. Anyway, it's all right for you,' she nodded towards Sylvie. 'You're one of those people who'll be fine wherever they go. Not all of us can just sail through life on raw talent, you know.'

Sylvie grinned but didn't demur, and not for the first time Eva experienced the treacherous sensation that her sadness at going their separate ways was tinged with a hint of excitement about finally wriggling out from Sylvie's shadow.

'When do you set off on your travels, anyway? Is your mum picking you up?' Benedict asked the others, and Eva glanced over to see Lucien's features assemble themselves into a sort of sneering bravado. It made her think, as she had a thousand times since the night they'd spent together, about how much he hated his vulnerabilities being exposed, and how maybe the reason there had never been a repeat of that night was that he couldn't quite forgive himself for having revealed them, or her for having seen them.

'Do be serious,' he told Benedict. 'She's working off her latest drink-driving ban. And she wouldn't have come anyway, I'm *persona non grata* with her current bloke, remember?'

'We're catching the train up to London this afternoon and staying the night with a mate in Fulham,' Sylvie said. 'Our flight doesn't leave till tomorrow morning.'

'How about you, Eva? What time does Keith get here?' Benedict had met Eva's father, a lecturer in Gender Studies at what he still insisted on referring to as Brighton Poly, on a number of occasions but was still clearly uncomfortable with calling him by his forename. Keith had always eschewed

'Dad' as a title, imbued as it was with patriarchal associations of authority. He was another one who had received the news of Eva's nascent investment banking career with less than unequivocal joy. He'd been so torn between paternal pride and Marxist disgust when she told him, that she thought he might implode in a puff of cognitive dissonance. But, as she'd explained, there was a third way now, a route between the heartless conservatism of old and the unavoidable impracticalities of socialism; a new world order was coming and Eva intended to be a part of it. The Berlin Wall had come down, the Soviet Union had dismantled itself, and while calling it the End of History might be over-egging it a bit, it didn't feel too grand an assertion to say that it was the dawn of a new era, and not just for a freshly minted graduate.

'Well, your mother would have been proud,' he'd allowed eventually, and Eva had swiftly changed the subject, as she always did when that quality of gruffness entered his voice.

'We'd better get going or we'll miss the train,' Sylvie said to Lucien, and Eva looked round at her friends with a sudden sense of something precious sliding away from her.

She didn't have her camera with her – it had already been packed up with the rest of her things – so instead she tried to snatch the scene out of the air and etch it onto memory: Lucien, eyes darkly gleaming, Sylvie, hair flaming like a radioactive halo in the sunlight, and next to them Benedict, silhouetted against clear blue sky, turning towards her now and, catching her looking at him, breaking into his broad, lopsided smile. Hold it right there, she thought. Everything's about to change, but just let me keep this moment.

And now there was no putting it off, it was time to say goodbye to Lucien. Eva urgently wished she could have a minute alone with him but Sylvie and Benedict were watching expectantly, so she just sat there as he leant down and dropped a kiss on her face, not quite on the mouth but not quite on the cheek either.

'See you around, kiddo,' he said with a grin, and it was all she could do to stop herself reaching up and pulling his face down towards hers, but already Sylvie was tugging at him and off down the hill they went, turning back to wave but still heading inexorably away from library days and party nights and mornings-after and endless afternoons spent huddled together laughing and clutching steaming cups of terrible coffee and everything else that had formed the fabric of their old lives together and which had seemed all along as if it would never end but was now, suddenly and irrevocably, over.

3

Corfu, August 1997

'Minuscule, isn't it?' yelled Benedict cheerfully above the roar of a landing plane as he tossed Eva's rucksack into the boot of the battered old Peugeot. 'Best sort of car to have out here, though, you'll soon see why. The air con doesn't work, I'm afraid,' he added as they lowered themselves into their seats.

It had definitely been the right decision to come, she thought, as they swept clear of the garish sprawl of Corfu Town and shot out along the coast, the plastic car seat hot beneath her legs and salty air buffeting her through the open window. When Benedict had suggested she join him for a week at his family's place in Corfu she'd wavered, but it was her only chance of a holiday in an otherwise tedious summer that would be spent living at home and working in a shop before she took up her traineeship in September. A whole holiday for the cost of a cheap flight was too tempting, even if it did mean the slightly intimidating prospect of staying with Benedict's family.

'Wouldn't it be a bit strange, though?' she'd asked as they walked back from Brandon Hill at the end of their final afternoon in Bristol. 'Your parents will probably think we're girlfriend and boyfriend or something.'

'Of course not,' Benedict assured her. 'The whole family takes guests there. More than likely my brother Harry will have a pal with him too.' Then, sounding just a little offended, he added, 'It's a genuine offer from a friend. I'm not going to jump on you if that's what you're worried about. Besides, who knows when we'll have another chance to really hang out together? You'll be off doing your thing and I'll be back in Bristol on my own. Think of it as a last hurrah.'

So she'd accepted, and now they were charging north along the twisting coastal road bounded on one side by the cliff wall and on the other by a sheer drop down to the glittering Ionian Sea below. The journey was spellbinding and hair-raising in equal parts; every time a car zoomed towards them they were forced perilously close to the road's edge, leaving Eva clutching the sides of her seat.

'You see?' bellowed Benedict above the roaring air. 'You wouldn't want to be in a Hummer on these roads.'

'Christ!' she yelped as they rounded a hairpin bend and swerved to avoid an oncoming coach. 'Are those things really allowed on roads like this? Couldn't they erect some bloody crash barriers or something?'

'It's all part of the distinctive Corfiot charm. You get used to the roads and, anyway, it's part and parcel of being in such an undeveloped place. No crash barriers but no McDonald's either, at least not where we're going. Don't worry, staying on the road's a simple matter of friction and momentum.' He grinned, seeing Eva grab the dashboard to avoid being thrown against the door as they rounded another sharp bend. 'Trust me, I'm a physicist.'

'Yeah, well, there's theory and then there's practice,'

muttered Eva, but her words were lost in the wind. She did her best to sit back and enjoy the journey, soaking up the sparkling expanse of water and the unfamiliar abundance of light that drenched the air and bounced playfully off every available surface. The further they travelled, the fewer cars they passed, and the white-walled shops and houses gradually gave way to a more sparsely populated landscape in which gnarled olive trees grew at improbable angles on steeply ascending terraces. Eventually they turned off the coastal road and started to climb a hill of nerve-racking gradient.

'Mount Pantokrator,' said Benedict. 'Nearly there.'

They pulled onto an unsurfaced road, bounced over a series of potholes and finally slowed to a halt in front of a pair of huge iron gates, which, prompted by the wave of a key fob, swung open to reveal a large sand-coloured villa. Around the side of the building Eva glimpsed the same captivating seascape that had provided the backdrop to most of their journey.

'Better go and say hello to the olds and find out where you're quartered,' said Benedict, clambering out of the car and stretching. 'I expect they'll be on the terrace.'

He led the way through an open gate at the side of the house and along a dusty gravel path running through a herb garden. The late afternoon air was heavy with the scent of thyme and hummed with cicadas. They wound their way around the building and up a flight of stone steps onto an enormous terrace overlooking the sea, where a willowy, fair-haired woman was gazing out over the railing. As she turned and came towards them, arms outstretched in welcome, Eva realized she must be Benedict's mother.

'Hello, darling. That was quick,' she said as they reached her. 'And you must be Eva.' She released her son from a brief embrace and turned towards her.

'Very pleased to meet you, Mrs Waverley,' replied Eva, adopting her best meeting-the-parents manner, and was surprised to notice Benedict shift uncomfortably. Was she imagining it or had Benedict's mother almost imperceptibly raised an eyebrow at him? What possible blunder could she have perpetrated so soon and with such an innocuous greeting?

'Oh, plain old Marina is fine. How wonderful of you to join us, we've heard so much about you. Bunny, why don't you go and give Eva's things to Eleni so she can sort out her room?' she said, spotting the rucksack in Benedict's hand. Eva struggled to convert her mirth at the pet name into something resembling a grateful smile, but if Marina noticed Benedict's glowering face and Eva's faint snort she showed no sign of it. 'Eva, come, and I'll make you a drink. Did you fly Sleazyjet? Frightfully convenient I know, but leaves you feeling quite soiled and in need of a tipple, don't you find?'

*

Standing at the edge of the terrace, clutching the cold glass that Marina had pressed into her hand, Eva was finally able to take in the scenery that terror had prevented her from fully appreciating during the drive. The calm sea stretched across to another coastline, where a flat plain led from the water's edge to a mountain range behind. Here and there, clusters of white buildings were scattered across the plain and the foothills. The azure sky was cloudless and yet just a little hazy.

'This view,' she exclaimed. 'It's breathtaking.'

Marina smiled. 'Isn't it? In all my travels I've never found one more perfect. That's Albania over there across the water. In the mornings the mountains look as if they're rising up out of the mist like an enchanted land. You almost expect to see unicorns bounding across them. I know everyone bangs on about the light in the Greek islands but, really, there's nowhere on earth quite like it.'

She took Eva's arm, led her to the wall at the edge of the terrace where the land dropped away and pointed down the hillside. 'Down there, you see that peninsula with the house and the beautiful bay? The owners have taken out a hundred-year lease on that bit of the Albanian coast you can see there, just so that no one can build on it and spoil the view.'

A tall man immediately recognizable as Benedict's father ambled out of the house and joined in the conversation. 'Of course, they don't have half the view that we have up here. It's all very well being down by the water, I suppose, for the swimming and all that, but I'd rather be up here in the heavens.' He dropped his voice dramatically and turned towards Eva, gesturing towards the vast expanse of sky. 'Wouldn't you?'

She nodded. It felt as if she were being drawn into a conspiracy, in fact this whole place felt like a marvellous secret that she had stumbled upon, a world she hadn't quite known existed. She wasn't at all sure what she had imagined whenever Benedict had mentioned spending summers at his family's holiday place, but it certainly wasn't this. It was utterly dreamlike, otherworldly, like being suspended in a thousand shades of blue.

'We like to think that our grandchildren and great-grandchildren will be coming here long after we're gone, don't we, Hugo?' said Benedict's mother. 'It's wonderful to know that all this beauty will be preserved for them.'

Was Eva mistaken, or had Marina cast a twinkling look in her direction?

'Indeed,' agreed Hugo. 'And one does so need a bolt-hole to escape the unwashed hordes every now and then. Far from the madding crowd and all that.'

Eva responded with a non-committal smile. She wasn't wholly confident that if the world was divided up into the Hugos and the unwashed hordes that she herself wouldn't fall into the latter category, and was relieved to spot Benedict making his way back across the terrace towards them.

'I see you've met Dad,' he said as he joined them.

'Well, sort of,' said Eva, blushing as she realized she hadn't actually introduced herself.

'Oh, silly me for not doing the introductions,' said Marina. 'This old curmudgeon is Hugo, dear,' and then, turning to her husband, she continued, 'and Benedict's young lady here is Eva.'

'Ah, I'm not exactly Benedict's young lady, we're more, you know, friends,' Eva said as she shook Hugo's proffered hand and felt her cheeks further redden.

'Bloody hell, just ignore them,' muttered Benedict. 'They marry me off to every girl I so much as glance at. It's supposed to be an old family tradition that the Waverleys marry young, but they've got more chance with Harry than me. Come on, let's go for a swim before they start planning the nuptials.'

'Better unpack and grab my bathing suit,' Eva said, glad

to be extricated from the situation but cursing Benedict silently for his false assurances.

'Eleni's already unpacking for you,' he told her. 'She's the housekeeper and she'll do all of that while you're here. Woe betide you if you attempt to put her out of a job by making so much as a sandwich for yourself. Come on, I'll show you where your room is.'

*

Her 'room' turned out to be more of a suite, composed of a capacious bedroom, a dressing room big enough to comfortably house a sofa and several wardrobes, and a generous bathroom with a free-standing tub in front of French doors looking out towards the sea.

Eva stood and boggled at her surroundings. 'Sweet Jesus, Benedict. *This* is what you've meant all this time by your family's holiday pad? Not exactly a flat in Benidorm, is it? I mean, I've always known that you weren't a pauper but seriously, just look at this place.'

Benedict shuffled his feet awkwardly. 'Well, obviously property doesn't cost half as much here as in England.'

Watching him squirm it suddenly all made sense: the reason that Benedict had never invited her to his home despite visiting her in Sussex several times during university holidays was not that he was embarrassed by her but by his own background, which was apparently far more opulent than the others had imagined even in their wildest flights of speculation. Eva found herself feeling somewhat sympathetic; Lucien was already prone to calling him Gatsby, and he would have a field day if he could see this place.

An awful thought occurred to her. 'Shit, what am I going

to wear?' She grimaced at the memory of Marina in her crisp white linen dress and silver butterfly necklace. 'Look at these cushions, and this bedding, and these sofas. The entire place is colour-coordinated. It's all white and . . . what would you even call that? Taupe?'

'I know, terrifyingly tasteful, isn't it? My mother's in her element here. She likes to think of herself as dreadfully modern, so she considers it a welcome escape from all the mahogany furniture and gilt mirrors at home, the old family stuff that my father would never dream of parting with.'

'It's impeccably, immaculately tasteful,' Eva agreed, thinking of the peeling lino at home and feeling faint with embarrassment at what Benedict must have made of her determinedly unsophisticated father. 'But the point is, I flew hand-luggage only and here's what I packed: a swimsuit, a pair of jeans, some T-shirts and an acid yellow sundress with two of the buttons missing. Oh God, I bet your parents have dinner in top hats and ball gowns.'

'Nah, don't you know understatement's where the real money's at?' teased Benedict. 'Seriously, don't worry about it. Your sundress will be fine, no one will care. Besides, Harry's arriving later with his girlfriend. Sit next to her and I guarantee that whatever you wear, you'll look like a nun.'

*

On this point at least, Benedict was as good as his word. Harry and Carla made their entrance at dusk in a whirlwind of kisses and handshakes, half-hugs and backslaps, so that it somehow seemed as if ten people had arrived instead of two. They swept off to their room to change for supper, leaving

Eva with the impression of a more solid version of Benedict and a lissom, barely clothed goddess.

Examining the pair more closely as everyone gathered on the terrace for dinner, Eva was struck most by the uniformity of their skin. They both appeared unnaturally smooth and unblemished. Were there really humans without a single freckle or mole? And Carla's limbs – her legs flowed for miles from shorts so short they could reasonably be referred to as hot pants. There wasn't even the usual consolation of tall, slim girls being flat-chested and sexless; Carla's gravity-defying breasts threatened to escape their orange halterneck at every dip and sway.

It was impossible for Eva not to feel dumpy in her old sundress, held together by several safety pins rustled up after a desperate plea to Eleni, but then, she comforted herself, it didn't really matter, at least not in the way it would have if Lucien had been there. She could just picture him leaning in towards Carla with a predatory smile, as much a feat of memory as imagination, having watched him do just that with what seemed like an infinite number of girls in countless bars over the years. Benedict, on the other hand, seemed more amused than anything by Carla's indecorous outfit, while his father appeared intensely appreciative, surveying the acres of exposed flesh with the manner of someone savouring a fine painting. Marina gave every impression of having failed to even notice Carla's near-nudity, bathing her in the same gracious warmth she had bestowed on Eva when she'd arrived.

'Eva, you simply must try the souvlaki,' she urged as they sat down at the candle- and flower-strewn table on the terrace. 'It's Eleni's specialty, she makes it with swordfish.'

'Ah,' said Eva, shooting a furious look at Benedict. 'Did Benedict forget to tell you that I'm a vegetarian?'

'Oh, one of the Latter Day Saints lot, you mean?' boomed Hugo. 'With the funny underpants? I met a chap like that at the Athenaeum a while back. Queer sort of a fellow actually, but I'm sure you're not all that way.'

'No, darling, that's not what she means at all,' said Marina. 'She's not a cult member, it's more like being a sort of hippy. Don't mind him, Eva,' she continued, placing a restraining hand on her husband's arm. 'He's not very modern. I don't mind telling you that I once danced naked around Stonehenge on the summer solstice myself. Well, it was the Sixties,' she continued in response to Benedict and Harry's appalled stares. 'Everyone was doing that sort of thing back then.' She turned to Eva. 'Now, why don't you try some of these meatballs? They're simply divine.'

*

Benedict lay face down on his lounger next to the pool and peered at Eva through the crack in his eyelids. The sun was too bright to open them any wider, and besides, it was a great opportunity to scrutinize her in a swimsuit unnoticed. Make the most of it, he told himself. Their week together was almost over; her flight was the following day and he didn't even know when he'd next see her, let alone in a bathing costume. What exquisite agony it was to let his eyes roam over her body, especially on a rare occasion when she appeared to be lying there unselfconsciously. All week she'd seemed to be hiding under a towel or pulling her dress on just to go from the pool to the bathroom. Was she making sure he didn't get any ideas, or did she genuinely not know how beautiful she was?

He'd thought it as long as he'd known her, right from the moment they'd met at the icebreaker party during Freshers' Week, when she'd spilt a pint of cider down his trousers and then spent half an hour drunkenly apologizing. Was it possible to be both clumsy and poised at the same time? Eva embodied a strange contradiction both in looks and temperament, shambling but upright, uncertain but determined. She wore an unfashionable selection of outfits, long flowing skirts and big boots and slogan T-shirts. Sometimes he suspected she was hiding behind her voluminous clothing, but her naturally straight-backed posture belied her five-feet-five-inches and made her stand out like a peacock in a flock of geese, at least to his eyes.

It was her face, though, that really got to him. He often had to remind himself to stop staring at the way her green eyes seemed to flicker from humour to concentration to determination at a second's notice, in a face framed by silky, tangled brown hair that gave the impression of never being brushed. Her mouth, too, was perfect, wide and upturned at the corners, though he'd noticed that she often kept a hand in front of it to hide the crop of spots that invariably broke out on her chin whenever she had an exam or a heavy night.

They'd met at a party in his hall of residence so he'd guessed she lived nearby but hadn't been able to believe his luck when she'd turned out to be studying physics too. They'd quickly fallen into the habit of going to lectures and then grabbing a coffee or three together afterwards. They were naturally on the same wavelength; he never got tired of talking to her and she seemed to feel the same way. She was interested in everything, wanted to experience all that life had to offer. He worried that he would seem boring to her by comparison, too focused on physics and narrow in his horizons, and he rued the fact that their natural rapport had translated so quickly into matey familiarity, the shackles of which had proven impossible to throw off even once he'd broken up with Emily halfway through the first year.

Emily: what a mistake that had been, and the consequences still echoed with him now. She'd been his back-home girlfriend, approved of by his parents and slotting frictionlessly into his group of friends from school. When he'd left for university and she'd been shipped off to finishing school in Switzerland he'd gone along with her assumption that they would stay together without giving it much thought, but his error had quickly become apparent after arriving in Bristol and meeting Eva. At first he'd avoided the subject, but their friendship had bloomed with an intensity that left him with no choice but to mention his girlfriend, which he'd done with a studied casualness designed to imply the relationship wasn't serious. He'd hoped and expected that Eva would give him the shove he needed to end it, but instead he found himself watching helplessly as something slammed shut behind her eyes. Then before there had been time to redeem himself, Lucien had appeared on the scene and all he'd been able to do was look on miserably at Eva's transparent attempts to make him notice her.

The thing with Emily had finally met its grisly and inevitable end during the summer after the first year, and the night he returned to Bristol he'd girded himself with a few pints and then gone to see Eva with the intention of confessing his feelings. That night, trudging back to his room after

Eva had pleaded tiredness and he hadn't even made it past the door, it began to dawn on Benedict what a high price he was going to have to pay for his cowardice and indecision. Had he simply missed his chance or was there some other undercurrent, something going on with Lucien, despite their studied indifference around each other? She'd never told him and he'd never plucked up the courage to ask.

How could it be so easy to talk about some things and not others? He flattered himself to think that he was Eva's closest confidant, or at least a close second to Sylvie. He knew her hopes and dreams and fears, how she was in turns insecure and defiant about her unconventional upbringing alone with her father and how unwilling she was to let herself use it as an excuse for anything. He'd opened up to her too, in ways that he'd never done with anyone else. Only yesterday they'd got up really early and walked all the way to the top of Mount Pantokrator, where they found a gaggle of floppy-eared goats mooching about the ruins of an ancient church.

They sat side by side on a dusty boulder looking out across the water, legs aching and eyes dazzled by the sunlight, and it had felt so natural to voice his excitement about the research he would be beginning after the summer and his hopes that it would eventually land him a job at the particle accelerator at CERN. As they sat together high above the world, he heard himself explaining how he loved particle physics because it gave him a different sort of perch, one that granted him the ability to see far beyond a normal human lifespan, back to the beginning of the universe and perhaps even forward to the end. There was no one else he talked to like this, no one with whom it would even occur to him to share these thoughts that he'd barely articulated to himself and yet now tumbled from his lips like poetry.

'Wow. That's quite the motivation for choosing what to do with your life,' Eva told him when he finished his breathless outpouring. 'It almost makes me feel bad about my own choices. Sometimes I wonder if I'm more motivated by fear than anything else. I'm scared that I'll make a mess of this new job and never succeed at anything, and I'll just go back to being Eva Nobody from Sussex, boring and unexceptional, which perhaps is just what I really am deep down,' she concluded with a smile that was only half ironic.

How ridiculous that sounded as he replayed the conversation in his head now, lying next to her by the pool: Eva Nobody. Everything about her was exceptional, and how she didn't know that he couldn't imagine. The afternoon air was lavender-scented and vibrated with the buzz of industrious insects. Through the gap between his eyelids Benedict watched as Eva opened her eyes, then rolled lazily onto her side and looked at him. At first he thought she was about to speak, but she remained silent and he suddenly realized from the unfaltering manner in which her eyes were making their way up and down his body that she didn't know he was watching her. Was she . . . could she be . . . ?

'Eva Andrews, are you checking me out?' he demanded.

Eva started. 'No, I'm not checking you out!' she yelped. 'I was admiring the view. Anyway, how would you know who was checking you out even if anyone was, which they absolutely weren't? You didn't even have your eyes open.'

'How would you know whether I had my eyes open if you weren't looking at me?' He turned over to lie on one side and posed with one hand on his hip and his head propped up on the other. 'You carry on. Don't worry about leaving me feeling soiled by your naked lust, I can handle it.'

Eva threw her magazine at him and stomped off towards the pool. He watched the way her breasts jiggled as she stomped and the way she emerged seal-sleek after diving into the water, and then found he had to roll onto his front and think about differential equations for quite some time before he could join her.

4

Goa, August 1997

Dearest Sylvie,

Greetings from Corfu, where the sun is shining, the scenery is breathtaking, and the grasshoppers are huge and bitey. Oh, and did I mention that I'm basically staying in a palace hewn from the mountainside? Okay, so I exaggerate un soupçon, but Benedict's clan are LOADED. I mean, obviously we always knew he was a posho but this place is ridiculous. His brother Harry and his girlfriend are here too, and she's some sort of supermodel who barely bothers with such trivialities as clothing. Obviously I showed up with not much more than a pair of flip-flops and that lurid old yellow sundress (which yes, I confess, I have 'borrowed' from you). His parents are lovely and have generously overlooked my being a peasant to make me feel very welcome. I do worry though, that that's just one of those rich people things. I have a slight suspicion that I could have turned up dressed as a banana and they would simply have embraced me warmly and pressed a drink into my hand without mentioning it. (I may have to test this hypothesis if I'm ever invited back.)

What else? Benedict's brother is terribly good-looking. I started out by loathing Carla, the girlfriend, on principle for being so exquisitely beautiful that she makes me look like a goblin by comparison (I've spent the entire week draping a towel over my wobbly bits whenever she's around), but we got totally sloshed at dinner (sorry, 'supper') the other night and stayed up chatting after everyone else had gone to bed, and it turns out she's really nice. She says she knows perfectly well that Benedict's family think she's a vapid exhibitionist, so she makes a point of wearing minimal clothing and talking about how great it is that Tony Blair won the election just to watch the steam rising off Hugo.

I feel a bit sad for her though, because you get the impression that she adores the brother but is scared he won't stick with her because his folks don't think much of her intellectual or social credentials. I don't know whether she's right about that, they seem pretty indiscriminately friendly to me, but she reckons she's the only one of his girlfriends that Hugo and Marina haven't attempted to march him up the aisle with. They're only in their mid-twenties but apparently getting hitched ludicrously young is a thing in Benedict's family.

And now, a small confession. Today the sun must have gone to my head, because for a moment Benedict started to look . . . well, you know. I'm leaving tomorrow and we spent the afternoon swimming and lounging around by the pool. So anyway, there I was, um, checking Benedict out in his budgie-smugglers. You know, for science. And don't laugh but he's sort of not all that bad with a tan, and you don't usually realize it, but under that awful green jumper he's always wearing there's a pretty decent bod. He's much more chilled out in his own environment too, not half as gawky as he seems back home. There was a moment today when I thought *he was going to kiss me, and I have to admit I actually wanted him to. We both went to walk back into the house at the same time and sort of got wedged in the doorway together and, honestly, if he'd kissed me then . . .*

Oh well, no point going on about it. It's not like I'm going to have time for a boyfriend seeing as how I'm going back to a new life that's going to be chock-full of glamour and excitement, plus it's not like he actually had the guts to kiss me today. So what really happened is absolutely nothing, which is just fine because my flight leaves first thing in the morning. I must confess that I'm fantasizing about staying here forever instead of returning to the real world. However, it has become apparent to me that I'm <u>very</u> cut out for a life of luxury, and I'm going to need the scary new job to pay for it!

Right, I'm off to collapse into my thousand-thread-count sheets. (Tosses shining mane of hair and sinks into billowing cloud of Egyptian cotton.)

Much love to you, and to Lucien.

Eva xx

In an insalubrious room in a hostel in Goa, Lucien carelessly tossed the letter onto a crowded table, unconcerned by its landing in a pool of beer dripping from an overturned bottle, before returning to the task of carefully counting out a pile of blue pills into little plastic bags.

'Well, well,' he said. 'So Fauntleroy really was born with a silver spoon in his gob. He plays that down, doesn't he? And he still hasn't got the *cojones* to kiss Eva after making puppy-eyes at her for three years.'

Sylvie, who was sprawled across a seamy mattress on the

floor on the other side of the room, looked up from the paperback she was reading.

'Give the poor guy a break. They can't all be Lucien-style lotharios.'

'I know, but he's so wet it's comedy. I mean, I like the guy, but . . .'

Sylvie looked thoughtful. 'Interesting, though. I thought it had all died down but if it's still going on after all this time . . . I wonder if those two might actually end up together one of these days. You know they were all flirty with each other when they first met?'

'Not really. Vaguely, I guess. Just tailed off, didn't it?'

'Sort of. He had a girlfriend back home that he'd carefully omitted to mention. Eva was spitting blood when he finally owned up. He broke up with her in the summer after the first year, but we were all good mates by then, so Eva kept things that way. You know what it's like, you can't have two people in a group like ours getting it on, it would have totally wrecked things.'

Lucien didn't answer immediately and fidgeted self-consciously, but Sylvie had resumed reading and didn't notice.

'Well, he's blown it now, hasn't he?' he said finally. 'She's off to her job in London and he'll be stuck in Bristol. It's not like they're going to be seeing much of each other.'

Sylvie frowned. 'It's only temporary, all of this though, isn't it? Everyone scattering to the four winds? You and I will go and live in London when we get back, and Eva will already be there, and Benedict will wash up there sooner or later and then the whole gang will be back together again. And then in, like, fifteen years' time when we're all grown up and our idea of a good time is drinking cocoa and doing jigsaws, Eva and Benedict can get married and have a couple of kids—'

'– called Tarquin and Octavia—'

'– and a golden Labrador. And I'll be a famous artist with my own gallery and you'll be, oh, I don't know, a mid-level advertising executive or something . . .'

'Oh, do fuck off. I'll have some really cool business empire and I'll sit in my corner office every day wearing sunglasses, with women feeding me peeled grapes and fanning me with palm fronds . . .'

Sylvie folded over the corner of the page she was on and put down her novel. 'Doesn't it drive you insane sometimes, not knowing how it's all going to turn out? Like, literally anything could happen.'

'Not really.' Lucien shrugged. 'I just figure that whatever adulthood's like, it's got to be better than our childhood.'

She hated the split in her loyalties that opened up when her brother said things like this. 'It wasn't all bad, though, was it? We've always had each other, and I know Mum was pretty useless but she's got a good heart, just a lot of her own problems too. There are some happy memories in there.'

'Like what?'

She gave it some thought. 'Summers in the Languedoc with Mamie and Papi? I mean, obviously they were a bit boring but at least it was sunny and we could swim in the river and go on bike rides.'

'Yeah, well. That was the upside of having grandparents in France. On the other hand, the downside of having grandparents in France is that they were nowhere to be seen when Mum was barely functioning enough to do the shopping so that I could pack you a proper lunch for school, or when she had another one of those fucking boyfriends who'd give me a clout whatever I did. I'm not saying you had it easy, but I did protect you a fair bit. Maybe that's why you feel more forgiving about it all than I do now.' Lucien yawned and stretched his arms. 'Anyway, I can't be bothered to have this conversation again. We're never going to agree on this stuff. Let's get going, these pills aren't going to sell themselves.' He stood up and pulled a dirty cotton vest on over his bronzed shoulders, only partially obscuring a recently acquired tattoo of a Chinese dragon, snarling face reaching over his collarbone and tail running halfway down his back. 'Full moon party, here we come.'

5

Docklands, July 1998

The obelisk towers of Canary Wharf, gleaming monuments to financial might, flashed bright semaphores in the morning sun as Eva walked towards them from the station, the block heels of her smart new court shoes clicking satisfyingly against the concrete. Almost a year into her new job she still experienced a frisson of excitement as she stepped into the cavernous lobby of the Morton Brothers building and swiped her security pass at the turnstile before striding towards the lifts. Her internal monologue was still that of an impostor: *tee hee, look where I am, do they really think I belong here?* But the pass that got her into the building and onto the trading floor said otherwise; she was an insider, and today would be her first day as a *real* insider now that she had been promoted to a seat on a proper trading desk and was no longer a graduate trainee on a boring government bonds book.

The lift doors glided open at the thirty-second floor and at 6.52 a.m. Eva stepped out and walked along the aisle past the banks of flickering screens. There were three seats in her new section and only one was occupied, with the ample form of a gently steaming derivatives trader. As she drew closer she realized the steam was actually rising from the enormous mug of coffee he was clutching, but even so the alcohol fumes rolling off his body seemed to render the air around him as watery as the inch of air above the tarmac on a very hot road.

Eva knew exactly who he was: Paul Costanzo, one of the two other members of her new team, whose legendary reputation in the market preceded him mostly in the form of tales of his night-time exploits. On his desk she could see a framed photo of a younger version of him in a yellow-and-black striped blazer, looking for all the world like a disgruntled bumblebee. This was no doubt an intentional reminder to those around him that he had been working in the financial markets since the days of the old open-outcry exchanges where garishly jacketed traders had screamed orders for runners to fill with paper tickets, before electronic trading had ushered in a quieter and more efficient era.

Eva drew to a halt by his desk, plastered a friendly but businesslike smile onto her face, and stuck out a hand. 'Hi. I'm Eva Andrews.'

The dishevelled bulk turned slowly towards her. 'Oh. Right,' he said, ignoring her outstretched hand and reaching for his coffee instead. 'No one told me the new minion was arriving today.' He peered at her through bleary eyes. 'Let alone one of the female persuasion.'

Eva glared at him, annoyance overriding expedience. 'Is that going to be a problem for you?'

'No need to get feisty now.' He perked up a little, apparently cheered by the hint of combat. 'It's no problem for me. I'm a feminist, you see.' Then, catching her sceptical look, added, 'You got a problem with that?'

She smiled despite herself. 'Not me, fella.'

'Good. So. Let's do the introductions properly. I'm Big

Paul, so called to distinguish me from Little Paul, that short-arse three desks over, who, incidentally, will have a fucking coronary if you actually call him Little Paul to his face. Yeah, that's you I'm talking about, small fry,' he called out to the man shooting a filthy look at him from across the aisle. Ignoring this, he continued, 'You presumably already met our boss Robert in the interview. He's not in yet. As you may be able to tell from my, ahem, beleaguered demeanour, we had a heavy night at the Rhino with Icap last night and my best guess is that he's still balls-deep in a stripper. So I suppose that leaves me to do your induction.' He ran a hand across his oily brow and took another swig of coffee. 'Do you want the HR-approved version, or the unvarnished truth?'

Eva eyed him with trepidation. 'I guess I'd better have the truth.'

'Right answer. See, I'm a good guy who's been around for a long time and probably the only one here who's going to tell you the things you really need to know. The first rule is: do not shag the traders. It's almost a sport to see who can sleep with the female jubs, that's what you are, right, the desk junior, but don't make the mistake of thinking it's going to lead to the blossoming of great romance because it's not. That includes Robert too, by the way. He's bound to have a pop at you sooner or later. Be firm but civil and he'll respect you for it. There's no such thing as sleeping your way to the top here. Only money talks in this place.'

'I'll do my best to restrain myself,' said Eva drily.

'What else? Aside from that, Robert's a great boss because he's a mercenary, a total fucking pirate, and he knows how to corner a decent share of the pie for his team come bonus time. He got so pissed off about his last bonus that he threw his toys out the pram and they added an extra half a million onto it. Can you believe that? An extra half a million. That's sterling, not dollars, mind.' Big Paul's eyes held a distant, wondering look for a moment, then refocused on her with a shrewder glint. 'Still, don't go getting any ideas. You're not going to be wearing Prada and turning left when you board a plane for a while yet. For the next couple of years you'll work yourself into the ground, thank the Lord for every day you don't get fired and feel pathetically grateful for whatever crumbs you get thrown from the bonus pool. Though obviously, however big your bonus is, you should always act like you're pissed off because you were expecting more,' he added.

'Right. Because other people take you at your own valuation?'

'Exactly. Value yourself highly and fight your own corner, because no one else is going to do it for you. Now, what else do you need to know?'

'Well, it would probably help if you talked me through the desk's trading books?'

'Yeah. But that's not going to happen till I've had at least another three cups of coffee. Did they send you on the Capital Markets course yet?'

'Yes, a month ago.'

'Where did you come?'

'In my group? Top.' Eva delivered this information blandly, secretly gleeful but figuring it was even more impressive to appear casual about it.

'Ah, brains as well as beauty. Good. But that's not all it takes to do well in this game. It helps of course, but it's about relationships too. You won't be in front of clients for a while, but you're going to want to put yourself about the market a bit, get to know the brokers. They take us out a couple of times a week, all top-notch places.' He peered at her again through bloodshot eyes. 'Nobu and Chinawhites will probably be more up your street than the Premier League and SophistiCats. Brokers have vast expense accounts to lavish on us because they want our business, so don't hold back. But, remember, they may act like your new best friend but you're not their only client and they'd sell their grandmothers for a chunk of commission, so don't drink too much and be indiscreet. That's rule number two: brokers are not your friends.'

Eva stifled a sigh. She was well aware that the City was more geared towards barely suppressed competition than companionship. The year since she'd arrived in London had been busy but tinged with a sort of loneliness, and she felt a quiet sense of shame that in a city where any night of the week the streets were lined with crowds of people clearly having the time of their lives, she had struggled to properly connect with anyone. If only her old friends had been around, but Sylvie and Lucien were still travelling in India and sending only sporadic and barely legible missives (*Hi, we are in Kerala something something sorry this letter is written on Rizla papers stuck together, it's all we had something something beach party blah blah . . .*), and a strange gulf had opened up between her and Benedict in the time since the holiday in Corfu. The intimacy of the trip, the one-on-one time without the others, the kiss that almost-but-didn't-quite happen, had raised the unanswerable question of what they really were to each other and then left it hanging, palpable in the air between them.

The silly thing was that she really missed him; she looked

forward to his calls with a surprising intensity but whenever she put the phone down she always seemed to be left feeling despondent, like they each wanted something from the other that they weren't quite getting. There was nothing to be done about it, of course. She wasn't an idiot; she wasn't in the market for a long-distance relationship with one of her best friends. But she couldn't help wishing that things would just go back to normal.

'I reckon the best place to start is for someone to talk you through the pricing models,' Big Paul was saying. 'Stefan can do that. He's your predecessor and he's just moved onto the Swaps desk. That's him, Swiss guy, over there by the yucca plant.' He gestured towards a man who appeared to be sitting at a desk wearing a wetsuit and flippers.

'Um. The guy in the wetsuit?'

Big Paul blinked. 'Yeah.' He turned back to his bank of screens.

Eva took a couple of steps away and then stopped. 'Er, Paul? Why is he wearing a wetsuit?'

He didn't even look up. 'What do I look like, the Grand Poobah in Charge of Wetsuits? Who knows? Who cares?'

Eva made her way over to Stefan's desk and cleared her throat. 'Hi, I'm Eva.'

He swivelled round and half stood to take her outstretched hand but was impeded by his flippers, causing him to abruptly slump backwards into his chair.

'I'm the new junior on the Interest Rate Derivatives desk,' she explained. 'Big Paul said you'd show me the pricing models?'

'Oh, right. You're the new me. Best of luck with that fat bastard.' He raised his voice loud enough for Big Paul to hear him, but although his target raised his head an inch or two, he maintained the air of a grizzled old lion unwilling to make the effort of swatting a fly. 'Sit down. Are you good with spreadsheets? Can you program VBA?'

'I'm not bad. I did some Visual Basic on my physics degree,' she told him, and then unable to resist any longer, 'Can I just ask, why are you wearing a wetsuit?'

Stefan scowled at her. 'The Swaps desk traders paid me two grand to come into work like this today. They want to film me on the way home on the Tube. They think it's funny. So what? They get their laughs, I get two grand. Who's laughing now?'

'You came in to work like that on the Tube?'

'Yeah. You think I'm an idiot?'

Eva grinned. 'For two grand? I'd have done it for five hundred.'

Stefan's frown finally reassembled itself into a smile. 'You, I like. Sit down. I'm going to show you all the tricks. And then, because you're a physicist, as a special treat I'm going to tell you about my thesis on Black-Scholes and how volatility in markets is predictably random, like the movement of particles.'

Now she had his measure; Stefan was a geek, her favourite type of person and by far the most useful in the building because geeks couldn't bear to leave a problem unsolved. One of the quants had even once stayed up all night sorting out a particularly thorny pricing issue she'd gone to him with, unable to bear going to sleep without answering her question. She'd come in the following morning to find him at his desk in the same clothes, surrounded by coffee cups and twitchier than ever, but triumphantly wielding the solution.

Sometimes it felt as though the cream of a generation was packed into this building, the Oxbridge engineers and rocket scientists. (So who was building the bridges and making the rockets? It didn't bear thinking about.)

'A treat indeed,' smiled Eva, half joking but mostly just relieved to have found a friendly face.

6

Vauxhall, August 1999

Lucien looked out across the swaying sea of his people and smiled benevolently. The bass thumped, smoke swirled, and several hundred pairs of hands reached for the roof of the warehouse in south London where his weekly club night, Candy, was rapidly becoming a raging success. Technically he was the promoter rather than the DJ, but he'd picked up enough know-how to mix a few records together while he was in Goa and he liked to take a half-hour slot early in the night just to get this feeling. Plus, the visibility helped with picking up girls. If they'd already seen him up here behind the decks it meant he didn't have to shoehorn being the promoter into every conversation. Not that he really needed the extra boost; success with women came easily to him. He knew he was slightly effeminate-looking, tall and slender with long sooty eyelashes and chiselled cheekbones, but he didn't care. If anything, it worked in his favour. He was non-threatening in appearance, the antithesis of your common-or-garden meathead, so he tended to get a friendly reception when approaching girls. And Lucien liked girls, liked them a lot, although of course it could be said that he didn't like them very deeply, or rather, he liked many of them very deeply but only for very short periods of time.

Lucien had a gift: to see straight into the souls of people and know what they needed to hear, right at that very moment. He'd explained this to a girl named Star he met at a beach party in India, and she told him that she could feel him reaching inside her as he looked into her eyes, so he carried on looking into her eyes all through the tantric sex they had when she took him back to her hotel room. At least, he'd done what he imagined tantric sex was supposed to be like, sitting up and facing each other, and it had taken him forever to finish because he'd drunk too much and done too much speed. He'd got an infection afterwards, maybe because it had gone on for so bloody long or maybe because she'd given him something. Either way, it had been a nightmare finding a doctor who spoke enough English to prescribe him antibiotics and it had cost a packet, so he felt a sort of karmic justification for never paying back the two thousand rupees she'd lent him the night before.

He was a free spirit, really, different from the others with their conventional outlooks and tedious career aspirations. They'd been back for six months now and even Sylvie was starting to talk about getting a proper job. Benedict was still a student, avoiding the real world for however many years it would take him to complete a PhD that would apparently land him some boring job that paid bugger all at the end of it, while he, Lucien, was doing better than any of them, because he had an entrepreneurial attitude and also because he was just the type of person who attracted good things by giving off the right vibe. The years they'd spent slogging away in the library, he'd spent selling overpriced drugs to the clueless but affluent students of Bristol and making more money in a weekend than the others could make in a month even now.

Still, it seemed as if Eva was doing quite well for herself these days. Apparently she'd been promoted twice in the two years she'd been in her City job. He didn't know exactly what she did, something stultifying to do with finance, but by the sound of it she made a decent amount of dosh. She'd changed quite a bit in the time that he and Sylvie had been away travelling, losing the old pudginess and dressing better too, less of the tie-dye and Doc Martens. And apparently she didn't drink pints anymore; in the bar where they'd all met up before the club she'd ordered a white wine spritzer and he'd almost laughed out loud. The newly constructed Eva seemed faintly absurd to him, but he could see that she had a bit more of an edge to her now, an attractive aloofness. There had always been a kind of connection between the two of them but there was just something offputtingly wide-eyed about her. She was the sort of girl who sucked you in and then started trying to get you to open up about your feelings, always trying to have conversations about *the big issues* or find out *what made you tick*. Lucien hadn't come this far by being the sort of person who dwelt on such things, and he wasn't about to start now. She'd suckered him into talking about his childhood once, looking at him with wounded eyes as she told him her mother was dead. For some reason it had made him blurt out a bunch of his own private stuff and he'd regretted it ever since, because after that when she looked at him he felt weirdly naked, and not in a good way.

Still, there was definitely something about her. There had been that one drunken fumble years ago in Bristol, but he'd had to avoid her for ages afterwards because it had been obvious she was hoping for something more, which he most certainly wasn't. She seemed much cooler towards him now, though, and that had always been like catnip to him. Should he, could he, talk her into a rematch tonight? Might be tricky, because she had Benedict staying at hers, but still, Lucien wasn't one to baulk at a challenge.

At that moment his eyes happened to alight upon Benedict standing in the far corner of the room, intermittently visible in the strobe light, engaged in animated conversation with a man who appeared to have a tattoo of a cobweb covering half his face. Probably shouldn't have given him that pill, on reflection. It had just been a bit of a laugh, offering a pill to Benedict, who'd always been so straight. Lucien hadn't thought he'd actually take the bloody thing but apparently there was a contagious recklessness in the air tonight, because when Benedict had seen Eva doing one he'd swallowed audibly and said, 'Go on then, before I change my mind,' and grabbed it out of Lucien's hand, gulping it down with a swig of Evian. They were decent pills tonight too. Lucien was coming up pretty hard and he'd only taken one so far. He was going to make a good bit of wedge on this batch, a lot more than the take on the door by the time he'd paid the DJs and lighting guys and bouncers.

Better go and do the honourable thing, he supposed. In any case, it probably wasn't a bad idea to get off the decks before he made a total twat of himself. He'd messed up that last mix as the pill kicked in, and for a horrible moment the hands had stopped waving and sort of lowered to half-mast. He'd managed to pull it back by dropping in 'Blue Monday' fast and hard, relief washing through him as the semiquaver kick-drum reverberated through the crowd and lent renewed vigour to the pumping fists; a good recovery, but still, better to quit while he was ahead.

'Bill, take over here, would you?' He motioned to the real DJ who was sullenly awaiting his slot at the end of the mixing desk. 'Got a bit of business to sort out.'

Lucien clambered down the steps to the dance floor and pushed his way across to the far corner where Benedict was by now having his neck massaged by Spider-Face.

'A word, mate.'

'Ah, Lucien. Superb night, thanks for sorting me out with . . . you know. This here is . . . this is . . .'

'Killer,' Spider-Face interjected helpfully, his warm smile revealing a mouthful of discoloured and broken teeth.

'Yes, um, Killer here was just telling me about this biker festival he was at last weekend. There's another one coming up in a few weeks, great fun, open to all-comers and not at all what most people expect apparently. We should—'

'We should and we will, mate,' assured Lucien. 'Let's all swap numbers before the end of the night. But right now we need to chip off for a few minutes. Eva wants a word. Don't mind do you, Killer?' He steered Benedict away from his beaming companion towards the back of the club.

'What does Eva want? Where is she?' asked Benedict, pushing his hair back off his face and peering about.

'Ah, well, that was a bit of a lie to get you away from your new friend, you see. This being your first pill, I should ex-plain a few things to you. When you're loved up on Ecstasy everyone seems like your best mate, but of course what really happens is you wake up the next morning with a Hell's

Angel named Killer asleep on your sofa and wonder what the fuck you were thinking. That's if he hasn't stabbed you to death in the night and nicked your TV.'

Benedict attempted to raise an eyebrow but succeeded only in generating a series of seemingly random facial twitches. 'It's not like you to be so judgemental. You're condemning the man based solely on his appearance and we all know you can't judge a book by its cover. You'd miss out on some very good books that way, all those Penguin classics with the orange covers for starters because they all look alike, not to mention—'

Lucien raised a hand to cut him off. 'Yeah, yeah. Call me a judgemental conformist, but I'm going to stick my neck out here and say that having a spider's web tattooed across your face is not intended to send the message, "I'm a cuddly, peaceable member of society who under no circumstances would stove in your face with a shovel for the change in your pocket."'

A hint of doubt finally crept onto Benedict's face. 'Ah. Well. When you put it like that. So, do you know where Eva's got to?'

*

Where Eva had got to at that very moment was wedged into a tiny toilet cubicle with Sylvie, who was struggling to break a pill in half between her fingers.

'Shit, I've dropped it. No, there it is.'

'Oh God, not on the floor. There's wee all over it. We can't take that now.'

'Oo, hark at you, princess. Here, I'll wipe it off. There, all better. That's your half.'

'I don't know whether I should do another one anyway. I need to be compos mentis for work on Monday.'

Sylvie glared at her through eyes lavishly caked in kohl. 'Eva. It's forever since we had a proper night out with the whole crew. Even Benedict's dropped a pill, bless him. For one night, take off your metaphorical power suit and relax. We've hardly seen you since we've been back, it's all work, work, work with you. You'll have the whole of Sunday to recover.'

Eva hesitated. She was being pretty reckless by her prevailing standards, but the markets were dead in August and next week would be a quiet one at work. And Sylvie was right: they hadn't seen enough of one another since she'd arrived back from travelling. There wasn't much Eva could do about that; a job like hers came at a price, and that price was putting it before everything else in your life. When you worked fourteen hours a day it didn't leave much time for anything else, and if you were half-hearted about it, well, there were plenty of people lined up behind you ready to take your place.

Still, at least the hard slog was finally starting to pay off. Many of her cohort were falling by the wayside, culled for underperforming or simply buckling under the pressure, and those left standing were finally being promoted to jobs where they wouldn't have to fetch anyone's coffee and would start to get paid the big bucks. Eva was beginning to understand that half of being successful was just staying in the game longer than anyone else. The great surprise of the adult world had been that no one really knew what they were doing, and especially not the people who exuded impenetrable confidence. The first year in the job had been soul-crushing; every time she'd asked a question she found that she didn't understand the answer. At first she assumed that this was because she was failing to grasp things that everyone else just magically understood, but lately she'd begun to realize that the reason her questions were often glossed over was that the people around her didn't actually know the answers.

Nobody really knows what they're doing. This was an epiphany that had scared the bejesus out of her but had also expanded her confidence tenfold, because if the big beasts of the markets didn't have all the answers, then if she could make it her business to be the one who did she would surely be ahead of the game. She'd quietly gone back and examined the fundamentals: there are two sides to every deal, every profit made by one person equates to a loss for someone else, every loan has to be either repaid or defaulted upon at some point in the future, a single dollar is a single dollar and if it's being counted in two places at once then sooner or later there'll be a shortfall. Simple truths, often overlooked.

Understanding everything from first principles gave you a certain confidence that other people could just smell on you, she found. And it wasn't only that; it was also knowing she could pick up the phone to her brokers and get a table at any club or restaurant she wanted in London that night, or tickets to Wimbledon, or pretty much anything else that her heart desired. It might not be finding a cure for cancer, but being greeted by name and given the best table by the maître d' at Coq d'Argent still had a way of making you feel like somebody.

Even Lucien was looking at her differently tonight, with a sort of hungry air about him. After all the times she'd had to quell the stabbing feeling she got from watching him look at countless other girls that way, she recognized it when it was directed at her, and savoured an inward glow of satisfaction. The balance of power was shifting between them; she had a new allure and they both knew it. It felt like the stars were starting to align for her at last.

She made a decision and grinned at Sylvie across the toilet cubicle. 'Go on then. But not that half you just dropped on the floor. Give us a clean one, I know you've got a bagful. I might as well have a whole one anyway.'

Sylvie fished around in her bra for the little bag of pills. 'Okay, sod it, flush that wet one down the loo. If you're doing another whole one then so am I.'

7

Primrose Hill, August 1999

Seven hours later, a hazy sun was rising above Primrose Hill and a blade of long grass was tickling the side of Eva's face. She propped herself up on her elbows and looked out across the city towards St Paul's Cathedral. Eva had meant to go home with Benedict after the club closed but somehow she and Lucien had ended up in the back of a crowded van headed for an after-party in north London, and they'd been halfway across town by the time she'd realized that Sylvie and Benedict weren't with them. Eva hoped Benedict wasn't annoyed; he knew where the spare key was and, really, it wasn't her fault they'd got split up. He was bound to be okay. She could make it up to him, take him out for breakfast before he caught his train. Eva was actually feeling quite straight now, not in a paranoid, scratchy way, just warm and mellow. She had been surprised and pleased when Lucien had tugged her out of the party, insisting that since they were in this part of town it would be a crime not to watch the sun rise from the top of Primrose Hill.

'I wish we had something to drink,' Eva thought as they lay side by side in the grass, and she must have said it out loud without realizing, because Lucien peeled himself up off the ground beside her and reached inside his jacket to produce a bottle of brandy.

'Ask, and ye shall receive.'

'Oh, you didn't,' she exclaimed, knowing it could only have come from the party they'd just left.

'No, I bloody didn't nick it, if that's what you mean.' Lucien sounded aggrieved. 'He gave it to me, all right. Said I had limpid eyes and that I should help myself to his drinks cabinet.'

'I think he meant to a drink, not a bottle.'

'Whatever. He left it open to interpretation. Anyway, a flat around here costs squillions so he's hardly going to miss a bottle of booze. And he wouldn't have invited a bunch of randoms back to his place if he was that worried about it.'

'You're incorrigible.' Eva laughed. 'Limpid eyes?'

Lucien leant across and held his face very close to hers. 'Yes, limpid. Like a rock pool. Can't you feel yourself being pulled in by their limpidity?'

'I don't actually think that's a word,' she said, wriggling out from under him. She'd seen him employ weapons-grade flirtation on at least five other people this evening regardless of age or gender, including the guy whose brandy he'd stolen, so she wasn't kidding herself that this behaviour meant anything.

'Did you have a good time tonight?' Lucien said, casually shifting back onto his side but still facing her. She looked up at the lightening sky, where the sun was rapidly burning away the early morning cloud. It was going to be one of those perfect summer days.

'Yes,' she said, 'I really did. I haven't had such a good time in ages. It's great the way your club night's taking off, seems like it's really working out for you.'

He stretched, causing his T-shirt to ride up so that a couple of inches of flat white stomach were exposed. 'I've got big plans for it, actually. I'm talking to a couple of other club owners about putting on similar nights for them. They love what I'm doing, bringing back proper old-school house and techno, none of that grungy Britpop shite. I'm hoping to put on a really epic night for the millennium.'

'If the millennium bug doesn't bring the world to an end, you mean?'

'Then it really would be the party to end all parties. Maybe I'll call it Chaos or something. That's a good angle, maximize the marketing potential.'

'Listen to you, Richard Branson. Marketing potential?'

Lucien turned a suddenly serious gaze upon her. 'I'm not messing about here, Eva. It might look like I'm just having fun but it's hard work and I'm planning on going places. You're not the only one making something of yourself. I've grown up a lot these last couple of years. I'm not just the same old Lucien you used to know.'

He was staring penetratingly into her eyes as he spoke, and was it her imagination or was he leaning in towards her again? Was he trying to tell her that things had changed, that he wanted her and wouldn't treat her the same way again? Or was that just the residual effects of the pills making her utterly stupid? Oh God, his face was really close now.

'We're not like other people, are we, Eva? What you're doing with your career, it's really impressive. And I'm going places too. We're really on the brink of something. Can you feel it?'

And she *could* feel it. The world was changing. She was standing on the edge of a cliff. But that sounded like a bad thing, so maybe she was at the foot of a mountain, but no, that made it sound like she had a mountain to climb whereas things were actually going to get easier. So a clifftop it was, but the sort of cliff where falling off was a good thing. She felt Lucien take her hand and slide his fingers between hers and suddenly he was standing next to her at the cliff's edge and they stepped off together and they were floating in the air as his mouth came down on hers and as he kissed her he shifted his weight so that his body was almost on top of hers and it felt . . .

'Get a room, why don't you!'

Eva jerked her eyes open and found herself looking straight into the contemptuous gaze of an early-morning dog walker. She buried her own burning face into Lucien's shoulder, which was shaking with laughter, until the man had passed.

'We could you know,' he whispered into her ear.

'Could what?'

'Get a room. We wouldn't have any problems with Sylvie or Benedict that way. Just you, me and an enormous bed . . .'

Could she really do this after spending years swearing to herself she wouldn't fall for it again? It did feel like she was learning new things about him. He was in some ways much more complex than she'd ever realized. Or was that just the pills?

She sighed. 'Oh, Lucien. I'm not even sure if this is . . . real. You know?'

He shifted further on top of her and nudged one of his legs between her thighs. 'Reality's overrated. It's for people who can't handle their drugs. Go on, there's a Travelodge just by Regent's Park. We could check in there.'

Her hands were inside his jacket, separated from his skin only by a T-shirt's width of cotton. She could feel the contours of his body against her palms. How many times had she imagined this? Not half as many times as she'd had to force herself not to, because what was the point in wanting something you couldn't have? And now here she was, in a situation where she *could* have it. Have him, Lucien. Was she really going to throw it away? Oh, but then there was Benedict, waiting at home for her, and she'd been so looking forward to seeing him. He wouldn't easily forgive her if she went off with Lucien instead of spending the morning with him, and she didn't even know if he'd made it back there okay, now she thought about it. He could have been mugged or anything. And he'd done his first pill tonight too. There really ought to be someone with him. She could just about be excused for the mix-up over who was in the van, but it would be unforgivable if she didn't get home soon.

She reached up and kissed Lucien slowly on the mouth, then pulled away. 'I can't. I want to, but I've ditched Benedict and I don't even know whether he's okay.' She kissed him again. 'You could call me. Next week.'

Even as she said the words she sensed a barely perceptible shift in his features, the strained quality of lust dissipating and being replaced by his usual easy confidence, the affect of a man who knows that what he wants is there for the taking. The world jolted into focus, and in that moment she knew that he wouldn't call her next week, or the one after. They weren't Eva and Lucien, kindred spirits floating on a bed of clouds through a celestial skyscape. They were two drugged-up idiots lying on the cold ground in a public park at six o'clock in the morning. She was the biggest idiot, of course. Lucien was a complete bastard, but there was almost no point in even thinking about that because Lucien was just doing what Lucien did, taking his chances and hoping to get laid. It would be like criticizing a scorpion for stinging you. Yes, it wasn't pleasant, but its sting was on display, so if you picked it up and got stung then *you* were the idiot. She looked at him. *Do I look like that?* she wondered, staring at his bloodshot eyes with their wildly dilated pupils. There was a crust of greyish scum gathering at the corners of his mouth and his teeth and gums were stained dark from the red wine they'd drunk at the party, or maybe from the lollipops he'd been handing out at the club all evening.

Lucien sat up and brushed the grass from his clothes and Eva followed suit, grimly picking a piece of chewing gum off her sleeve. The new distance between them, in reality only a few inches, might as well have been a mile for the gulf that had opened up in the wake of the evaporated intimacy. What was she doing here when she could have gone home with Benedict and sat on the sofa with a duvet and a bottle of wine and finally caught up? They'd barely had a chance to chat this weekend and he was leaving in a few hours. It wasn't that there was anything specific they needed to talk about; it was just that there were so many things she'd made mental notes to tell him, nothing of consequence, just anecdotes she'd been saving up because she knew they'd make him laugh. She didn't really have that in her life anymore, and she missed it, really missed it. Eva looked at Lucien and tried to imagine talking to him about her job, or the book she'd just read, or her hopes and dreams. He looked back at her, grinning and dead-eyed.

'Right then,' he said. 'Time for the walk of shame.'

8

Spain, August 2000

'Okay, here's one,' said Sylvie. 'If you were offered the gift of immortality, would you take it and why?'

The four friends were trudging through a forest seventeen miles west of Baladas in Galicia, where they'd spent the previous night in a hostel dormitory. It was the penultimate day of a week spent hiking the last ninety miles of the ancient pilgrimage route of the Camino Frances to reach the cathedral at Santiago de Compostela. They made an unlikely band of pilgrims, with Sylvie's fluorescent orange hair and Lucien's aviator sunglasses and velvet trousers setting them apart from the other walkers in their sensible hiking gear, but having spent months arguing over where to go on a joint holiday they'd all finally agreed when Benedict had suggested this trip. It suited Sylvie because walking and staying in hostels was an option she could actually afford, and Eva had figured it would be useful for losing a bit of the extra weight she'd put on over a few too many boozy broker dinners and takeaway lunches. Lucien had agreed because he was up for anything that promised an adventure, and also because he'd reached the point where he would have said yes to a caving holiday in Timbuktu if it meant they didn't have to have any more tedious debates on the subject.

'Wow. I think this might be the hardest question yet,' said Benedict, taking a swig of his rapidly dwindling water supply. He'd started the trip the best prepared of the group, with a tiny rucksack weighing less than the recommended ten per cent of his body weight, but had ended up carrying most of Eva and Sylvie's possessions. Both of them had over-packed: Eva with sensible things like suncream and raincoats and perhaps one or two more books than strictly necessary, and Sylvie with an extensive supply of paper and pencils, paints and pastels. 'What a choice. You'd get to see every bit of incredible technology we develop and learn about every scientific discovery, and whether we ever find aliens and manage to colonize other planets, then eventually watch the sun go supernova.'

'Yeah, but picture this,' said Lucien, going into doomy voiceover mode. 'The sun is dead, the human race has drawn its last breath, the aliens never arrived . . . it's just you . . . alone . . . in a vast, cold tract of dark, empty space.'

'Well, yes, there is that,' said Benedict. 'Plus you'd get to watch everyone you love die. But on the other hand you'd get to see to the end of the universe and beyond. I can't decide. What about you, Sylvie?'

In truth, Sylvie hadn't been particularly enjoying adult life so far and the prospect of an eternity of it wasn't remotely attractive. Job opportunities had been thin on the ground since she and Lucien had returned from travelling, and accommodation expensive. She'd been reduced to signing up for office temping, and even debasing herself in this way hadn't exactly resulted in a flood of offers. What's your typing speed? Do you have any experience with spread-sheets? Those were the sorts of things they wanted to know, not whether the candidate was passionate and creative and fun to work with.

For the first time in her life, she was starting to feel like she was at the bottom of the pile. At school and university she'd always been in demand; she was good-looking and confident and naturally subversive, and that had always been enough to keep her high in the social hierarchy. The academic side of things wasn't her forte, but Mr Nolan, the art teacher at one of her secondary schools, had said she had a rare talent, confirming her sense that her destiny lay in being an artist. But a lot had changed since the days when her star had been so firmly in the ascendant, even within her immediate group of friends. These days Eva was glowing with a new confidence, and more, an overarching sense of purpose, which only compounded Sylvie's growing feeling of being adrift. Lucien, too, was raking it in on his club nights and Benedict at least had a direction in life, even if it wasn't one that she much envied. But she wasn't about to admit any of this out loud.

'Never mind immortality, I'm going to top myself if I have to listen to Lucien moaning about his feet for much longer,' she said.

Her brother glared back at her. 'Have I mentioned in the last five minutes that they're agony? And that this whole trip was a shit idea? I was promised sunshine and naughty Catholic girls, not blisters and hostels full of stinking Germans. And that's if we're lucky. I'm telling you, if we don't find somewhere with vacancies soon we're going to have to sleep under a tree.' He waved a hand at the darkening air around them; the last three hostels they'd passed had no free beds, forcing them to keep walking. 'Look at these shoes, they're completely ruined. And what about these trousers, eh? Three hundred quid they cost me, and now they're covered in mud.'

'I did tell you that you wouldn't be able to walk a hundred miles in suede shoes,' snapped Sylvie. 'Why on earth didn't you bring proper hiking boots?'

'Because I'm not fucking forty?'

Eva, who was walking a little way in front of the rest of the group, suddenly drew to an abrupt halt in the road. 'Halle-bloody-lujah!' she called back to them. 'A hostel with a sign saying they've got beds.'

Sylvie, the only one who spoke any Spanish, went in to check while the others sat on a wall to relieve their aching feet. She came out smiling a few minutes later.

'Good news?'

'Good news and bad news. Which do you want first?'

'The good news,' the others yelled in unison.

'The good news is that we are not going to be sleeping in a ditch tonight. We have beds.'

'As long as we've got beds, I don't even care what the bad news is,' said Eva.

'That's lucky,' said Sylvie. 'Because the kitchen's closed and there are only two rooms left. I'm in the single and you three are sharing the double.'

Even before she had finished the end of the sentence she had flung a room key at them and started to run towards the converted stable block nearby. By the time the others had picked up their rucksacks and chased after her she had already slammed and locked the door to her room, leaving them banging on the door and protesting feebly, which only seemed to increase the volume of her laughter emanating from within. Eventually they gave up and trudged off to find the other room.

'Just when I thought it couldn't get any worse,' groaned Eva as the three of them stood looking down at their bed for the night, a standard-size double. 'I barely slept in that dorm last night. My bunk was above that Franz guy we keep running into. He snored like a tractor and smelled like something had crawled up his bum to die.'

Exhausted and out of options, they silently munched their way through the sandwiches left over from lunchtime before stripping down to T-shirts and pants and collapsing onto the bed, with Eva in the middle and Benedict and Lucien either side of her. Benedict rolled over to face the door and started snoring almost immediately. Eva turned face down and stuck a pillow over her head, but after a few minutes she became aware of Lucien wriggling closer.

'Well, hello-o there,' he whispered, sticking his head under her pillow and flinging an arm across her body. 'Fancy a quickie?'

'Stop grossing me out, Marchant,' she hissed. 'I'm wise to your slutty hit-and-run ways, remember. Now go to sleep, we've got an early start tomorrow.'

Undeterred, he poked a lively erection into her thigh.

Eva shoved him away. 'Really, Lucien? In the same bed as Benedict?'

'Oh, don't be such a prude, I've done this sort of thing loads of times. He's fast asleep, won't even notice, and anyway, it'll be a treat for him if he wakes up.'

'No it bloody won't,' said Benedict grouchily, rousing himself from sleep and clambering over the top of Eva to the middle of the bed so that he was between them. 'Keep your pervy paws off her.' Then a few moments later: 'And no wanking, you fucking reprobate. I can feel the bed moving, you know.'

*

Eva was woken by her alarm at 6 a.m. She switched it off quickly and lay back against Benedict's warm bulk beside her. He smelled good. Really good, actually. She'd been seeing a management consultant called Jeremy in London for the last few months, but all he talked about was spreadsheets and he definitely didn't smell as good as this. She closed her eyes and found her mind drifting towards a scenario in which it was just her and Benedict in the bed together. As if sensing it, he shifted closer to her in his sleep, exhaling softly onto her neck. For a moment, in the darkness, none of the multitude of reasons not to – Jeremy, their friendship, living in different cities, Eva not wanting to be tied down – seemed to matter. If Lucien hadn't been in the bed with them . . .

What the hell was wrong with her? She shut down her wandering mind and slid out of the bed to retrieve her washbag from her rucksack and head for the shower, which for once she wouldn't mind being cold.

After predictably bracing ablutions, Eva returned to the room to kick the others out of bed and make a start on the day. She opened the door to their room and burst into laughter as she took in the scene illuminated by the light from the hallway. This woke Benedict, who opened his eyes and, seeing Eva, broke into a sleepy smile that rapidly gave way to an expression of dawning horror.

'Hang on. If you're over there . . . who's spooning me?'

Lucien groggily raised himself up onto the elbow of the arm that was trapped under Benedict, looked down at him and grinned. 'I've woken up with some uggers in my time, mate, but this really takes the biscuit.'

Grimacing, Benedict rolled out of the bed, leaving Lucien to slump back onto the pillows. 'God, I'm tired. Do we really have to get up at sparrowfart today? Let's just get a bit more sleep, eh? It's unnatural, getting up at this hour.'

'No chance.' Benedict tugged the sheet off him. 'The pilgrim mass at the cathedral at Santiago de Compostela is at twelve thirty, so we need to set off early to make it. That's the whole point of the walk.'

'Not for me it's not, what with my not being a religious nutjob,' grumbled Lucien. 'And it's Catholic, right? Are they going to want me to confess my sins? Because that may take some time.' He winked at Eva, who turned away in mock disgust.

'It doesn't matter,' insisted Benedict. 'Half the people walking the Camino aren't religious. But to have a journey you've got to have a destination and this is ours. Now come on.' He lifted the edge of the mattress and rolled Lucien off onto the floor. 'We've come this far, only fifteen more miles to go.'

*

It was an unseasonably chilly morning and even as the day grew lighter, the air remained clouded with mist. The group trudged quietly along a pathway through a eucalyptus forest, each of them subdued by the knowledge that they'd be back in England and back to real life tomorrow. Benedict was trying to untangle a problem with energy ranges for his thesis but found his mind kept straying to thoughts of how good it had felt to spend the night with Eva in bed beside him, and then reminding himself tetchily that she had a boyfriend. Eva found herself resolving to end things with Jeremy when she got back; he just didn't smell right, and no amount of working at things could fix that. Sylvie was deciding to visit every art gallery within a twenty-mile radius and beg for a job when she got back – it was time to carve out a proper life for herself. Even Lucien seemed lost in thought, limping along without the usual complaints.

Eventually the scent-filled woodland thinned and gave way to fields and then roads, until finally they reached the bridge to Santiago de Compostela. They joined the steady trickle of walkers following the brass shells inlaid in paving stones into the narrow streets of the old town, and eventually right up to the looming Baroque facade of the cathedral itself.

Lucien made a few token protests about preferring to go to a bar but Benedict rounded everyone up and in they all went, inching into a pew at the back just as the service started. A hush descended on the cathedral packed with pilgrims with dirty clothes and dishevelled hair, people from every corner of the globe and yet nevertheless all giving themselves up to a service in Spanish and Latin which somehow communicated everything it needed to through its sonorous rhythm. Once it was over, Lucien got chatting to a man sitting next to him who had made the journey on crutches and Sylvie wandered off to sketch some of the icons and altarpieces. Eva ambled through the side chapels and surprised herself by slipping a couple of euros on impulse into a bank of electric candles and thinking of her mother.

Benedict strolled away casually, then, after checking that none of the others were in sight, furtively slipped into a pew on the other side of the building and bowed his head in prayer.

As the four reassembled in the square at the front of the cathedral, they were each so wrapped up in their own thoughts that it took a while for anyone to notice Lucien dabbing at his face with his sleeve.

'Lucien,' said Benedict after a while. 'Are you . . . blubbing? Are we witnessing a miracle? The most cynical man on earth having some sort of religious experience?'

'Oh, fuck off. I'm not blubbing, mate.' He rubbed his eyes. 'It's just . . . that Spanish guy I was chatting to, the one next to me in church with the withered leg and crutches. He came all the way from Sarria like that, just to be blessed here. Can you imagine doing the walk we've done, but on crutches?'

'Wow. That must have been tough,' said Eva, whose legs were so sore she wasn't certain she'd ever want to walk anywhere again.

'It's taken him over a month and he said it was the hardest thing he's ever done. His leg's been like that all his life. Seemed really happy to have made it. Look, he gave me this.' Lucien pulled a shell out of his pocket with a loop of string hanging from a hole drilled through it. 'Said he'd worn it round his neck for the journey, that it had brought him good luck and now he wanted to share it. Don't you hate it when people do stuff like that? I can put up with any amount of arseholes but that shit just pushes my buttons.' Lucien's voice grew husky again.

Benedict stifled a laugh. 'Seriously? You're crying because

someone did something nice for you? I've seen it all now. Come on over here, Snugglepops, you look like you could use that cuddle you were trying to give me this morning.'

Lucien glared but allowed Benedict to envelop him in a bear hug, quickly followed by Eva and Sylvie, who threw their arms around him too. The four of them stood like that for a long time as pilgrims and tourists bustled around them, huddled together with arms stretched out to encompass as many of the others as possible, each of their bodies aching with tiredness and elation and relief and sadness that it was over.

9

Bristol, June 2001

Benedict rubbed a hand across his unshaven chin and cast a gloomy look around what he loosely referred to as his office. It was rather an aggrandizing term for a cluttered desk in the corner of the basement of the physics department. True, the basement was the right place to keep the experiments, what with its being easier to control light and temperature, but spending so much time down there was getting a bit much. Every time he left the building he would emerge squinting into the light, like coming out of a daytime showing at the cinema and with much the same feeling of discombobulation.

In winter it hardly bothered him, but now that another summer had rolled around it was wearing a bit thin. At least he was about to have a break. He was mostly tying up loose ends now, archiving data and annotating his code for when he came back to finish writing up his thesis in the autumn. The university would be dead over the summer and in a few weeks' time he'd be off to Corfu for a lengthy holiday, more at the behest of his parents than through any great desire of his own. It would be pleasant enough, he supposed, so long as he manoeuvred himself into a room as far away as possible from his brother and Carla and their noisy new baby, but he was feeling restless and ready for a change.

He'd moved back into the postgrad hall this year to avoid having to find another flatmate now that the old one had decamped to Fermilab to immerse himself in the heady world of high-energy particle physics, leaving Benedict behind tinkering around in the dungeon and dining nightly on Pot Noodles in the shared kitchen that was barely more hygienic than the one in his undergraduate halls of residence.

Doing a PhD forced you into a sort of extended adolescence, he thought ruefully. He was working at the cutting edge of particle physics, and yet there was just something uniquely infantilizing about the student lifestyle. The email he had received that morning from Eva – an increasingly rare occurrence – had only served to underline this. The picture she painted was, as ever, very much one of bright lights, big city; big deals, big nights out. She mentioned Sylvie but not Lucien, making Benedict wonder whether she saw much of him these days. The email hadn't really felt as though it was from his old friend. It contained none of the shared jokes they used to shoehorn into their messages to show that nothing had changed, that underneath it all they were still the same old Benedict and Eva. Of course, they had never really been Benedict and Eva, at least not in the way that he would have liked, and perhaps she really had changed. Certainly it sounded as though Eva was more excited by bonuses than bosons these days.

There had been that moment, a few years ago, when he'd thought it might actually happen between them. She'd joined him in Corfu the summer they'd graduated, and over the course of a week she'd grown browner and more relaxed until the last day when they'd come in from the pool together and made to enter the house at the same time. They'd got sort of wedged in the doorway, he in shorts and she in a bathing suit, and though their bodies hadn't actually been touching electricity had seemed to crackle and arc between them.

Benedict shifted uncomfortably in his chair, relieving the pressure from the fly of his jeans. Just thinking about it gave him a combined flush of desire and humiliation even now. He should have just kissed her. This wasn't a new thought; it was the same one he'd been having, oh, four or five times a day in the several years since, give or take. He should have kissed her but instead he'd stepped back out of the doorway, almost but not quite brushing her body with his own, and the spell had been broken and he'd mumbled an apology and she'd darted off to her room.

He wondered whether he'd die an old man still cursing himself for not having taken what could easily turn out to have been his best shot at happiness. After three long years of watching Eva pining for Lucien and being roundly ignored himself, he'd finally had his chance and he'd blown it. The savage rage he'd felt at himself for the first year afterwards had largely subsided, but the thought of it was still enough to make him cringe at his own inadequacy.

He glanced up at the clock: 9 p.m. He might as well head home, picking up a Pot Noodle from the Spar on the way. He'd just write his data back down ready for the morning, and make a start on a reply to Eva's message while he was waiting for the job to finish. Benedict sent the command and listened for the telltale signs from the cupboard in the corner of the room, where Boris the data-management robot would be busying himself. The sheer volume of data for his PhD on the search for first-generation leptoquarks in decay channel collisions was so enormous, petabyte upon petabyte of the stuff, that it couldn't be stored on local computers and was instead written onto cartridges which were lifted in and out of the reader by the robotic arm. Most of what he spent his days doing was writing computer programs to sift through massive datasets looking for signature patterns of his particle, isolating traces in amongst all the other distracting and irrelevant data and allowing him to zero in on these tiny signals and separate them out from the background noise.

He opened the email from Eva and read it again. New York, *blah blah*, client dinner, *blah blah blah*, broker night, *blah-di-blah*. He was losing her, that much was clear. She was jetting around the world attending important meetings, hobnobbing with movers and shakers, while he festered in a basement. She never mentioned men these days but he knew they must be there, coming and going. He probably wouldn't know until one day a wedding invitation would plop through his letterbox, and then it really would be too late.

A thought was coalescing in his mind as he hit Reply. If it would be too late then, didn't that imply that it wasn't too late now? What if some future version of himself in a parallel universe was looking back at him sitting here now and cursing him for a bloody fool, just as he was doing with the version of himself of a few years earlier?

'Eva,' he began to type recklessly.

Sounds like all you do is work! Do you have any holiday you can take this summer, and if so, do you fancy joining me in Corfu again like you did a few years ago? It's been ages since we spent any decent time together and I don't want to sound utterly soppy but I miss you. I never tell you that even though I often think it because I don't know how you'd feel about it. But what the hell: I'd love us to spend some time together this summer. Do you remember how great it was last time? This is going to sound crazy but there was a moment, do you remember it, when we got sort of lodged in a doorway together? I've kicked myself so many times for not kissing you then.

He was distracted by a crunching noise coming from the data cupboard. Benedict glanced up but couldn't see anything amiss, so he turned back to the screen and continued.

Anyway, I don't want to jeopardize our friendship so if this is totally unwelcome then just say so and I'll never mention it again, but I'm reading your messages and realizing that your life is moving on and I don't want to end up kicking myself even more for just letting that happen and never being man enough to say what's on my mind.

The noise from the cupboard was growing worryingly loud now, more of a thudding than a crunching sound. Irritated at being distracted but sufficiently unnerved by the possibility of something being wrong with what was, after all, a cupboard full of very expensive equipment, he pushed his keyboard aside and went to investigate.

*

Benedict opened his eyes and watched as the polystyrene ceiling tiles and strip lighting of the office swam into view.

There was something else too, dark and blurry and closer to his face than the ceiling. He struggled to focus on the inorganic arm protruding from a hole in the cupboard door. Boris. There was a sharp pain in the side of his face, he realized, and he lifted his hand to touch it.

'Don't move,' a woman's voice barked. A female voice was in itself an unusual phenomenon in his office. He tried to turn his head and focus on the face as it hove into view above him.

'What did I just say? Don't move.' Now the face moved directly into his line of vision and he recognized it as belonging to Lydia, another PhD student, from the Solid State team along the corridor.

'What happened?' His voice came out as an embarrassing croak.

Lydia appeared to stifle a smile. 'I'm afraid your robot appears to have gone rogue. I'm using my powers of deduction here, Watson, but it looks like it punched through the door and hit you in the face. I was just checking my gallium arsenide cells when I heard a load of banging and then a squeal, and I found you lying on the floor and Boris hanging halfway out the door of his cupboard. I've turned the power to your room off at the fuse box, by the way – hope you didn't have anything unsaved on your computer but Boris was still twitching rather alarmingly.'

Benedict started to peel himself up off the carpet.

'You stay right there. The ambulance will be here any minute.'

'Ambulance?' he groaned. 'That's really not necessary.'

As he clambered to his feet waving away Lydia's restraining hand, two green-clad paramedics appeared in the doorway.

'The patient's in here,' Lydia called to them. 'I did tell him not to move. He was knocked out by a robot, you know.'

'Robot attack, is it?' said the first paramedic, a large grey-haired man of about fifty, in a thick West Country burr. 'We don't get many of those, I don't mind telling you.'

'Honestly, it's nothing,' Benedict said. 'Look, I'm fine now, really, it's just a graze.'

'We'll be the ones to decide that,' said the second paramedic, a skinny young man with a large nose. 'Sit yourself in this chair and let me have a look in your eyes. Bright light, try not to blink. Now, this young lady said you were out for the count. How long was he unconscious?' This last addressed to Lydia.

'Not more than a few minutes, I'd say,' she told him. 'I heard a loud noise which must have been the robot arm punching through the door, and found him out cold on the floor. I phoned for the ambulance but he opened his eyes almost as soon as I put the phone down.'

'You've got a bit of a bruise but it doesn't look that bad,' said the older man. 'Still, can't be too careful with a head injury. We'd better take him in.'

'No really, I'm absolutely fine,' Benedict protested. 'I certainly don't need to go to hospital.'

'Well, we could release you into her care, I suppose. Will you be with him all night, young lady? Take him straight to A&E if there's any vomiting or strange behaviour?'

Benedict looked pleadingly at Lydia and she sighed. 'Yes, I can take him home with me tonight. I'll keep a good eye on him.'

This seemed to be enough to placate the paramedics, and they picked up their bags to leave. As they reached the doorway the older man turned back towards them.

'So that's what you lot get up to down here, is it?' he said disapprovingly. 'Shenanigans with robots? And then they get a mind of their own and something like this happens? I'll tell you the name of a film you should watch, young man. It's called *2001: A Space Odyssey* and it will teach you a thing or two about just how far you can trust computers. Mark my words, it never pays to go against nature,' he added darkly, before stalking away along the corridor.

Benedict and Lydia looked at each other and covered their mouths with their hands, both waiting until they heard the double doors along the hallway swing shut before exploding into laughter.

'Do you think Boris has achieved consciousness?' asked Lydia when she'd stopped laughing long enough to catch her breath.

'What, and set out to cause the downfall of his human masters and take over the world?' Benedict guffawed, and then winced at the pain in his head.

They both glanced over at where Boris was hanging limply from the door of the data cupboard, looking not at all like a supreme, humanity-crushing intelligent life form, and cracked up again.

'Right, that's enough shenanigans with robots for one night, young man,' said Lydia. 'Come on, get your stuff together and we'll head back to mine. There's nothing we can do about this now. It'll have to be sorted out in office hours.'

'Oh, you don't actually have to look after me tonight, you

know,' Benedict said. 'I just needed you to say that so they wouldn't insist on taking me in. I'm fine, see, perfectly all right to head home now.'

'What, and have it on my conscience when they find you dead in the morning from a blood clot on the brain? Not likely. You're coming with me, and that's that.'

*

When Benedict woke the next morning his head still hurt, but he couldn't have said whether it was due to Boris's assault, Lydia's cheap plonk, or the rather vigorous pounding it had taken on her headboard.

Crikey, he thought, looking over at her naked body, only partly obscured by sheets. Not timid old Benedict after all, eh.

Okay, so she'd done most of the running. Or all of the running if he was honest, but he hadn't put on a bad show. The first time he'd been a bit trigger-happy, but surely the second, third and fourth times would have made up for that? Perhaps there were some advantages to a build-up of sexual frustration.

She'd been surprisingly kinky, way beyond any real-life experience of his own. His cheeks glowed remembering that thing with her finger. God, you'd never have thought it to look at her. Actually, he realized, he barely had looked at her until now. He knew she did something or other to do with solar cells but it wasn't his field and he rarely went into the Solid State office. He looked at her again, taking in the curly brown hair and freckles. The freckles were on her arms and back too, he could see now. They made her sort of friendly-looking, and were more than a little sexy. Why had he never noticed any of this before? Partly because she usually had more clothes on, of course, but also because he was usually too busy thinking about Eva to notice what was right under his nose.

Eva. The thought gave him a jolt. He'd been typing that email to her when Boris had started to malfunction . . . had he hit Send? No, he'd gone to see what Boris was doing and hadn't finished the message. And then Lydia had turned the power to the whole room off, so it would have been lost. A wave of relief washed over him. What on earth had possessed him? What sort of idiot sends a declaration of love when it couldn't be any clearer that it wasn't reciprocated? And anyway, looky here. There were other fish in the sea.

Lydia seemed to sense his appreciative gaze on her and rolled over sleepily, exposing her breasts (large, also freckled). She opened her eyes and gave him a lazy smile. Galvanized by her boldness, he reached out and ran his fingers over the left breast, tracing the outline of the areola.

'What are you doing this summer?' he asked, rolling towards her. 'Have you ever been to Corfu?'

10

London, September 2001

The thick cream envelope was lurking in the stack of post that Eva grabbed from the communal entrance table as she arrived home from work, on top of a pile of takeaway menus and exhortations to apply for credit cards. She noticed it immediately: her name and address handwritten on the front in black ink, the calligraphy stylish and precise. Hand-addressed letters were becoming rarer these days and usually meant a treat, or at least not a bill, so it was the first envelope she opened once she'd let herself in and put her bag down. She slid the card out of its envelope with a pleasant sense of anticipation, and read it three times before bafflement gave way to astonishment. It informed her that a Mr and Mrs Jeremy Price-Kennington requested the pleasure of her company at the marriage of their daughter Lydia Sarah to the Hon. Benedict Michael Waverley, at a church in the Cotswolds some three weeks hence. She was still standing in the hallway staring down at it when her phone started to ring.

'Have you got one of these?' she demanded before Sylvie had a chance to speak. 'An invitation to Benedict's wedding? Is this some sort of a joke?'

'Nope, deadly serious apparently,' Sylvie told her. 'I just got off the phone to him. We only spoke for a moment

before his paramour whisked him away to discuss the intricacies of table decorations but apparently he's known her all
of about ten minutes, which makes sense, because I wasn't
even aware he was seeing someone. Did you know?'

'I had no idea. The only thing I can tell you is that getting
married ridiculously young isn't considered weird in his
family, they all do it. But it says here it's in three weeks' time.
What's that all about?'

'Apparently the unseemly haste is because they wanted to
do it before the weather gets cold and so it doesn't interfere
too much with writing up their theses. You know he's about
to finish his PhD?'

Eva turned this over in her mind. 'I bet he's got the CERN
job and needs to do it before he leaves for Switzerland.'

'Who is she anyway, this Chlamydia Princely-Cameltoe?'

'Lydia Price-Kennington? She's another physics PhD, I
knew her a bit when we were undergrads. A horsey sort, a bit
ostentatiously sloaney, but then I suppose Benedict's hardly a
pleb himself. Still, he always wore it more lightly than she
did. The word in the lecture theatre was that she boinked
half the guys on our course, for which I'm sure they were all
eternally grateful since that would have been all the action
most of them saw in their undergrad years. She should probably be given a medal for services to desperate physicists.' Eva
found herself growing more despondent as she spoke. 'She
had a certain reputation for kinkiness, if I remember rightly.'

'Pah, the physics crowd wouldn't recognize kinky if it
danced in front of them wearing a gimp suit and waving
an armful of tentacle hentai porn. I bet she's dull as ditch-
water and the wildest they get is him rubbing one out in the
corner of the bedroom while she recites prime numbers to

him. Which come to think of it *is* kind of kinky, but not in a good way. But listen, are you okay with this? I always sort of thought that you two would get together eventually.'

'I don't know, really,' said Eva. 'The whole thing's a bit of a shock, isn't it? And I always thought . . . I mean . . .' What did she mean? That she had secretly assumed Benedict would always be there, that the thought of his actually being in love with somebody else created an unexpectedly forceful ache in her chest? She let the sentence tail off. 'I'll just have to get used to it, I suppose. Anyway, it's been a while since we caught up. How's it all going with you?'

'Oh, you know. Still tiding myself over with bar work till I actually manage to sell some paintings.' Sylvie sounded morose.

'It'll come, you'll see. And wouldn't you be better off in an art gallery or somewhere till then? You might make some decent contacts. Or at least be something like a designer or illustrator, use your artistic talents?'

'I've been trying but all that's really on offer is unpaid internships, so you've still got to pay your rent and feed your-self while working for nothing. And even they seem to require experience. It's catch 22: you can't get experience till you've got experience. I actually went for an interview at a gallery in Chelsea yesterday, figured I could do an intern-ship in the day and then go straight to my bar job at night. I mean, who needs sleep, right?' She let out an unconvincing laugh. 'Don't think I've got it though, they seemed rather underwhelmed by my 2:2 in art history. The fuckers. I mean, I could swallow it if they were actually going to pay, but to be sniffy about your degree when they expect you to work for free . . .'

'Just you wait,' soothed Eva. 'When you're a famous artist you can go back and buy the place and fire them all. See how sniffy they are then.'

They carried on chatting for a few minutes, each trying to inject a bonhomie they didn't feel into the conversation, before giving up and saying their goodbyes. Eva hung up and sat at the kitchen table looking down at the wedding invitation. That was it then. She was losing Benedict, who'd always been there for her. There had been that moment, towards the end of their holiday in Corfu, when they had very nearly kissed. How different things might be now, if only one of them had actually made a move. Maybe she should have, but it would have been such bad timing, just as she was moving to London and starting her new life. Even as she'd been finally giving up on Lucien and growing closer to Benedict, there had been a part of her that hadn't really wanted her old life hanging around as she headed off on new adventures. She'd wanted a blank slate and the opportunity to recreate herself however she chose. But over the last couple of years she had started to realize that there weren't a whole lot of men out there with Benedict's qualities: his rumpled good looks, his kindness, his gentle humour. She had never met anyone else she found it so easy to talk to. He was one of those people who knew everything and had read everything, so that you never had to stop and explain yourself.

Anyway, what was this Honourable Benedict business about? He'd kept that flipping quiet all these years. What did it even mean? That Hugo was a lord or something? She suspected she'd find out at the wedding; clearly Lydia and her social-climbing family weren't planning to allow Benedict to maintain his discretion. Catty, she reproached herself. You don't know a thing about them. Sour grapes, that's what it is, and you've got no right. If Benedict's found someone he loves you should be happy for him. Being your safety net shouldn't be a lifelong project for him.

Eva didn't feel happy though. She felt stunned and nauseous.

★

'So are you really not having a stag night?' Eva asked Benedict as they picked their way through the long grass on Hampstead Heath ten days after the invitation had dropped through her door.

He smiled. 'This is it. This is my stag do. I can't think of anything I'd rather be doing. Besides, I'm not risking letting the Plasma Physics boys organize something. It's all good fun till you wake up in Utah in bed with a dead Girl Guide.'

'Oh, come on.' Eva gave him a gentle shove with her shoulder. 'A walk on the Heath isn't a stag do. At least let me invite Sylvie and Lucien out for drinks. Who knows when you'll next get the chance to spend time with us once Lydia has the old ball and chain around your ankle.'

'Well, yes, it could be a while,' he admitted. 'I've got another bit of news, you see. After the wedding we're moving to Switzerland.'

Eva stopped walking and looked at him, the cheerful expression she had been effortfully sustaining slipping a little. Not only was he getting married, but he was emigrating. She couldn't be losing him more completely.

'So you got the CERN post? Congratulations,' she said bleakly. 'You deserve it. And Lydia's going with you? Doesn't she mind putting her own life on hold?'

'She's decided to take some time off. She's just finishing her PhD too, and even for a Solid State bod it's a pretty exciting opportunity to spend time at CERN. We're at a stage where the theorists don't know which direction to go in and the results from the Large Hadron Collider will determine that. It might come up with a real surprise but whatever we find, it's going to keep physicists off street corners for a long time to come.'

They were walking past the Highgate ponds now, the water gleaming in the autumn sunshine, and through the hedge they glimpsed an old man of perhaps seventy diving into the men's swimming pond.

'What a nutter,' commented Eva to save herself having to think of something positive to say about how exciting it would indeed be for Lydia at CERN. 'I know it's warm for September, but can you imagine doing that?'

Benedict laughed. 'I can because I have. My father used to take us when we were kids. The house where I grew up is just the other side of the Heath, though my parents spend more time in the country than here these days. The real hard-core swim in there all year round you know.'

'Hugo used to take you? I thought the men's pond was a bit of a gay pickup place? No offence, your parents are great, but I can just imagine him fulminating against the queers. God, do you remember how he thought that being vegetarian meant I was some sort of cult member?' Eva laughed.

'Funnily enough he doesn't seem too bothered by that sort of thing. I know he's a bit of an old reactionary but you have to bear in mind that he was at Eton in the bad old days of fagging so a spot of homosexuality would be unlikely to shock him, though of course he'd think it terribly bad form to actually speak about it. She'd never admit it, but my mother would probably be more scandalized. She's enquired rather pointedly about what she calls my lifestyle more than once over the last few years, so I think Lydia has come as quite a relief to her. She was no doubt trying to convey that she'd love and support me even if I did bat for the other team, but she looked like she was about to have an attack of the vapours. I've tried to explain often enough that I'm just crap at girls.' He let out what seemed to Eva a rather sad little laugh. 'God knows, it took long enough after that Corfu holiday for her to stop asking hopefully after you.'

She jabbed him in the ribs with her elbow. 'And after all the reassurance you gave me about how they wouldn't think anything of it if you brought a friend.'

'Well, I wanted you to come, and you wouldn't have if I'd told you that my family had been asking to meet you for ages and would descend on you like a pack of raptors, would you?'

The thought of that summer seemed very far away to Eva now, part of a more innocent era when the world sat more lightly on her shoulders. They wandered on, weaving away from the tarmacked path and across the spongy grass until they neared the crest of the hill.

'Shall we sit down for a minute?' Eva said. 'I love the view from up here.'

They lowered themselves onto the grass and looked out past the ponds towards the old Witanhurst mansion and St Michael's church spire. It was only four in the afternoon but already the sky was hinting at dusk with a streak of purple, a gentle reminder that a warm week in September didn't mean that autumn could be staved off forever.

'I guess there won't be many more chances to do this,' said Eva, leaning back and propping herself up on her elbows. 'Hanging out just the two of us, I mean, doing nothing in particular, just wandering around talking about anything and everything. I guess this is what happens when you grow up. People drift off in their own directions. Sometimes I look around at my job and my flat and my car and can't believe that people have mistaken me for an adult and let me have all of this. But this is it, isn't it? We're the grown-ups now.'

Benedict shifted so that he was facing her instead of the view. 'Yes, I suppose we are. I probably shouldn't admit this, but some days I'm petrified. I've spent the whole of my adult life to date as a student and now I'm going off to a new job in a new country with a new wife.'

Eva sighed. 'It really is the end of an era, isn't it? Or maybe the era already ended without our quite having realized it. I'm going to miss you, Benedict. In a funny way, I think I already do even though you're right here beside me.'

They suddenly seemed to be very close together without either of them having moved.

Are you really going to do it again? Benedict was asking himself. Let her walk away? You've spent years regretting not kissing her – do you want it to be the rest of your life? Shit, but Lydia, you're marrying Lydia, and you love her and she's . . . she's . . .

And all the time he was thinking these things his mouth was inching lower and Eva was raising hers and once their lips were touching it would be crazy, impossible not to kiss her, was he expected to just sit there with his face on hers and not move his lips like some sort of mad statue, he wasn't made of stone and now he was kissing her and it felt . . .

'Shit!' yelled Benedict and he sprang back, pushing Eva away so hard that she almost rolled backwards into the grass.

'What?'

'This! We can't do this! What are we doing? We can't do this.'

'God, I thought you'd been stung by a bee or something. Okay, look, calm down, let's sit on this bench and talk.'

But Benedict was up on his feet and pacing now, hands pressed to his temples.

'Benedict, this isn't all bad. It's not great timing, but it's happened. And we both wanted it to happen.'

'It's not that simple.'

Eva took a deep breath. 'No, I know, there's Lydia. And the wedding. Benedict, I know this is the worst possible time for me to say this, but do you really want to go through with it? I've got no right to tell you this, but since I knew you were marrying her I've felt, well, bereft. I thought you'd be there forever but now I'm losing you and I haven't been able to sleep for wondering, what the hell are we doing? Should we be together? And I know it's impossible, that there's Lydia and the wedding and CERN, but . . .'

Benedict stopped pacing and swung round to face her. 'Fuck you, Eva, fuck you,' he shouted, bringing startled tears to her eyes. 'Why would you do this to me now? You could have done it any time in the last seven years and I'd have been the happiest man on earth, but now?'

She reached out and tried to take his hand. 'Benedict, I know there couldn't be a worse time but, oh God, do we want to regret not doing this for the rest of our lives?'

He wrenched his hand away. 'Actually there could be a worse time, or at least, this is a worse time than you can possibly imagine. Lydia's pregnant, Eva, she's pregnant. We're having a baby. And I love her, and I love that baby and no matter how many years I've spent pining for you, it was never *real*. You were always off doing something else, looking for something else, and you always will be. But this, Lydia, the baby, this is real. You've never been anything more than a fantasy for me and now it's time to grow up.'

Eva felt a chasm open up inside her chest. 'God, Benedict, I didn't know. I swear if I'd known she was pregnant . . . Why didn't you tell me?'

'We haven't told anyone, not our families, no one. It's the twelve-week scan on Thursday. You don't tell people till after that.' He rubbed his eyes in a suddenly crumpled-looking face. 'Look, I just can't do this. I've got to go.'

'You don't have to do that.' Eva was crying now. 'Please don't go, we can talk about this. I'm so sorry. I'm not going to make this hard for you. I don't even have to come to the wedding.'

'How's it going to look if you suddenly pull out of the wedding? If you've ever been a friend to me you'll come and you'll be happy for me, for us. And for God's sake don't tell anyone about this, not even Sylvie, just forget it.' His voice grew quieter as he spoke, and she watched as his anger was replaced by calm resolve. 'You know I care about you, Eva, but it has to be just as a friend now. Things have changed and this is how it has to be.'

He leant down and kissed her forehead, then turned and walked away. She watched him go, racked with shock and shame, heart pounding painfully inside her ribcage. Eva lowered herself onto a nearby bench and watched him grow smaller as he strode away from her down the hill. For a long time after he'd finally disappeared she remained sitting there alone, letting the air darken around her and her hands grow cold and her mind go numb.

11

Cotswolds, October 2001

On the day of the wedding Eva drove out to the village in the Cotswolds with Sylvie in the front passenger seat and Lucien and his plus-one in the back. Chas, as she'd introduced herself whilst clambering into the back of Eva's car, was a six-foot podium dancer from one of Lucien's increasingly successful club nights.

'As in ". . . and Dave"?' Eva had joked. 'Seventies pop-rock duo credited with popularizing the musical style colloquially known as "rockney"?' she added in desperation when that failed to elicit a laugh, but Chas had just stared at her blankly and then shifted over to allow Lucien to ooze in beside her with a cat-that-got-the-cream look on his face.

Lucien and Chas were in an extremely intimate relationship. Eva knew this because they'd spent much of the two-hour drive being extremely intimate on the back seat of her car, until she'd been forced to tilt the rear-view mirror away and turn up the radio in order to stifle the steadily building urge to swerve into a tree.

They were booked into the country spa hotel where the reception was taking place, and as they approached the Georgian manor house along the gravel drive, sandstone walls glowing golden in the sun, Lucien let out a low whistle.

'They're certainly doing it in style. Not bad for a shotgun wedding.'

Eva had to admit that he was right. She had certainly never been the sort to fantasize about her wedding day, what with growing up with Keith's lectures on gender oppression and the patriarchal nature of marriage, but if she'd given it any thought this would have been just the sort of place she'd have wanted to do it.

It was a relief to finally arrive so that she could escape the car to go and get changed in the room she was now apparently sharing with Sylvie. Eva had booked two rooms for the trip, waving away Sylvie's faint mutters about repaying her. She knew that Sylvie couldn't have afforded to come if she'd had to pay for the hotel so taking care of the booking had seemed the easiest way to avoid any awkwardness. But what hadn't occurred to her was that Lucien would bring a date, so that she would end up sharing a twin room and shelling out the best part of two hundred quid for him to get his rocks off. The thought made her seethe. Dressed for the wedding, they reconvened in the hotel lobby, where Lucien, clad in a foppish sky-blue designer suit, was leaning against an enormous carved wooden fireplace, somehow looking at once utterly ludicrous and devastatingly handsome.

'Shall we?' he said, proffering Eva the arm that didn't have Chas hanging from it in a gold lamé dress.

The ceremony took place in an old chapel half a mile away, sunlight trickling in through stained-glass windows and threadbare prayer cushions hanging from the backs of the pews. Eva had lain awake in her bed the night before with a knot in her stomach thinking about what it would be like to watch Benedict say his vows, but sitting here now she found herself feeling remarkably detached. It was all so surreal and removed from their real lives, Lydia with her bump just visible through her roman-style gown, luminous with pregnancy or bridal joy, Benedict stumbling over his words but generally looking happy and a bit dazed. Eva found herself feeling strangely peaceful, perhaps because of the calm of the chapel, or perhaps because of the finality of Benedict actually being married to somebody else, the relief that comes of being behind a closed door.

*

After the wedding breakfast Benedict's brother Harry, who was his best man, made a speech that trod a deft line between joking that the marriage had been prompted by the imminent arrival and implying that it would have been only a matter of time anyway, and then the music had started up, allowing Eva to take a much-needed breather to compose herself in the bathroom. She stood at the basin washing her hands and examining her weary face in the mirror, assessing the cumulative damage from an eighty-hour working week topped off with a good four or five glasses of champagne. Even to her own eyes she looked tired and sad. She pulled a few faces at her reflection and then practised a smile. Only a few more hours to get through before she could slink off to her room and then the whole ordeal would be over and she could go back to her life, which would, after all, be much the same as it had been before the wedding invitation had arrived.

It didn't feel like it was going to be the same, though. It felt as though she was staring down the barrel of a long, lonely winter, and perhaps even a long, lonely life of regretting having been too stupid to know what she had until it was lost. This too shall pass, she reminded herself. She wouldn't always be drunk and tired and emotional. New days would roll by, new men would come and go. That was life: you put one foot in front of the other. She was just steeling herself to rejoin the fray when a cubicle door swung open behind her and Lydia staggered out.

'Oh hi,' squeaked Eva, sounding artificially bright. And then, because she couldn't think of anything else to say, 'Congratulations. How does it feel to be Mrs Waverley?'

'The Honourable Mrs Benedict Waverley, to be precise,' said Lydia, coming over to the sink next to her and rinsing out her mouth with a handful of water from the tap. 'And right at this moment, it feels utterly nauseating, if you must know.'

Eva tried a joke. 'Well, Benedict has been known to have that effect on women.'

'Ha ha,' said Lydia without actually laughing. 'No, it's the morning sickness. Except that's the biggest lie in history, because it doesn't begin and end in the morning, or if it does it's followed by the afternoon sickness. Which lasts just until the evening sickness kicks in.'

'Oh. Sorry. You'd never know it to look at you. You were positively radiant today in church.'

'That's just the sweat.' Lydia wiped her brow and underarms with a paper towel. 'Another thing they don't tell you about pregnancy, the amount you perspire. Plus, I gained a certain sheen from throwing up five minutes before the ceremony.'

'Oh dear. In any case, the chapel was beautiful,' Eva said, clutching at straws.

Lydia brightened. 'It was, wasn't it? If it had been up to me we'd have just run off and done it in Vegas, but I'm really glad that we did it this way now. I wasn't sure about going for the whole church thing at first, but you know how Benedict is about all that.'

Eva shot her a quizzical look. 'I don't, actually. I mean, I didn't know it was a big deal to him. It was Benedict who was keen to have a church wedding?'

'Oh yes. Hugely important to him. I found it a bit strange at first because let's face it, you don't meet many religious physicists, but he absolutely insisted. I thought that your little gang was as thick as thieves, I'm surprised you wouldn't know that about him.'

'Well, I suppose we don't know him as well as you do, obviously,' Eva said, adding internally, *or anything like as well as I thought I did, as it turns out.*

The first few bars of Spandau Ballet's 'Gold' floated in from the dance floor.

'God, this DJ. Where did my mother find him? Still, it seems like everyone's up and dancing so he must be doing something right. Better get back out there.' Lydia took Eva's hand and gave it a squeeze. 'I'm glad we had the chance to have a chat, I do want to get to know my husband's friends better. You'll have to come out for a weekend once we're settled in Geneva.' She swept away, leaving Eva mumbling something about how nice that would be.

*

Back in the ballroom Marina was working the room like a pro, towing a visibly reluctant Hugo behind her. The long, cowl-necked russet dress she had chosen for the occasion was draped glamorously over her shoulders, a rather fashion-forward selection for the mother of the groom, Eva thought, but of course perfectly in tune with the season, and beautifully offset by a messy chignon of grey-blonde hair.

'Eva, my dear, how lovely to see you again,' she cried on spotting her. 'Benedict tells us you're a rising star in the City these days. It's always marvellous to see one of us ladies giving the other side a run for their money.'

'Well, "rising star" might be a bit of an exaggeration.' Eva smiled, genuinely pleased to see them. 'But yes, the job's going pretty well. Exciting that Benedict's off to CERN.'

'Isn't it? We're terribly proud of him, and of course it's lovely to see him so happy with Lydia. It's been a bit of a whirlwind, of course, but aren't all the best romances?'

Was it Eva's imagination or was this just a little too pointed?

'Thought it might be you, actually, at one point,' chuckled Hugo.

Eva struggled to prevent her facial features from arranging themselves into a look of mortification but Marina had already dug a sharp elbow into her husband's ribcage and begun to tug him away, reaching back to pat Eva's arm and say that they would have to catch up again later and, oh, was that Martin Wentworth-Oxley over there?

Out on the dance floor, Lucien and Chas were grinding their pelvises together to a medley of Eighties classics. Eva looked around for Sylvie but couldn't see her anywhere so she wandered out onto the terrace, moving to the far end away from the muffled thud of the music and the glow of the lights from the ballroom doors. She dug a cigarette out of her handbag and lit it, blowing the smoke in satisfying jets out into the darkness. Eva had barely smoked in the last couple of years but she'd had a premonition that she might need a cigarette before the day was up, and had bought a packet of Marlboro Lights and a cheap lighter when they'd stopped for petrol on the motorway. Now she savoured the treacly rasp of tobacco hitting the back of her throat and the welcome light-headedness that followed.

'Room for one more?'

The voice startled her, making her jump and spin round so fast that she almost knocked the lit end of her cigarette on the morning-suited figure behind her.

'Benedict! Christ, you startled me, creeping up like a bloody ninja penguin. I thought I was alone. What are you doing out here?'

'Just getting some air. I wasn't sure I had the stomach for "Agadoo" hot on the heels of "Love Shack".' He reached out and gently extracted the cigarette from between her fingers before taking a long pull on it.

'You won't be able to do that for much longer.'

'I know. Not once the baby comes. Lydia would kill me now, actually, if she caught me,' he added, exhaling through his nostrils so that the smoke emerged in two swirling streams.

'She looked lovely today,' Eva told him, trying to inject some sincerity and goodwill into her voice. 'You both did. I'm really happy for you. I don't know if I should even be saying this on your wedding day, but, Benedict, I know things got a bit awkward there for a moment, but I've got my head straight now. You're leaving soon and I so want it to be on a good note.'

'Thanks.' He nudged her with his shoulder. 'Thanks for

saying that, and for coming today. I'm really happy and I'm glad you're happy for me.'

Eva shrugged. 'How could I not be? It only hit me today how close you must be to Lydia. She mentioned something about how important it was to you to get married in a church. I didn't even really know you were religious, Benedict. After all these years.' She tried to keep her tone light and not allow a note of reproach to creep into it.

'Well,' he said slowly, 'it's mostly not been a big deal in my life, just something I grew up with, I suppose. Anyway, I'd never have mentioned it when we were at uni because I'd never have heard the last of it from you lot, particularly Lucien, who, by the way, appears to have brought an extremely drunk stripper as his plus-one. Last I saw she was practically giving a lap dance to my highly appreciative father while my mother expended all her energies pretending to be deep in conversation with Great-Aunt Gwendoline.'

'Ah. That would be Chas. She's a podium dancer, apparently. Just be thankful that you aren't the one driving them back tomorrow. If I have to put up with another two hours of dry-humping on my back seat I may be forced to set fire to the upholstery.'

Benedict took another drag and handed the cigarette back to Eva and they both stood in silence for a minute, leaning forward against the balustrade and looking out across the darkened gardens.

'I've been thinking about it a lot more recently, I suppose,' Benedict said eventually, prompting Eva to spend a confused few seconds trying to work out why he would have been thinking about Lucien frotting on the back seat of her car. 'The religious side of things, I mean. I'm about to become a father of an actual baby. As we stand here a tiny human with my DNA is growing from nothing. That seems like a sort of miracle. An everyday miracle to be sure, but then, perhaps the miracle is that something so astonishing, so remarkable, can just happen every day, that something so miraculous is available to everyone, rich and poor, no qualifications needed.

'I know you probably just find all this weird. Do I believe in the absolute specifics of Christianity, the virgin birth and the Resurrection and all that? Maybe not. But I do believe there's a mystery at the heart of human existence that I don't have the answer to, or even the tools to answer. I suppose I'm with Shakespeare: "There are more things in heaven and earth, Horatio, than are dreamt of in your philosophy."' He retrieved the cigarette from Eva's hand and took another drag before passing it back. 'And that's the nice thing about the Anglican Church, if you ask me. It doesn't really bother to insist that everyone subscribes to a rigid set of doctrines. Some people think that makes it a tepid, wishy-washy religion but to me that's actually its strength. Everyone has their own conception of God and mine is to do with a sort of awe at the balance of the natural world that only deepens the more I learn about the universe.'

Eva couldn't think of anything to say. She'd always assumed he was a default atheist of the same rather unthinking sort that she was, the sort who believed in things for which there was empirical evidence and didn't see any merit in giving much thought to anything else. How much more was there that she didn't know about Benedict? Somewhere out there in an alternate universe she'd have a lifetime to learn it all. In that universe, a woman very much like her would be waking up every day to continue this conversation, a conversation that she realized now they had begun years earlier and had carried on through days and nights, emails and phone calls, glances and laughter. That Eva, although she looked and sounded like this one, was just subtly different enough to have known a good thing when she saw it, and as a result hadn't just watched the man who might possibly be the love of her life get married to somebody else.

'Well, religion's not all good,' she said finally, for want of anything else to say. 'Look at what just happened at the World Trade Center.'

'God, yes. Your bank's American, isn't it? Did you have people there?'

'Several thousand. Six dead, no one I knew. It would have been a lot worse if it hadn't been for the security guy there. He's a legend among the staff now. An ex-military guy who took his job really seriously and managed to evacuate nearly everyone.'

'"Took?" Past tense?'

'Yes. He was still evacuating people when the tower went down. Presumed dead, though no remains have been found yet. Maybe they never will be. He was originally from Cornwall and apparently he sang Cornish songs from his youth to keep everyone calm as he evacuated them. In amongst all the chaos and destruction, there was this sixty-year-old guy standing in the stairwell, directing people down and belting out, "Men of Cornwall, stand ye steady, stand and never yield." And he phoned his wife and told her to stop crying, that he'd never been happier and that he loved her and she'd made his life.'

They stood quietly looking out into the night and thinking about this new world in which planes flew into towers and people fell from the sky, and in which there were men who so hated their world that they were willing to die a spectacular death to make their point. Eva thought, too, about who she'd have called as the tower went down, and whether if Benedict had been there he would have called Lydia and been able to say that to her, that he loved her and she'd made his life. She was sure he was thinking the same thing but she could only see his profile in the dark, and it gave nothing away. Eventually he broke the silence.

'I love it out here in the country, where you can still actually see the stars. You don't get that in the city, do you? Too much light pollution. When I was a child everything seemed to stop at night. I remember my father driving us to Gatwick to catch a flight at three o'clock in the morning and being the only car on the road. It was magical. You felt as if you were getting a glimpse of a secret world while everyone else slept. Now the cars never stop and the lights never go out. But out here you can still just about make out the constellations and it puts things in perspective, makes you feel like what you really are, a tiny mammal on the surface of a planet spinning through infinite space amidst a billion stars. Easy to forget that, don't you find?'

'I suppose so.' Why wasn't she saying anything? He was pouring out his innermost thoughts, and that was all she could offer? But if she started talking now she knew she wouldn't stop. She'd tell him how stupid and blind she had been, and try to convince him that his future lay with her. And what if she succeeded? What if he turned round and said, I feel the same way, let's run away together? Then for the rest of her life she would be the woman who had gone to a wedding and run away with the groom, leaving the pregnant bride devastated and the baby fatherless. Anyway, even if she was a terrible enough person to do that, Benedict had already proven he wasn't, that day on Hampstead Heath, and if anything she loved him more for it.

She leant towards him so that her arm was pressed against his and rested her head on his shoulder and felt him leaning back towards her. They stood like that wordlessly for a minute and then Benedict said, 'You're shivering. Come on, let's get you back inside.' He put an arm around her and leant down to kiss her on the top of the head, then led her back towards the lights and music and a world in which Benedict was married to Lydia and they were having a baby together and Eva was going back to her life tomorrow, alone.

★

Back inside, Lucien was slumped in a chair at the edge of the dance floor on his own, swigging from the neck of a champagne bottle.

'I think I'm going to call it a night,' Eva told him. 'Where's Sylvie?'

'She's already gone upstairs.' And then in response to Eva's questioning look he added, 'Chas drank too much and Sylvie found her throwing up in the ladies, so she's gone to put her to bed.'

Eva mustered a smirk. 'Ah. Looks like you won't be having a night of passion after all.'

'Looks that way, doesn't it. Unless you're offering to step in and fill the gap.'

'Not me, fella. Far be it from me to try to fill the size twelves of the lovely Chas.' Then, 'Why do you call her Chas, anyway? Bit of an odd name for a girl, isn't it?'

Lucien paused and frowned before finally answering. 'It's short for Chastity, all right. Her name's Chastity.'

A smile spread across Eva's face, wider and wider, until she was unable to stop the laughter from bursting out of her mouth.

'Priceless. Just priceless,' she gasped when she finally managed to take a breath, collapsing into the chair beside Lucien's and heaving with mirth until even he couldn't help but join in, and Eva and Lucien ended the evening of Benedict's wedding side by side beneath the coloured disco lights at the edge of the dance floor, crying with laughter.

12

Docklands, August 2004

Summer in the city: you had to love it. For nine months of the year London was relentlessly grim, but everything about it got better in the sunshine. The light twinkled on the river, sheered off the glass sides of the skyscrapers, and brought pallid, scantily clad city dwellers blinking out into the streets. Chairs and tables sprouted from the pavement outside pubs and cafes, immediately filling up with people sipping wine and nibbling snacks. Even the hazy pall of traffic fumes added a misty beauty to the place, Eva thought fondly as she walked along the riverside towards the gym. Feeling virtuous, she allowed herself a moment of satisfaction with her life. That day, a Saturday, had begun with a wheatgrass smoothie. She had phoned her father and tidied her flat, a smart rental in a converted warehouse with a balcony over the water in up-and-coming Limehouse, just three stops on the DLR or thirty minutes' walk from the office in Canary Wharf.

She'd even scheduled a personal training session at the gym, meaning there was no way to get out of going. Eva was getting the hang of it now, the female banking aesthetic. It was all in the detail. The hair a little lighter, the teeth a little whiter, the skin just bronzed enough to suggest outdoorsy good health but still far short of a couple of weeks in Maga-luf. Of course, all this was quite difficult to achieve when you were spending eighty hours a week at a desk on a huge trading floor so that you barely saw daylight between October and April each year. Big Paul claimed that trading floors were designed that way for the same reason that casinos never have windows: you want your traders and punters to be oblivious to the passage of time. You certainly wouldn't want them noticing that it was getting dark and thinking, *oh well, time to call it a day*, or spotting the sunshine outside and suddenly feeling that breaking for a spot of lunch might be just the ticket.

The other part of the alpha look was of course the gym body, the hardest of all to achieve because of the impossibility of faking it. While a few extra pounds could be considered characterful on a broker, they certainly weren't much in evidence on the female traders. After her last bonus Eva had signed up for a year's membership at the Canary Wharf gym with the subterranean spa and the swimming pool right on the edge of the river, so that as you pounded out your sixty lengths you could pretend you were actually swimming along the Thames, only without the risk of contracting Weil's disease from all the rat urine. Signing the contract had proven highly motivating; unable to bear the thought of the massive monthly subscription fee going to waste, she had sweated her way through spin classes, attempted to find her inner goddess in hatha yoga sessions, and almost given herself a coronary in the aptly named Body Attack, billed as a 'rocket-fuelled combination of music and hip moves'. As she'd lain groaning on the floor at the end of the previous week's class, the instructor had strolled over and peered down at her.

'Should I be calling an ambulance?' he enquired. 'Only I might get fired if I actually hospitalize the clients.'

Lying there gasping for breath in an old Pixies T-shirt and misshapen tracksuit bottoms, Eva looked up at the Lycra-clad vision of male beauty hovering above her, barely perspiring after an hour of savage exercise, and let out an appalled involuntary giggle.

'Well, you can't be dying if you can still laugh at my jokes,' he said, reaching out a hand to pull her up. 'Don't worry, it's a tough class, this one. What you should do is sign up for a few one-on-one sessions with me. You get them as part of your joining package, so if you haven't used them yet, and between you and me I suspect that you haven't . . .' He paused and winked at her. 'Ask at the front desk for them to pop you in Julian's personal training diary.'

'Julian being you.'

'Julian being me. Hi.' He shook the hand he was apparently still holding long after he'd finished using it to haul her upright.

'Hi. Eva,' she told him, withdrawing the hand, which was as embarrassingly hot and sweaty as the rest of her. 'And I may have humiliated myself enough already, thank you. I don't know whether my ego could withstand more scrutiny of my athletic prowess. Or lack thereof,' she continued, but it was beginning to look as though she was losing him so she allowed the gabble to trail off.

'Hey, don't worry about it. If you were an Olympic athlete we'd have nothing to work on, right? Tell them I said to put you in my diary. I'll see you soon then, Eva?'

He was backing away from her now, and doing that thing

where you make your hand into a gun to point at someone, so she smiled and half-nodded, half-shook her head in what she hoped was an ambiguous gesture of possible agreement but almost certainly just made her look like a lunatic. Safely back in the changing room and under a pounding hot shower, she wondered whether he was encouraging her to book a free session with him because he got paid by the hour or whether he might actually have been flirting. Figuring that the worst that could happen was that she got fit and made the most of her gym membership, she found herself standing at the front desk on the way out.

'Does it have to be the weekend?' asked the flicky-haired receptionist, drumming long pink fingernails on the counter.

'Yes, sorry, I work long hours in the week.'

'And it has to be Julian and not one of our other trainers?' Hair flick. 'He's *very* popular you know, particularly among our female clients,' she continued, giving Eva the once-over with a meaningful smile. 'It does make it difficult to find an opening with him.'

*

Having eventually been granted the honour of being booked into Julian's special 5 p.m. reserve slot the following Saturday, Eva had taken herself off to buy some new gym kit, arriving at the checkout with a pair of soft charcoal yoga pants and a sleek black support vest with fluorescent pink panels at the sides. The sales assistant assured her that this was de rigueur for the well-turned-out gym-goer these days and ignored Eva's wince as she rang up the total. Even now that she was making good money by most people's standards, Eva hadn't quite got used to casually spending on a gym outfit what she would have been able to live on for several weeks during her university years.

As she waited for Julian in the reception area, she shuffled about in her new outfit feeling self-conscious and trying to catch a glimpse of herself in the glass cabinet fronts. It had seemed okay in the changing room, but under these unforgiving lights she looked like a sackful of oranges, she thought with a grimace. Not only that, but it was such a drastic transformation from the previous week that he was bound to notice and conclude it was for his benefit, which it most certainly wasn't since they had nothing in common, what with his being a Greek god who spent his days stretching out the hamstrings of perfectly toned gym-bunnies. Yes, she'd been anticipating this session with rather more relish than she'd usually feel at the prospect of exercise, but that was just the inevitable frisson of having some rare one-on-one time with an attractive man, even one in whom she had no romantic interest.

In the three years since Benedict's wedding, Eva's love life had been a barren wasteland, home only to drifting tumbleweed. Most of her time and energy went into her job, and her social life consisted mainly of work events or nights in with a bottle of wine, which was Sylvie's usual preference as she was now working as a receptionist and always skint. Once in a while they got Lucien to put them on the guest list for one of his club nights, but Eva didn't enjoy them much anymore; whether it was watching Lucien seduce his way through an endless supply of pneumatic dancers, or just that it was hard to summon up much enthusiasm for hundred-decibel house music when one preferred not to addle one's brain with pills, the shine had gone off clubbing for Eva.

*

Forty minutes later Eva had long since ceased to fret about her clothing, but only because it was the least of her worries.

'Twenty-four! Twenty-three! Twenty-two! Keep going!' Julian was bellowing at her, counting down from fifty stomach crunches.

'I . . . can't,' she panted, letting the medicine ball slip from her grasp and roll away across the floor.

'You can! Come on, just another few to go! You can do it!'

'No, you don't understand.' Eva collapsed onto the mat. 'I physically can't. I'm telling my body to carry on but it's staging a mutiny.'

'Keep going!' Julian hollered. 'It's all about mind over matter!'

'No, it's bloody not,' she snapped back. 'I've got a bloody physics degree and I'm telling you that my matter is utterly impervious to my mind. You can yell at me as much as you want but it won't change the fact that I can't bloody do it.'

'Oh.' Julian stopped and looked crestfallen and she felt her anger dissipating and being replaced by the urge to ruffle his light brown hair. 'Too much? Am I pushing you too hard? I was just trying to be motivational. And I don't get many clients who can't do a bit more than that, if I'm honest. Well, maybe the odd pensioner.'

She laughed at his cheek. 'Look, it's not you, it's me. I've spent the last five years working on a trading floor in the conditions of a battery chicken and my body has withered.

And I wasn't exactly Linda Hamilton in *Terminator II* to begin with. I think this whole thing may have been a mistake.'

'Please don't give up,' he begged. 'We can take it more slowly. Your pace, I promise. The first session's always the hardest. I have to push you to establish your limits, and now that I know them I can ease up on you. Let's wind down with some assisted stretching and massage, then you'll see it's not all misery.'

At that point she'd have agreed to gnaw off her own limbs if it meant she could stop, so she meekly allowed herself to be led to a mat in an alcove at the rear of the gym, where he ground his elbows into her buttocks 'to release trapped nerves' and then practically lay on top of her to pull and stretch her leg muscles into a sort of agonizing bliss. She had to admit that some of it felt good, but she was far too tense to enjoy it. Lying on the floor sweating profusely under the most attractive man she had ever been within ten metres of was a lot less sexy than she would have imagined. Finally the clock ticked round to the hour and he released her to limp towards the showers. Apparently his day was over too, because he followed her down the stairs to the changing rooms, chatting about the triathlon he had coming up. She was about to scuttle into the ladies' changing room when he put a hand on her arm and said, 'You're not coming back, are you?'

'Um, no. Probably not. I think maybe I'm cut out for more cerebral pursuits. Life of the mind, and all that.'

Julian looked mortified. 'Look what I've done. My job is to make people love exercise and instead I've put you off for life. You must think I'm a total sadist.'

'No, really, it's fine,' Eva stuttered, embarrassed.

'At least let me take you for a drink to make up for it. You're my last client today. Are you free after we shower?'

'You mean like an alcoholic drink? Do you fitness freaks actually do that?'

'Well, not that often, to be honest,' he admitted. 'But I can make an exception this once. You'll come then? That's great! I'll see you out the front in ten, okay?' He bounded away without waiting for her answer.

13

Hampstead, September 2004

'Actually, do you mind if we go to Pizza Express instead?'

Eva and Benedict both turned to look at Lydia in bemusement. They were standing at the entrance to Hampstead tube station, where they had arranged to meet. As Eva had pushed her way out of the lift and through the turnstiles her initial cheer at spotting Benedict's face had turned to surprise as she panned down to the baby snuggled in a carrier against his chest, then finally dissolved into horror as she'd spotted Lydia a few metres away grappling with an enraged toddler, who seemed extremely unhappy about being impeded from hurling himself under the feet of the crowd marching towards the exit. With a show of force from Benedict, the group managed to assemble in front of the ticket machine, shuffling uncomfortably close together each time a glaring traveller needed to purchase a fare.

'Though maybe Giraffe would be better,' Lydia continued. 'They'll have crayons and stickers for Josh. And a kids' menu. Trust me, we'll be in a world of pain if we go to Jin Kichi, there's nothing for little ones and nowhere to put the buggy. We can hardly expect Josh to eat raw fish.'

'I don't eat raw fish either, remember?' parried Eva. Judging by the last thirty seconds, during which Josh had turned his demonic attentions to battering her shins with a plastic digger, they were going to be in a world of pain wherever they went. 'There's plenty of vegetarian stuff on the menu at Jin Kichi.'

Maybe if she stood firm and insisted they go somewhere unsuitable for children Lydia would get the message and decide to take the kids back to Benedict's parents' instead.

Benedict shot her a pleading look. She knew that he hadn't planned this but it still rankled. When he'd suggested lunch she'd assumed he meant the two of them, and had pictured a leisurely afternoon lingering over coffee and catching up with everything that had been happening since they last saw each other almost a year ago. She'd imagined telling him how well her job was going, mentioning the *very* handsome personal trainer she'd been seeing, flirting a little, making him laugh, and generally savouring the bittersweetness of a love affair that never was. She'd hoped it would be . . . was *healing* too strong a word?

Eva had wondered after the wedding whether a clean break might not be best but time had softened the sense of shame and rejection she felt until it was an almost pleasurable sore spot, like pressing a bruise. She and Benedict hadn't spoken for several months afterwards and the first time he'd called it had been a bit strained, but after that he had diligently emailed and phoned every week or two and it hadn't taken long for them to slip back into their old friendship and for her to conclude that her life was the better for having him in it in whatever capacity he could manage.

'I suppose we *could* go somewhere else,' Eva relented after another pleading look from Benedict, who, she couldn't help noticing, appeared tired and rumpled and generally deserving of pity.

They shuffled out of the station and made their way down the high street towards Giraffe, a chain restaurant that Eva normally made a point of avoiding because of the unpleasant preponderance of children. It was a short walk, during which Josh nevertheless managed a couple of passable attempts at hara-kiri by wriggling free and charging towards the traffic at random intervals. They'd only just sat down at a sticky table in the heaving restaurant when Benedict announced that he needed the loo.

'Do you fancy holding Will for a minute?' he asked Eva, not waiting for a response before unfastening the sling and depositing ten pounds of squishy, drooling infant onto her lap. Eva held the baby awkwardly under the arms and looked at it. The baby looked back. He had deep blue eyes and a solemn expression on his face. She forced her face into a smile.

'Well, hello there,' she tried.

Will gazed up at her intently and then broke into a huge gummy smile. Emboldened by this early success, Eva poked out her tongue at the baby, who looked appalled and promptly screwed his face up into a ball of angry wrinkles before turning an improbable shade of puce and emitting a piercing wail.

'How about you, Eva? Getting broody yet?' Lydia shouted above the continuing screams, which by now were competing with the noise of Josh's concerted efforts to demolish his high chair with his truck.

'Strangely not,' Eva shouted back, holding the writhing

infant at arm's length. A pungent smell was now wafting upwards.

'It'll hit you, don't you worry. What are you now, twenty-eight? I give you another two years. So many of my friends said a few years ago when we were having Josh that they didn't want their own, and now they're all procreating like mad.'

Eva's expression grew steely. She was long-accustomed to variations on this speech from supposedly well-meaning acquaintances but it was particularly galling coming from Lydia, who was apparently labouring under the misapprehension that her family was straight out of a Boden catalogue and blissfully unaware that in actual fact Eva couldn't think of a single better advertisement for the judicious use of contraception.

Was she merely being insensitive, or was this an act of passive-aggression intended to underline what Lydia saw as her superior status as wife and mother? Either way, it was just as infuriating as all the other times she'd had to tolerate speculation on when her body clock would kick in. It was surprisingly difficult to deflect the pitying assumption that she was putting a brave face on not having a man to do it with rather than the true reason, which was that she had absolutely no aspirations to join the ranks of breeders stacked into Giraffe on a Saturday. Any idiot could pop out a sprog, while she had a career that most people could only dream of. Plus, it wasn't as though she was sufficiently optimistic about the future of the world to want a stake in it. Having a baby would be like going long human race futures in a position that you had to constantly monitor and could never hedge or close out. That wasn't a trade she'd want on her book.

'I expect your friends changed their minds when they saw your two,' said Eva sarcastically, and then immediately felt mean-spirited when Lydia looked up from trying to prevent Josh hurling the salt cellar onto the floor and beamed at her.

'Eva, what a lovely thing to say. Gorgeous, aren't they? Hard work, obviously, but worth every minute. Don't you worry, your turn will come.'

At that moment Benedict came back to the table and Eva wasted no time in thrusting the yelling baby into his arms.

'Ew, Will ponks a bit, Lydia. Do you mind doing the honours? Give me and Eva a few minutes to catch up?'

'I suppose so. What about you, Josh? Might as well do them both I suppose, while we're somewhere with proper changing facilities.'

Benedict sat down and looked at Eva across the newly silent table. 'Sorry about this,' he said. 'I know it's not what you bargained for but Lydia really wanted to join us. She hasn't seen you in ages, and we're staying with my parents so I think she fancied getting out of the house. My mother's driving her a bit mad with her parenting advice. Which mostly amounts to "why on earth don't you get a nanny?"'

'That's okay, it's nice to meet the new baby,' muttered Eva, sounding as insincere as she felt. 'He looks like you,' she added automatically, having grown accustomed to what was expected of her in these situations.

Benedict's tired face brightened. 'Do you think so?'

Eva grinned. 'Well, if you're going to force me to be honest, mostly he looks like Jabba the Hutt. Have you considered a paternity test?' For a split second she worried that she'd overstepped the mark, but Benedict didn't miss a beat.

'We're booked onto Jerry Springer next week. You can

catch us on the *I Think My Wife was Impregnated by a Gargantuan Space Monster* episode.' He caught her eye and they both laughed, their old rapport returning at last.

'Seriously, though, how's it going with two of the little blighters?' she asked. 'Looks like a handful.'

'Fine, mostly. I'm well aware that it looks like the seventh circle of hell from the outside but so much of it is wonderful. You can't really explain the joys of parenting to non-parents, but they're there and they more than make up for the copious excrement and deadly assaults with diggers. Lydia finds it a bit tough at times, what with living away from friends and family. And my having to work such long hours doesn't help. But it's just the early bit that's hard, when you don't get much sleep. It'll get easier once Will's a bit older.'

'And have you glimpsed any wondrous particles lately?' Eva asked.

'No, we're still a way off firing up the hadron collider. How about you? How's being a Master of the Universe working out?'

'Work's going great. Done a few big trades this year, looking forward to a big bonus.'

'Yes, I've been hearing about those City bonuses,' chirped Lydia, arriving back at the table with the boys. 'It's a bit obscene, isn't it, the way they pay millions to you lot just for shuffling money around when there are people starving in the world? Just don't become one of those awful people who are obsessed with money and status, Eva, whatever you do. There's more to life than making money.'

Eva couldn't believe what she was hearing. She saw Benedict look from her to his wife and back again and open his mouth to say something placatory but she didn't wait for him to speak. 'Well, Lydia, some of us have to work for a living. And I work bloody hard for mine.'

It was Lydia's turn to bridle. 'Yes, well. Raising kids is hard work too. It doesn't come with a big bonus, but then, not everything that counts can be counted. You know who said that? Albert Einstein.'

'For fuck's sake,' Eva blurted out, more forcefully than she'd intended, causing several parents at the surrounding tables to glare at her. 'Those of us who didn't grow up with our own pet pony don't have the luxury of swanning through life pretending that money doesn't matter. It does bloody matter. It dictates where you live, what education you get, whether your cancer is diagnosed before it's the size of a walrus and whether you get a thrombosis flying economy. Yes, there are things that money can't buy, but I'd still rather cry about them in the back of a Mercedes than on a bicycle.' Eva glanced at the mother still tutting at her from the next table and lowered her voice to a growl. 'And by the way, if you understood anything about basic economics you'd know that my bonuses aren't taking money out of other people's pockets. A rising tide lifts all boats. I make money, and then I pay other people to clean my flat, and buy a new jacket that I wouldn't otherwise have bought, and that creates jobs and puts money in the pockets of the people who clean flats and make jackets.'

In the time she'd been speaking, Lydia's expression had progressed from shock to defensiveness to grim-faced rage. Had she gone too far? Benedict leant back from the table, perhaps bracing himself for Lydia's response, but this time Josh beat her to it.

'Forfucksake,' he shouted joyfully, and hurled the salt cellar onto the floor where it shattered into tiny pieces.

*

'So that went rather well, I thought,' said Eva sheepishly as she said goodbye to Benedict in the street outside the restaurant after the most interminably long lunch of her life.

'You think?' he asked. 'I mean, you only managed to mortally offend Lydia and teach Josh his first swear word, which, if I know my son at all, will be his absolute favourite word from here on in. If you really wanted to be sure I didn't turn up for lunch with my family again you should have gone for the hat-trick and shown Will how to stick a fork in a plug socket.' He grinned, but also glanced nervously over his shoulder to where Lydia was herding Josh out into the street to join them. 'Are you walking back up to the station?'

'No, I think I'm going to stay and do some shopping. Cheerio then!' Before Lydia had a chance to reach them, Eva bustled off down the high street with a jaunty wave and darted round the next corner into an alleyway, where she remained gently and repeatedly banging her forehead against the side of a building for the several minutes it took for her to be certain the coast was clear.

14

Docklands, March 2005

Eva put down her bag in the hallway and closed the door quietly behind her so as not to wake Julian. She didn't feel as bad as she could have done, a little bleary perhaps, but she could definitely have been excused for feeling worse. She'd managed to sleep on the plane and in the taxi from the airport so that helped, and of course there was a certain amount of euphoria at the trip having been so successful. Eleven client meetings in six countries in eight days was close to the limits of human endurance, but it was finally over and she was pretty sure she had set up a decent pipeline of trades for the year, meaning a decent bonus with a bit of luck. That would be good news professionally, and helped to ease her mind about the ridiculous amount she had spent on this place.

This place, her new home, was a penthouse in a tower in Docklands with an impressive view of the east London skyline and beyond. Big Paul and Sylvie had both said she was crazy spending such an enormous sum on a new-build in Docklands, but she considered it a sanctuary, an investment that enabled her to keep doing such a demanding job. Of course, she needed the job to pay the mortgage so in one sense the argument was circular, but still. Most of the men at her level of seniority had wives who did their laundry, stocked their fridges and bought their mothers' birthday gifts, leaving them free to concentrate on making the big bucks. Eva didn't have a wife but she did have the apartment, and she felt a far more sensual connection with it than she suspected half of those men did with their spouses. She ran her fingers over the Corian worktop, sank her stockinged feet into the deep pile of the rug and then stepped onto the terrace and looked out over the city, its buildings gently blurred by the evaporating vestiges of last night's mist.

The apartment (she'd taken on the Americanism and no longer called it a flat, a word redolent of council estates) was designed specifically for people like her, short on time and long on cash. You could actually order room service, proper meals on china that you didn't even have to wash up. There was a laundry service, and she'd given the concierge a key so that her washing simply disappeared and then reappeared a day later hanging in her walk-in wardrobe, perfectly pressed. The concierge service didn't quite stretch to buying her mother a birthday gift but then, she didn't have a mother, and her father barely knew when his own birthday was. In any case, there were plenty of high-end shops in the commercial precinct willing to wrap anonymous trinkets with expensive-looking ribbons when the occasion called for it, and she could reach them through a tunnel from her building without ever having to set foot outside in the open air.

Eva glanced at the clock: 6 a.m. Better grab a couple of hours' sleep and then head into the office. She checked her phone and groaned when she saw she had four voicemails, two work calls and two messages from Sylvie, who sounded dejected. Eva felt a pang of guilt. She hadn't had an awful lot of time to spend with her friend lately, what with the demands of her job and her boyfriend, and whenever they did get together these days the disparity in the success they were each having in realizing their dreams was an unspoken barrier between them. While Eva's career trajectory had been little less than meteoric, Sylvie's was resolutely earthbound. Over the last five years her increasingly desperate attempts to earn a living had seen her working as a casino croupier, a drug-testing guinea pig and very nearly a lap dancer at one point, which Eva had only just managed to talk her out of by insisting on buying several of her paintings at grossly inflated prices, claiming that they were a sound investment in a great artist.

Eva wasn't being entirely disingenuous; she always had believed in Sylvie's talent, she just no longer believed that talent was always recognized and rewarded. The first time she'd gone back to Sylvie's room in halls a couple of weeks after she'd arrived in Bristol she had been agog at the canvases and portfolio books stacked against every wall. Sylvie's sheer obsessive devotion had astonished her and made her wonder whether something similar was lacking in her own make-up. The room was dominated by a large canvas on an easel in the corner, a detailed study of a face which at the time she didn't know to be Lucien's. Eva had been even more impressed by a meticulous pencil drawing of a snake coiled around the branch of a tree, with each individual scale picked out and the texture of the tree's bark so intricately rendered that it defied the viewer to believe that the page was flat. Sylvie had dismissed that picture as showing off, a mere technical exercise, but Eva remained in awe of her ability to sit down in front of a blank sheet of paper and create something so lifelike with nothing more than a pencil.

Now both of these pictures as well as several other original Sylvie Marchants adorned Eva's walls, and she enjoyed holding forth to visitors about her friend the up-and-coming artist. True, she wasn't certain that having a painting of Lucien on her wall was entirely psychologically healthy, but she honestly felt it was one of Sylvie's best and in occasional maudlin moments told herself that it was a good reminder that being too trusting often meant making an idiot of yourself.

Still, in these days of pickled sharks and soiled bedclothes, Sylvie's oil-on-canvas had few cheerleaders. Eva had always loved her work, but then, it wasn't really her field of expertise. Even Sylvie had called her 'parochial' and 'overliteral' when she'd laughed at Sylvie's description of a painting of a house in a storm as a self-portrait.

There had been a few flares of hope over the years, in particular the show at a Hoxton gallery just around the corner from White Cube, which Eva had felt certain would be the start of something big. In the event the private view had degenerated into a melancholy evening in which she and Sylvie had hoovered up the excessive quantities of cheap wine left over after the last of a meagre handful of punters had passed through.

*

Eva undressed and padded through to the bedroom, where the curtains were letting in just enough light for her to see that Julian was fast asleep with his legs tangled up in the sheet. Stumbling over his jeans in the gloom, she reflected grumpily that she might as well let him move in properly if having his own cupboard would mean he wouldn't throw his stuff on the floor. They'd been together for about seven months and he was starting to make increasingly insistent noises about living together, and her generally making more room in her life for him.

She stood for a moment admiring his sleeping form in the dim light. In the early days of the relationship she had basked in the envy of other women and felt flattered that someone like him would fall for someone like her. A solid seven with plenty of make-up on, Big Paul had once teased her after several drinks, and though she'd retaliated with a furious torrent of insults centring on his own expanding belly and receding hairline, afterwards she admitted to herself that she couldn't honestly disagree with his assessment.

Still, the full effect of Julian's looks wore off after a while. Eva wasn't the first girlfriend he'd met at the gym, he'd admitted sulkily when they'd eventually had 'the conversation' about their sexual histories, and though he clearly didn't want to talk about it at length she gleaned enough information to suspect that more than one had viewed him as a quick fling and then dumped him once they'd shown him off to their friends.

Eva slipped into bed beside him and he stirred and rolled towards her.

'I missed you,' he mumbled sleepily, throwing a warm, heavy arm across her and tugging her towards his side of the bed. 'Come here, you little minky.'

Eva cringed internally. This was a recent and wholly undesirable development. She wasn't actually sure what a minky was, some bastard chimera of 'minx' and 'sweetie' she presumed, but she was very sure that she didn't want to be called either of those things, and she was absolutely certain that the place in the world that she least wanted to be called them was in bed.

'I *said*, get over here, my minky-minky,' he said, moving his weight on top of her just as she felt every last ounce of sexual desire drain out of her body.

'Mm, not now, babe. I'm exhausted and I've just got time for a bit of sleep before I head into the office for a meeting.'

It was true; she was exhausted. But somewhere at the back of her mind lurked the uneasy truth that for the first few months of the relationship she had found ways to make time for sex, and it had always taken precedence over her tiredness. A brush of the hand had been enough to send them hurtling towards the bedroom (or the kitchen or, on one particularly daring occasion, the balcony) at every opportunity in the early days. But you couldn't survive on caffeine and lust forever.

*

Of course, she reflected as she levered herself out of her now empty bed a couple of hours later, it was inevitable that any relationship would calm down a bit after the initial shag-fest. It didn't mean he wasn't the right man for her. There were still the days when he turned up on her doorstep wearing that old grey T-shirt, with his hair tousled and damp from the shower and holding a flower he'd picked for her on the way over between his teeth, and she'd think, why wouldn't I want him to move in with me? She wasn't always certain she loved him, not exactly, but what was love anyway? The intense, almost obsessional passion she had once felt for Lucien? That could hardly be the foundation of a functioning adult relationship. Or the painful sense of loss that had been present in her life ever since Benedict had got married, fading, true, but never quite disappearing? Much good that had done her. And it wasn't as if there was a queue of eligible men at her door clamouring to make her life complete.

No, relationships were a compromise and the people who were prepared to compromise were the ones who didn't end up dying alone and being eaten by their cats. Benedict, for instance, had almost certainly compromised: she doubted that he'd been in love with Lydia at the outset but he had got her pregnant, married her, and was now, judging by his occasional emails, perfectly content. Could she be happy with Julian?

She wished she could talk to Benedict about all this, ask him if he really was happy and what he thought she should do, but they hadn't spoken much lately. Things had been awkward since that disastrous lunch with Lydia and the kids; he'd mentioned being in London a number of times since, but with Lydia in tow neither of them really fancied meeting up. She hoped he'd be over on his own sometime soon, so that they could get together and have a good laugh about the awfulness of that lunch and smooth things over properly. Putting things right was hard to do by email, and whenever she phoned it was clear from the slight but detectable stiltedness in his voice that Lydia was within earshot. Still, at least she could talk things over with Sylvie. Eva picked up the phone and dialled.

'Hi, this is Sylvie Marchant. Leave a message.'

'Sylvie, it's me, Eva. Sorry, I only just arrived back from my trip and got your voicemail. Let's meet up tonight, somewhere near my work if that's okay. Say seven thirty in Smollensky's?'

15

Docklands, March 2005

Eva was running late, as usual. Sylvie sat scraping the remainder of a layer of chipped blue varnish off one of her fingernails with a broken cocktail stick, then finished her second extortionately priced glass of wine and ordered another. She didn't know why she bothered sometimes. What she should do was give Eva a taste of her own medicine, stop phoning her until she wised up and realized that she needed to be a bit more considerate and put a bit more effort into the friendship. But if she did that, it would probably be at least a year before Eva even noticed, Sylvie thought bitterly. She was feeling increasingly like a small adjunct to her friend's life, an inconvenient scheduling problem. Everything always had to be on Eva's terms these days: do you mind coming up my way, are you free to get together in this ten-minute slot between my leaving my extremely important job and tumbling into bed with my ridiculously good-looking boyfriend? Okay, so Sylvie herself was between jobs again and had a bit more flexibility, and yes, Eva would probably pick up the tab for the evening, but was it really too much to ask for her best friend to consider the way it all made her *feel*?

God, you sound like a teenager, she chided herself. *No one understands me.* But it wasn't really surprising that she sounded like a teenager, seeing as how she was practically living like one despite having turned twenty-nine a few months earlier. Sylvie didn't have much to show for adult life so far. No husband, no kids, no career, no mortgage. Ten years ago that would have sounded like a good thing, a sign that she hadn't been sucked into conforming to society, so why was she beginning to feel as if she had taken a wrong turn somewhere along the line? These thoughts were enough to make Sylvie take another big gulp of her wine and start to wonder whether to order yet another drink, when at last Eva glided in through the glass doors.

'Finally,' she said as Eva reached the table. 'You're only fifty minutes late.'

'Sorry, I got stuck in a meeting. Thanks for waiting.'

'I didn't have much choice, did I? Seeing as it took an hour and cost six quid to get here on the Tube.'

'Okay, I get it. I'm late. I'm sorry.' Eva threw her jacket over the back of the chair next to her and sat down. 'How's it going?'

'Well, I just got fired from a job scraping chewing gum off school desks and I'm thinking of selling a kidney to make the rent. But apart from that, tickety-boo.'

'That bad, huh? Let me know if you need me to help you out again this month.'

'Nah. It's all life experience. It will feed my art and give me something to talk about in interviews once I'm famous. I'll have a ready supply of anecdotes about clambering over piles of unconscious junkies to get to the front door of the squat I'm going to end up living in.'

In truth Sylvie had long since given up the notion that adversity was the soil in which talent grew. What looked like glamorous squalor from a distance had turned out to be grindingly unpleasant to live day to day, and most of her twenties had been spent in the grey-hued no-man's-land between poverty and the level of financial security needed to stave off anxiety for long enough to flourish. Just having a stable place to live would have helped. She'd been longing for that since she was a child and now here she was, a fully grown adult, moving from one dodgy flatshare to another. It had become impossible to afford a decent place to live in London and paid work was getting harder to find. For anything more than a shop job she was up against all the people who'd got it right first time around, years younger and with all the optimism and confidence that life had already sucked out of her. Sylvie couldn't compete with that.

Was it London, though, or was it just her? She looked around at the other people in the bar, men and women in their twenties wearing suits and greeting one another with kisses and loud laughter and giving every appearance of thriving. Not everyone was having the same problems that she was. Take Eva. She had landed on her feet with her job and had spent some obscene amount of money on a horrible soulless flat that looked like a hotel room. Sylvie cringed every time she saw her own pictures on the walls of that flat, but at least Eva had a home, money, a job. Look at her now, casually raising a hand to attract the attention of an aproned waiter.

'Can I get . . . ?' Eva looked over at Sylvie.

'A bottle of the pinot grigio.'

'. . . and a Badoit over here, please?'

How times have changed, thought Sylvie. If you'd told her when they were at university that Eva would be there in her tailored suit waving down waiters and asking for mineral water by brand with practised confidence, she'd have laughed. Sylvie had always been the one who got most of the attention, and it had been all she could do to prise her friend out of her Doc Martens now and again. Did the fact that Eva had changed so much and Sylvie hadn't mean that Eva was inauthentic, a fake, or just that Sylvie was getting left behind, a loser who had failed to move on and carve out any sort of a coherent adult life for herself? Okay, there was the art, but really, what was the point if no one wanted to buy it? You could only get by for so long convincing yourself of your unrecognized talent, telling yourself that the whole world was wrong and you were right.

'There's something I wanted to talk to you about,' Eva was saying, interrupting her train of thought.

The waiter returned with the bottle of wine and two glasses but Eva held a hand over the top of hers.

Sylvie frowned. 'You're not drinking? Why did you let me order a bottle?'

'I figured you'd get through it. I'm sticking to water tonight. I'm a bit jet-lagged and I've got work in the morning.'

This was just another sign of where she sat on Eva's priority list. She couldn't even be arsed to have a drink with her. She would deign to spare her an hour or two, but only if she could be in and out as though it had never happened, with no hint of a hangover to interfere with her precious job afterwards. This was a new low, even for goodie-goodie corporate Eva. Unless . . .

'Oh God. You're not pregnant are you? You are, look at you! That's what you want to talk to me about, isn't it?'

Eva looked straight at her friend with a deadpan expression. 'Yes, Sylvie, I'm pregnant. With a massive food-baby.'

'Shit, sorry. I didn't mean you looked fat. It would make sense, that's all. What with needing to talk to me about something and not drinking. And you have to admit you've put on a few pounds lately.'

'I've put on a few pounds because I work fourteen hours a day and the only way to get through it is with junk food and sugar highs. I don't need you to remind me I'm overweight, I get enough of Julian hinting that I should work out more.'

'Well, you should make the most of having a personal trainer for a boyfriend.'

'I do, but in other ways.' Eva attempted a half-hearted leer, and then gave up and sighed. 'I mean, obviously he's *very* hot, and we do have fun together, but he's pressing me to let him move in properly and I can't put off a decision much longer. That's what I wanted to get your advice on, really. I mean, it makes sense. He's so lovely and he practically lives at my place already. It's just that I sometimes wonder whether there's a spark missing. And . . . I suppose there's a bit of me that's always felt like I was waiting for Benedict.'

'Benedict?' Sylvie hitched an eyebrow upwards a couple of notches. 'Eva, he's married. To Lydia. I thought you put this to bed before the wedding? Didn't you ask him to give things a go before he got married and he chose her? I know you were upset at the time, but I thought you'd got over it long ago.'

'I did. I had. But the thing is . . . I suppose in the back of my mind there's always been the thought that maybe he and Lydia wouldn't last, and that when they broke up we would have a chance to be together.'

'It's a long shot, though, isn't it? I mean, it's been what, four years? And they've got kids.'

'I know. I wasn't really thinking this stuff consciously, it's just always been lurking there, the knowledge that I've never met anyone else I could be as close to as Benedict, and I took him for granted because I was young and stupid. And now I have to decide whether to commit to Julian, and I want to but it means letting go, properly letting go of the idea that Benedict and I will ever be together. It just feels so final.'

'Steady on. He only wants to move in with you, right?'

'Well, yes, for now. I mean, if it was just that I could handle it, but it never stops there, does it? After that comes marriage and kids. Either that or you break up, which is much harder if you live together, and I'm just not sure I want to do any of those things.'

'Do you even have to worry about that now? Can't you just try living together and see what happens?'

'There's no point ignoring the inevitable, though. This stuff has consequences.'

'Christ, I don't know. There's no way of knowing, is there? You just have to decide whether you want to try it and then see how it goes.'

'Yeah, well, I'd like to have thought it through properly before I "see how it goes".' Eva laughed. 'Never mind, I know it's not really your scene.'

'How do you mean, not my scene?' Sylvie didn't join in

the laughter, but Eva didn't seem to notice the edge to her voice.

'Well, it's not your cup of tea, is it, all of this? Cohabitation, commitment and so on. Now, if I wanted to decide whether to have a bunk-up with the barman I'd know who to ask.'

Sylvie could feel the wine sloshing in her stomach like a ball of acid. 'When did you become so fucking smug?'

Eva's eyes widened. 'Are you kidding? It was just a joke.'

'Do I look like I'm kidding? I may actually have to stab myself in the face with this fork if I have to listen to your ridiculous problems a moment longer. "Oh no, my super-hot boyfriend wants to move into my million-pound apartment but I'm worried he might be too nice to me."'

'What on earth brought this on? I'm only saying that casual sex is more your field than committed relationships. It's nothing you haven't said yourself a thousand times before, but suddenly I can't say it? Suddenly you're jealous of my relationship?'

'Jealous? I'm not jealous.' Sylvie slammed down her glass, spilling a puddle of wine onto the table, where it soaked into her sleeve unnoticed. 'This is exactly what I mean about you being smug. Smug and self-centred. You love it now that you're on top and I'm your charity case instead of you being the gawky sidekick.'

'What the actual fuck?' Eva stared at her, open-mouthed. 'Your gawky sidekick? That's how you see me? And now you think I'm getting ideas above my station, is that it?'

'Well, you were hardly the Fonz, were you, when we first met? I introduced you to people, took you to parties. Back in the day, your idea of a good time was a lager top and a chat about relativity. But it was still better than the money-obsessed corporate clone you've turned into.' Her voice was loud and spiteful, and the couple on the table behind them fell silent and turned to stare.

Eva blinked. 'Are we even friends anymore, Sylvie? I know you're not happy with your life, but it's not my fault and there's no point resenting me for making a success of mine. I've worked hard for what I've got while you swanned about being all bohemian. I don't think you ever really appreciated how tough and lonely it was for me. You always had Lucien, and pretty much any man you wanted for a roll in the hay.

'So yes, fine, I used to be the gawky sidekick and no one looked at me and I'm not surprised that you don't like the fact that things have changed but that's how it is, so get used to it. I've tried with you, I really have. I pay for every-thing and spend about as much time with you as I do with my own boyfriend, and you're still always miserable.' Eva paused and waited for Sylvie to respond but she was staring pointedly out of the window. 'What I don't understand is, if you hate everything you think I stand for, the corporate world and material possessions and consumer society, why are you even still friends with me? And if you're so unhappy with your own life, why don't you think about changing it instead of sitting around resenting everyone else?' Eva stood up, reached into her purse and threw a couple of twenties on the table. 'I'm sure you'll have no trouble finishing that bottle on your own. I've got an actual life that I need to get back to.'

★

Walking home, Eva was half surprised to find that she was crying. It was indignation as much as hurt, she told herself. What Sylvie had said was just so *unfair*. Eva had always wanted nothing but the best for Sylvie, but it was impossible to help someone who refused to face up to reality.

She'd been right about one thing, though: Eva was crazy to agonize over the good things in her life. In a world where even her oldest friend could be that spiteful to her, having at least one person she could count on was crucial. What was she waiting for? Why wouldn't she want her devoted, gorgeous boyfriend to move in with her? There wasn't going to be a thunderbolt, but what she and Julian had together was pretty damn good. Sylvie can say as many horrible things as she likes about me, thought Eva, but at least I'm not the one going home on my own tonight.

⋆

As it happened, Sylvie didn't go home on her own that night. Just as Eva had suggested, she stayed and finished the bottle, and once it was finished she sat at the bar and chatted up the barman, who slipped her a free drink every time the manager wasn't looking. When his shift was over she went back with him to his flat in Canning Town and when she woke the next morning she had to slide her hand between her legs for the slimy, clotted confirmation that yes, they'd had sex and no, he hadn't used a condom. She managed to dress and sneak out without waking him, pausing only to vomit as quietly as possible in the kitchen sink on the way to the front door.

16

London and Languedoc, June 2005

After Phil the barman there had been Asif, then Clive, and then Piotr. There had been the sweet guy who had taken weeks to get the message and stop phoning her, and the not-so-sweet one with the whole, 'Oops, sorry, wrong hole,' routine. There had been the guy who'd panted, 'Call me daddy, call me daddy,' until she'd had to stop him and explain that while she was for the most part happy to call him whatever he wanted, she had to draw the line at anything that hinted at their being more closely related than, say, very distant cousins well above the age of consent.

A pattern quickly emerged, a cycle of about a week in which Sylvie went out with whoever was up for it, drank far too much and went home with whoever was still standing at the end of the night, then lapsed into a sort of psychotic depression in which she couldn't even face answering the phone. After four or five days it would lift a little, and she would think about all the changes she needed to make to her life and resolve to make them. By Friday or Saturday she would feel up to celebrating her fresh start with two or three drinks. But she would finish drink number three at 9 p.m., and what was she supposed to do then, go home and sit in her room on her own, half-cut? She needed to find a third way, a middle ground between total excess and having to become a hermit. So a fourth drink could be justified but maybe not a fifth, but then after the fourth drink she found herself feeling like the old devil-may-care Sylvie again, and besides, wasn't it someone else's round?

And on it went, week after week and month after month, until early one Sunday morning when she got back to her flatshare in Hackney and found herself standing in the bathroom in front of the stained avocado sink and looking at her yellow, baggy-eyed face in the mirror, and was suddenly so filled with self-loathing that the urge to slam her forehead into her reflection was overwhelming. The first impact didn't hurt but it also didn't break the mirror, she couldn't even do that properly, and that thought made the rage surge up even more strongly inside her, so she did it again and then again, harder and harder, until it finally smashed, leaving a constellation of cuts on her forehead that bled down her face and into her eyes. Then she got into bed and stayed there all day.

The next morning the bedding was cold and sodden with urine and her forehead really hurt. When she gingerly pressed her fingertips against it she could feel something hard under the skin. Sylvie waited until she heard her flatmates leave and then got up to examine the damage, but she couldn't see much because only a few shards of the mirror remained stuck to the wall. She put on her biggest, baggiest hoodie and sunglasses and walked to A&E at Homerton Hospital, where a tired-looking young doctor picked out the shards of glass with a pair of tweezers and put in a couple of stitches.

'Do you want to tell me how this happened?'

'I slipped. In the bathroom. Wet floor. Went face first into the mirror.'

'That doesn't explain why you waited so long to come in, though. I can tell you this: he's not worth it, whoever he is. Even if you don't want to file a complaint with the police, I can refer you to support services or give you a number for a women's refuge.'

'Honestly, it wasn't a guy who did this to me.'

The doctor shrugged. 'Well, the help's there if you want it, all we can do is offer. Hope I don't see you next time, that's all.' He snipped the end off the final stitch. 'Wait here and a nurse will be along with some antibiotics and your discharge form.'

Sylvie sat and watched the cubicle curtain flap gently behind him and then fall still. How come you never saw that exact shade of green anywhere other than a hospital, she wondered. Was it because it had become so deeply associated with hospitals and illness that no one wanted to use it anywhere else? And also, what had happened to her life?

*

When she got home, she phoned her grandfather in France and when he picked up she found that she couldn't speak, only cry, and so she sat on the floor in the hallway crying until he realized who it was and then they spent half an hour like that, her sobbing and Papi crooning French platitudes that she half remembered from childhood but didn't really understand anymore, and at the end of the conversation when she could speak again they agreed that she would pack her things and give notice on the flatshare and go and spend the summer in the Languedoc, and then they could decide together what to do.

*

Once she had made the call Sylvie didn't know why she hadn't done it sooner. She'd been so desperate for a way out and yet it had seemed impossible to risk losing face by asking for help. In the months since their row, she hadn't heard a word from Eva. She hadn't wanted to explain about the men to her brother, and though she'd half hoped Benedict would call he hadn't for ages and, anyway, the problems she had now weren't the sort of thing he'd understand. At university things had been different; they'd all seen one another nearly every day, so someone would always notice if you were struggling, and they were all living the same sort of lives so their differences hadn't seemed to matter. It had been the happiest time of her life, she realized now: a stable home, a network of friends around her, a future full of hope and possibility. Now those hopes and possibilities had fallen away one by one, and she was alone and adrift in a city that felt more hostile every day. She should have recognized sooner that it was time to get out. Sylvie could feel the weight lifting from her even as she packed up her stuff and made her way round to Lucien's to tell him she was going.

She hadn't seen him for weeks, since she didn't like to go drinking with him because he tended to scare off any man who tried to talk to her, and anyway, he was busy with his club nights at weekends. He opened the door in his boxer shorts, yawning even though it was three in the afternoon.

'Come on in. Jeez, sis, what happened to your face? You look like shit.'

Sylvie picked her way over to the sofa across a dense carpet of empty beer bottles, overflowing ashtrays and CD cases encrusted with powdery residue.

'Accident. Really. I'm not kidding, it was honestly an accident,' she repeated when he looked at her with narrowed eyes. 'I was drunk, I tripped and went face first into a mirror. Anyway, you don't look so great yourself.'

'Yeah, well. I had a big night last night. It's my job, remember.' He lowered himself into a chair, rubbing his bloodshot eyes.

'How are you doing? Really, I mean?' she asked.

'Fine. What's up? Not that it isn't always a delight to see you, but I'm feeling a bit jaded and you haven't been over for ages.'

'I know. I haven't been feeling great lately. To tell you the truth, I've been a bit of a wreck. I'm going to spend the summer with Papi and Mamie, try to sort myself out a bit.'

He looked up, surprised. 'What's been happening? Why didn't you tell me? I'd have helped you out. I know the job thing's been getting you down for a while but I didn't know things were bad enough for you to exile yourself to rural France with the relics.'

'I'm sorry. I haven't been talking to anyone really, just drinking myself into oblivion. It's all got pretty bad and I need a break, need to get away. I'll be back after the summer. Or maybe I won't. I need a plan, Lucien, a proper long-term plan for my life.' At that moment she noticed a trickle of blood making its way from his nostril towards his upper lip. 'Your nose is bleeding. Here.' She handed him a tissue from her pocket and he swiped it across his upper lip before discarding it on the floor.

'Sounds heavy. But whatever you need, sis. You know where I am. You can always come and stay here for a bit when you get back.'

She looked at him closely. 'Listen, Lucien, why don't you come with me? You've been caning it for quite a while now, and you're not looking great.'

'I'm doing just fine, thank you.' He sounded tetchy. 'Bought myself a new car yesterday as a matter of fact, a BMW. There's nothing wrong with me. Besides, that's the last place I'd go if I wanted to clean up. Do you remember how the old bastard thrashed me after I smashed that window in his precious greenhouse when we were kids?'

Sylvie sighed. 'Yes, and I don't think he should have done that but it was a long time ago. When I look back now, my happiest childhood memories were of the summers we spent with them. Which is weird, because remember how much we used to complain about how boring it was there?'

'Yeah. Because it *was* boring. And if those are your happiest memories it just means that being bored was marginally better than being miserable.'

'Well, I'm miserable now, so I guess I'm ready to trade it in for a dose of boredom. I know they weren't perfect, but there aren't that many people in the world who are there to help you out when you're on the ropes. You don't get to choose your family, you just make the best of what you've got.'

'Don't I know it, sis.' Lucien jumped onto the sofa beside her and pulled her into a headlock, dragging his knuckles across her skull until she screamed and wriggled away laughing. They settled back on either end of the sofa as the laughter subsided and a quiet came over them.

'You're right,' said Lucien suddenly. 'I do need to get myself together a bit. Lay off the blow a bit more.'

'Why don't you come with me then? Seriously.'

'Look, Sylvie, I know we don't have much in the way of family, but I just don't see it the way you do. For me it's way past the time when I could have done with their help. If they wanted to help me out they could have done it any time in the first fifteen years of my life. Anyway, I honestly don't need it now. I'm doing all right.'

'So long as you're sure you're really okay.'

'Haven't I always been here for you? You go and do what you need to do and I'll be right here when you get back.'

He pulled her up off the sofa and engulfed her in a hug, then pushed her towards the door.

*

I've made a terrible mistake, Sylvie thought to herself a thousand times a day. It was too hot, there were too many insects, the sun was too bright and scorched her skin, her eyes, her soul. Papi and Mamie were gentle but watchful. The first night she drank two bottles of wine and after that there had been no more wine in the house, and though she woke every morning with a clear head, as evening approached she felt restless and stunted and had to go out for long walks just to quell the urge to scream into the still darkness. They were miles from the nearest town, and Papi and Mamie drove there only once a week to do the shopping, so she couldn't have laid her hands on any booze even if she'd wanted to. She wondered how they didn't go mad without anything to drink or any company or even a TV. She herself cycled between being agitated and enervated, pacing and lying limply on the sofa. She'd stay for a few weeks and then leave, she told herself over and over again.

Then, during the third week, at the end of which she had decided it would be possible to go without appearing too rude and ungrateful, something began to change. Life began to get easier, almost imperceptibly at first, and then distinctly and noticeably as the periods in which she felt calm grew longer and longer. The days had an irresistible rhythm to them. Each morning, she woke early and walked down into the valley before the sun had fully risen. Where her surroundings had seemed oppressively still and quiet at first, she now found herself tuning in to more subtle sounds and movements, leaves stroked by the breeze, drifting butter-flies, warbling birdsong. Some days Papi walked with her, and though he slowed her down and quickly got tired so that they had to turn back much sooner than she would have done alone, she enjoyed his company. He was quick to point out and name some of the creatures they came across, the two-tailed pasha butterfly, the ocellated lizard, and as a spe-cial treat one morning, a short-toed eagle overhead.

During the day she helped with the laborious housework that was still carried out with little electronic intervention, sweeping floors and washing clothes by hand. When she wasn't doing chores, she was working her way through the eclectic selection of paperbacks that Mamie picked up for her in the second-hand bookshop in town. She read everything from P. G. Wodehouse to Jilly Cooper, eventually resorting to slowly ploughing through a battered copy of Albert Camus's *L'Été* with her rusty French when she'd run out of English books. In the last essay in the book, 'Retour à Tipasa', Camus returned to the Algiers of his childhood to wander among the Roman ruins and reflect on his life. One passage in particular kept niggling at her, so she sat down with a pen and translated it properly:

It seemed as if the morning were motionless, the sun stopped for an incalculable moment. In this light and this silence, the years of rage and night melted away. I heard in myself an almost forgotten sound as though my heart, long since stopped, began to softly beat again. Now awake, I recognized one by one the imperceptible sounds that made up the silence: the birdsong, the faint sigh of the sea at the foot of the rocks, the vibrations of the trees, the blind singing of the columns, the swish of the wormwood plants, the furtive lizards. I heard these noises, and listened also to the waves of joy rising within me. It felt as if I had finally returned to harbour, for a moment at least, and that this moment would never end. Soon after, though, the sun rose visibly by a degree in the sky. A magpie sang a brief prelude and at once the songs of other birds burst forth from all around me with energy, jubilation, joyful discordance, an infinite rapture. The day started up again.

She viscerally understood what he said about the light, the silence, the melting away of wrath and night. Was it ridiculously lofty to compare herself to Camus? He was writing about Europe after two wars whereas she was drying out at her grandparents after a drinking binge, but then again, weren't they both living lives shaped by forces greater than themselves? She lived in a time of great freedom, true, but also a time in which house prices, globalization, the threat of war and terrorism, pressed down hard on people. Art and music had mostly been replaced by shallow facsimiles of the real thing, she felt, ruled by markets and commercial imperatives rather than passion or anger or a thirst to reflect the world back at itself in a way that might change it. Wasn't she united with Camus by a longing for beauty, a search for a lost piece of their youth and innocence, just as all humans were? She went back to the essay and read it aloud to herself.

> I discovered once again at Tipasa that one needs to keep in oneself a freshness, a source of joy, to love the day that escapes injustice, and to return to battle having won the light. I found here an ancient beauty, a young sky, and I measured my luck, understanding, finally, that in the worst years of our madness the memory of this sky had never left me.

*

Late in the afternoon as the sun grew cooler, she would help Papi in the garden, learning how to tend the vegetable plot, before eating dinner and going to bed not long after dusk. She was surprised how easily she was thrown back into memories of childhood summers there, by the scent of her grandmother's lavender talcum powder in the bathroom, or the way the light trickled through the panes of blue stained glass in the porch. The sky here had never left her.

By the end of August Sylvie felt strangely both older and younger than she had when she'd arrived. She had brought no art supplies with her, and was full of the sort of urgent creative energy that she hadn't experienced in a long time. But she sensed, too, a stillness inside of her. She knew she couldn't stay forever, but she felt like she had gathered enough strength to go back and start over.

On the morning she was due to leave, she rose early and, still in her nightie, stepped out through the door that led directly from her bedroom to the garden. Mamie was sitting in a deckchair under the apricot tree at the far end and, spotting her, waved her over. Sylvie picked her way barefoot across the patchy, dried-out grass and sat on the ground next to her. Mamie reached down a hand and touched her hair.

'You look better than you did when you came, Sylvie. You can hardly see that mark on your forehead now. Do you feel better now?'

'Yes, I do. Much better. I just really, really needed a break from London. Thanks for giving me somewhere to escape to.'

'You know that London will be the same when you go back, don't you? If you want things to be different then you will have to be different, because the city, the people, they won't have changed.'

Her grandmother's voice was quiet and whispery, and sounded to Sylvie like leaves falling through the air from the tree above them.

'I know that. I know I'm going to have to work hard not to fall into the same traps again, but I feel strong enough to do that now.'

Mamie leant her head back and looked up into the branches and was quiet for a few minutes, so that when she spoke again it gave Sylvie a jolt. 'Sometimes I wish we had done more for you and your brother. Virginie was never a happy person, and I don't think she has been a very good mother to you. I don't know why she was never satisfied.

Some people are born that way, I think, and too much drink isn't good for anyone. We thought that if we gave her money or took over and looked after you children then she wouldn't bother to find her own way in the world, so we tried to encourage her to take responsibility. I wish we had let her send you and Lucien here after she left your father. But we did what we thought was best. I want you to know that.'

Sylvie blinked at her grandmother. They'd never had a conversation like this before and if she'd thought about it at all, she would have assumed that Mamie didn't reflect on such things.

'I know. Thanks.' She reached up and took the dry old hand that was still resting on her hair and squeezed it.

Then, as suddenly as it had arrived, the moment passed. Mamie stretched her arms and looked away.

'Now go and pack your things. Papi won't want to be kept waiting to drive you to the station.'

17

London, Autumn 2005

It was just as her grandmother had said: London was the same, but she was different. Or rather, London was changing with the seasons, as even cities must. A chill was creeping into the air and the leaves formed sodden heaps on the pavement, giving off an earthy scent as Sylvie ploughed through them, smashing the bigger piles with her boots when she thought no one was looking.

She stayed with Lucien for the first few weeks after she arrived back, but it quickly became clear that wasn't going to work out. On the weekends, which seemed to run from Thursday to Tuesday, the flat filled up with people drinking and smoking and snorting and groping. Even if it hadn't been for the constant temptation, the noise was maddening and set her nerves jangling, calibrated as they now were to the peace of the Languedoc hills.

Sylvie made a plan. She would move a bit further out to a quieter area, somewhere more affordable. As always, she'd have to offset the cheaper rent against the cost of travelling to anywhere she'd be likely to find employment, but for the first time that seemed like a reasonable trade-off. It was going to take a while to sort out housing benefit, but Papi had handed her an envelope at the station containing enough cash for a deposit and a couple of months' rent, and she found a basement flat in a Victorian house in Sydenham, little more than a studio really, but with its own tiny patio garden. It may have been the wilds of Zone 3, but it was a respectable twenty minutes on the train from London Bridge, so she could still apply for jobs in the centre. There was brown woodchip on the walls and the musty smell of the previous occupant's dogs, but she picked up some cheap white paint at a discount store and once she'd thrown a few coats of that around it felt much brighter and more cheerful.

She filled in job application after job application with no luck, so she put an ad in the local shops for babysitting and dog walking and a bit of work started trickling in. Then her landlord, who'd given her permission to paint her flat and been pleased with the results, asked if she'd like to earn a few quid by painting the communal hallway and the larger upstairs flat that the tenants were moving out of, so she'd done that too. She made a good job of it, and he recommended her to a friend a few streets away and she'd ended up painting their house as well. They let her do a robot mural in the kid's bedroom and he'd loved it, and loved her too, spending hours watching and asking questions as she painted, and so they'd started paying her for regular babysitting. Bit by bit, she built up a local client base of people who needed walls painted, or help with their pets and children, and eventually she found that if she didn't spend money on booze and cigarettes and kept her expenses low, she didn't need to go through the rigmarole of signing on anymore. Working like this suited her better than being a waitress or a shop assistant ever had, and without much of a social life she was left with plenty of time to paint, which she found herself doing with more passion and creativity than she'd had in years.

Outwardly her life was unglamorous, checking the price of bread and going to Tesco at the end of the day to buy food nearing its sell-by date that had the price marked down. She didn't have a TV and to use the internet she had to go to the library. New clothes would have to come from Oxfam, she supposed, but it was funny how little this stuff actually bothered her now it came down to it. Her inner world fizzed with an energy and inspiration that she'd thought was gone forever, and that mattered more than any of the rest.

*

There was still one really big thing that needed sorting out: Eva. She had been waiting to see how long it took her supposed friend to get in touch, the days ticking by filled with hurt disbelief that Eva was willing to just let ten years of friendship end over one stupid argument. Where had Eva been when she had hit rock bottom and sat in that A&E alone? Okay, she didn't know that had happened, but surely a friend should have been able to see that Sylvie hadn't been doing well and was heading for a disaster? The ball of pain in Sylvie's stomach disguised itself as anger, and every time she picked up the phone it bubbled up and said, you don't need a friend who isn't there when you need her, and then she would put the phone back down without dialling.

Then one day it occurred to her that it cut both ways: she also didn't know how Eva was doing. What if Eva was having a bad time too, needing a friend, and she hadn't been there for her? She had got so used to the new world in which everything always went brilliantly for Eva and badly for

Sylvie that she'd somehow developed a mental block about the fact that this wasn't an immutable law of the universe. That day she didn't put the phone down. She dialled the number and waited.

*

It was dark when Eva arrived home from work, as it would be every day for many months to come. It wasn't the cold that got her down in winter so much as the lack of daylight, she thought grouchily as she pushed the apartment door closed behind her. She arrived at work in the dark and left in the dark, making the days blur together. The sitting room was empty, and she remembered that Julian had mentioned this morning that he had a couple of evening training sessions booked, so she had the place to herself. Because so many of his clients wanted after-work slots, Eva often got home to an empty flat and was grateful to have an hour or two in which she didn't have to string a sentence together at the end of a hectic day.

Pausing only to retrieve an apple from the kitchen, she kicked off her shoes and sank down onto the sofa, at which point her phone started to ring from the depths of the bag she had dropped in the hallway as she came in. Cursing, she ran to the bag and dumped its contents on the floor in order to find the offending item. The shock of seeing Sylvie's name on the screen made her freeze on her knees on the carpet. It had been over six months since they'd argued, and neither had made any attempt to contact the other. Eva had thought about it numerous times, always concluding that if Sylvie hadn't meant what she said then she would have phoned and apologized, and if she had, well, then she was better off without her.

Should she answer? What if Sylvie had dialled Eva's number accidentally? But if she didn't answer she might be missing the chance to work things out with her oldest friend, something she wanted more than she cared to admit even to herself.

'Hello?' she said warily down the line.

'It's Sylvie.'

So she had meant to call.

'Yes, I saw. It's been a while, huh?' Eva tried to make her voice sound cautiously friendly.

'I know. Listen, do you want to meet up?'

Sylvie's own voice was neutral and it still wasn't clear to Eva what was going on in the conversation. 'I guess. This is a little weird though, isn't it? After all the stuff you said last time I saw you?'

'Look, I wanted to tell you that I was drunk and I'm sorry. I didn't mean any of it.'

'I don't know, Sylvie.' Eva sat back against the wall of the hallway and raked her fingers through her hair. 'It sounded a lot like you did mean it. You were pretty specific. About how smug I am and how I was always your gawky sidekick? Can you imagine how it makes me feel, knowing that was how you thought of me through all those years of supposed friendship?'

Sylvie groaned. 'You're really going to make me work for this, aren't you? Okay, look. I don't know why I said that stuff. The stupid thing is, it's not even true. I was always glad to have a friend like you because you were so down to earth.

Okay, you wore some pretty dodgy clothes, but you were so totally artless. In a good way, I mean, you were never calculating what was in it for you like most people always are.'

'Oh. Well, that's a nice thing to say . . . I think.'

'It's intended that way, honestly. You sort of anchored me to the ground because you used to look up to me and I wanted to be the version of myself that you reflected back at me. But things weren't always exactly how they looked. You used to be impressed by stupid things I did, like sleeping with random guys when I was off my face, when you should have been telling me to stop being such a fuckwit.' She sighed down the line.

'Well, I was always a bit envious of you,' Eva admitted, 'because everyone fancied you and you got all the attention. Everything always seemed to come so easily to you, which was the complete opposite to me. And of course I never told you to stop, because you always looked like you were having such a good time. At least, you used to. Maybe not so much in recent years.'

'A lot's changed though, hasn't it? And it *was* weird for me how different everything was after we left uni. Now you're doing so well and in a lot of ways I really admire you, but sometimes it feels like you've bought into all the City bullshit a bit too much, like you're not the old Eva anymore because the old Eva wouldn't bang on all the time about the size of her fucking bonus or how much her broker spent on a bottle of Petrus at Gordon Ramsay. She might have been a bit wide-eyed, but she would have known deep down that none of that really matters. You taught me that, and I don't think you even know it yourself anymore.' Sylvie paused. 'Anyway, this is starting to sound like I'm having a go at you again and that's the last thing I want to do, I'm just trying to explain and mainly what I want to say is that I had a really bad patch where I acted like a dick, but I'm sorry and I'm doing a lot better now and you're my best friend and I miss you.'

Her voice broke a bit when she said that, and Eva wondered whether maybe she was crying.

'I'm sorry too,' she told her. 'I'm sorry if I was boastful. I didn't mean to sound smug or make you feel bad. I've missed you horribly and I've been completely miserable without you, to be honest.'

Only now that she was saying it aloud did she realize just how true it was. Eva had allowed herself to feel anger and outrage, but mostly what this had been doing was masking sadness and now she couldn't understand why she hadn't recognized this and just called her friend sooner. She had been too proud, she realized, and would probably have carried on being too proud forever if Sylvie hadn't phoned. What a pointless thing ego was, how much damage it did. Suppose neither of them had ever called and they had both just carried on like that, stubborn and unhappy? The thought made her eyes well up with tears, and she let out an involuntary little sob.

Sylvie audibly blew her nose. 'How about meeting up and burying the hatchet? When are you free?'

Eva tried to think fast. Her schedule was full, but suggesting a day a week or two away would make it look as though Sylvie was at the bottom of her priority list, which was part of what had caused the argument in the first place.

'I'm going away with Julian for the weekend on Friday, but how about tomorrow night?' she suggested. 'I've got desk drinks straight after work, but I could escape by eight thirty. We'll be in the Canary Wharf Corney & Barrow, on the terrace overlooking the dock. Why don't you come and rescue me?'

*

Eva remained sitting in the gloom of the hallway for several minutes after they hung up, and had only just started to stuff the scattered pens and tampons and other assorted detritus back into her bag when her phone rang again. She sighed to see Big Paul's name on the screen, since it was nearly nine o'clock at night and presumably he was calling because something had gone wrong at work. Julian would be home soon and she could feel her precious minutes of downtime slipping away. She cleared her throat and carefully wiped her eyes with a grubby tissue before picking up, even though he couldn't see her.

'What's up, big guy? Are you still in the office?'

'Yeah. I've been stuck on a teleconference with New York for hours. I thought I better give you the heads-up on something I picked up from the sales guys at the end of the call. You know that Bellwether Trust order on tomorrow's close? You just got another one and it's double the size. Big day for you tomorrow.'

'Double the size. Okay, thanks for the warning.'

Eva hung up and sat back against the wall, suddenly alert. This was a big deal, a game-changer even, coming so close to bonus time in what was shaping up to be a decidedly unexceptional year. She was going to need a game plan. By the time she heard Julian's key in the door she'd forgotten all about Sylvie's phone call, and was pacing up and down formulating her strategy for the following day.

18

Docklands, November 2005

'Use the French clients,' advised Big Paul as he and Eva walked onto the trading floor the following morning. 'They're all cunts and it's not like we have much of a reputation to protect in France anyway.'

'But I'll never get close to the size I need from clients,' she told him as they made their way towards their section along an aisle of desks bordered by banks of blinking screens. 'I need nine hundred million bonds. That's huge, half a normal day's trading volume in BTPs. I've got no choice but to do most of it in the market.'

'You've got a point. Okay, here's what you do. Buy a third in the market over the course of the day, then use another third to ramp the price higher in the last hour before close, then go home short the final third and buy it back tomorrow when the market corrects what will in reality be a move based on no new information.'

'Isn't that, you know, a bit of a regulatory no-no? Market ramping?'

'Well, if you wanted to be really pernickety about it you could call it price manipulation or front-running client orders, but it's basically a grey area. Everyone does it. What are we going to do, just not make money? Because some other fucker will do it if you don't.' Big Paul shrugged. 'Anyway, it's your show. Just telling you how I'd play it.'

Eva pondered his words as she reached her desk and placed her coffee down on it, sending ribbons of steam swirling upwards in front of her six screens. He was really just echoing what she already knew. It was going to be hairy, but there was no other way to do it without risking getting her face ripped off in the market when the other banks got wind of the size she needed. She would have to start off quietly, taking care not to move the market too much, and then use her buying power to really push the price up towards the end of the day and fill the client orders at the higher closing price. She opened up her pricing spreadsheet and tweaked a few parameters, then watched with widening eyes as a cascade of calculations flowed across the cells. The numbers involved were not small. This was going to need a very steady hand, but she might just make a killing.

*

Things started well enough, with Italian government bonds opening up on the previous day's closing price without her having to buy a single one, giving her the feeling that the natural tendency of the market was to drift gently higher over the course of the day. With a bit of luck that meant she wouldn't encounter too much resistance when she went in all-guns-blazing to really push the price up towards the close. It would revert, of course; the more something goes up in a day, the more likely that it will correct and come back down the next day, when she could buy the rest of the BTPs she needed at a lower price. She took a deep breath, and opened up a line to her broker to buy the first ten million bonds.

'Graham. 95.00 bid in 10.'

'Working that,' came her broker's voice down the line.

She waited for him to come back to her, expecting there to be at least a few sellers taking profit on the overnight move, but there was nothing. Seconds and then minutes slid by before Graham came back on the line suddenly, his voice an octave higher than usual.

'95.20 lifted, 95.20 to 95.40 on the follow.'

That was unexpected, another buyer out there. Eva experienced a tingle of unease. She hadn't expected to have to raise her bid by thirty cents just to get into the game. Something felt . . . off. There was no choice but to buy the bonds, of course, but it was all a question of timing. The trick was learning when to listen to your instincts. Over the years she had gained a feel for how markets behave, observing the processes that went on within herself as she traded, the ebb and flow of fear and greed, elation and panic, and then generalizing outwards to all the other traders just like herself that in aggregate made up the market, all of them subject to the same basic motivations.

'Okay, I'm thirty bid, Graham,' she told her broker.

'Working . . .' came the broker's disembodied voice down the line. This time it was much quicker. 'Forty lifted, bid over there, seventy offer on the follow.'

'95.70 offer?' she muttered disbelievingly. The market was running away from her. She lifted the offer through clenched teeth. 'Mine at seventy, Graham, I take thirty million.'

On a normal day she'd have a sense of which way the ocean of trades was flowing, as if she were a grain of sand swept around by the tide, but with at least a feeling for the magnitude and direction of each force acting upon her. And on her best days of trading she would lose herself in the flow of numbers completely, nudging and shaping them according to her wishes. But today she was feeling like there were things going on beneath the surface that she could sense but couldn't see, leaving her unable even to call which direction things were headed.

Over the remainder of the morning things only got worse. Someone out there had started dumping bonds like they were toxic waste and by lunchtime Eva was long three hundred million bonds, the market was down to 94.30, and her trading book's profit was down well over four million euros. Since her entire trading desk had made fifteen million over the whole year to date, at best she would look like a complete idiot and at worst would wipe out the entire team's annual bonuses in a single morning. A day like this could make or break a career and Eva had the uncomfortable sensation of all the years she'd toiled clinging to her back, all of the slog and fourteen-hour days worth nothing without the combination of luck and ruthlessness you needed to stay afloat on a day like this. *Get a grip, get a grip*, she muttered to herself.

From her seat she spotted Brad Whitman, the recently appointed head of Fixed Income, wander out of his office and begin one of his strolls across the trading floor. He was an American poached from Morgan Stanley, and like all new appointees he was looking to make his mark and justify the multimillion-dollar golden handshake he'd almost certainly been given to join. That would be achieved through downward pressure, in the form of the tantalizing carrot of big bonuses and the stamp of approval, of being in the club, coupled with the stick of being seen as a failure if you didn't make money, with the invisible yet potently stigmatizing mark of a tiny bonus. She suspected Whitman would be successful; something of a personality cult had already sprung up around him, with even normally cool-headed traders namedropping him in conversation: 'So Brad was just saying to me the other day . . .'

He was a smoothly handsome man but there was something disconcerting about him, exacerbated by the fact that his eyes pointed in slightly different directions, making it difficult to know whether you had his attention when you spoke to him. Not that Eva had much call to speak to him anyway; she was too junior to deal with him on a day-to-day basis, and on a day like this, that was a blessing. She hunkered down behind her screens, waiting for him to pass. He was heading in her direction, though, stopping to exchange a few words here and there with the Sales desk then the Gilts team, before halting abruptly beside her desk.

'What's happening in BTPs?'

She looked around for Big Paul or Robert, but their desks were empty; it was definitely her he was talking to.

'Well, they opened fifteen basis points up on the back of the ECB announcement,' she told him.

He nodded. 'Feels like something's happening in the market. Ten-year Italy's as expensive as I've seen it in, what, four years? Haven't you guys got a big order today?'

'Yeah. Nine hundred million. I'm in the market for the first six hundred before today's close.'

He leant down with an arm on her desk, close enough to engulf her in a cloud of expensive aftershave, and read from her screen over her shoulder. '94.10 to 94.60. Where are we long?'

'A bit higher than that, but it's all under control. I'm just letting the market settle here before bringing out the big guns,' she lied.

He stood silently looking at her, or perhaps at something in the distance beyond her shoulder. Had he not heard her? Was something else expected?

'Should make a big number on this,' she continued, hearing the words fly out of her own mouth without meaning them to. What the fuck had she said that for? Did she have some form of impress-the-management Tourette's? God, she was pathetic, as pathetic as the Brad-cultists.

'Make sure you don't end up the wrong way on this, Evelyn.' He smiled broadly and vacantly in her direction, already beginning to glide away. 'Year-end cut-off is tomorrow, and it's touch and go as to whether we make budget. We need everything we can get.'

Eva slumped in her seat, half relieved at the conversation being over and half in despair at not having owned up to her losses, and worse, making it sound like she was going to make money. Still, she reasoned, she couldn't really make the situation much worse anyway. If she lost another half a million she'd have reached her stop-loss and she'd have to ring Market Risk and own up, and would be effectively barred from trading. Game over. You did occasionally hear of traders getting stopped out and then having their losses cleared and their trading book reset to zero but for that to happen you'd have to have friends in high places, which was in no way an accurate description of her own situation.

A broker was walking across the floor handing out takeaway food and she grabbed a couple of bags of greasy thick-cut chips, wolfing them down at her desk without taking her eyes off her screens. They sank to her stomach like boulders and stayed there, refusing to digest.

'How's it going?' asked Big Paul, arriving back from a meeting.

'I'm a bit underwater on those BTPs at the moment,' she mumbled, thinking that even if she was going down, she'd be damned if she was going to let him see how nervous she was.

He looked at the numbers on the screen and then back at her pale face and laughed. 'Just a bit, eh? Look at you, you're bricking it. This is all going to be fine, I'm telling you. You just have to hold your nerve.'

'Easy for you to say. Whitman's been walking the floor and I was the only one here. He asked about the BTPs and basically told me I better make him some money today. On the upside he called me Evelyn – he can't fire me if he doesn't actually know who I am, right?'

Big Paul smiled. 'Oh, don't worry about that, it's just how he keeps people on their toes. Graces you with some unexpected attention and then menaces you with his expectations. I worked under him at Goldman back in the day. He knows fuck all about markets, but he's supremely good at making people scared enough they'll do anything to make money for him. You notice how his eyes point in different directions? The rumour used to be that he'd had an operation to do that on purpose, the better to freak people out when he talks to them. You're never quite sure whether you've got his attention and then he pounces on you like a shark.' His voice was admiring. 'Has he done that other thing to you yet, where he makes a comment and then just stands there without saying a word until you start gabbling to fill the silence? God, it's effective. I've seen him break people with that in meetings. They end up telling him whatever they think he wants to hear, and then it's on them to go away and make it happen.'

'I'm still trying to picture a shark pouncing,' said Eva, to avoid admitting that that was exactly what had just happened to her.

'Like a fucking great-crested pouncing shark, I'm telling you. Anyway. It's what, one thirty now, so two and a half hours till close. Try not to get stopped out or lose our bonuses, eh.'

*

It was still a bit early to be trying to really work the market but Eva thought she might actually scream if she had to sit there fidgeting any longer, so she opened up the line to her broker.

'Put a forty bid in, Graham.'

Her bid appeared on the screen and she waited, expecting the seller from earlier to hit her out of sight. The seconds stretched out, warping and elongating in the air around her. She slumped in her chair with a clammy sense of inevitability, growing so resigned to her fate that she had to blink and double-check when suddenly the sixty offer disappeared from her screen. That was unexpected; could the market actually be shifting back in her direction or was it just a blip? A few trades and ten minutes later, the offer was back up to 95.10. Was it actually possible that the sellers were finally getting scared off?

All day the momentum had been against her, and momentum was almost impossible to reverse. But now it felt as though something was weakening, slackening. Was it really possible that this could turn from a career-ending day of humiliation and failure to a triumph? The sheer range of possible outcomes and their implications for her future seemed unfathomably vast as she sat balanced at what might just be a point of inflection. Things could still go either way. Eva felt a strange calm descend upon her. She opened up a line and began to trade.

*

'There, look, you're nearly back to flat,' came Big Paul's voice from behind her some time later, sweeping her attention out of the screens of flickering numbers that she had been entirely immersed in, and he was right, she'd forced the market back to a level at which her losses had almost completely evaporated. Her surroundings swung back into focus and she realized that he'd been doing nothing but sitting at his desk watching the BTP market move as she traded.

'Damn right,' she told him. 'Watch this. If we can just get back up to ninety-six, we'll be in business.'

It was three o'clock now, with just one hour to go before the market closed. Over the last few minutes two of the higher offer prices had disappeared from her screen, which could mean that people were finishing up for the day, or just that they wanted her to think that they were. Still, if there were ever a time to strike it was now. Eva kept buying steadily until she had about two-thirds of the six hundred million bonds she wanted that day and there were just twenty minutes to go. The sellers were pulling back and she could see the path to the finish line opening up in front of her. The best offer was now ninety-seven, allowing her to exhale.

'96.50 bid,' she told the broker. It was a high enough bid that she expected to trade immediately. Fifteen minutes to go.

'Can show you eighty offer,' came Graham's voice down the line.

'They're coming at you,' growled Big Paul from behind her. 'Hold your nerve.'

'Repeat my bid,' she told the broker. She was damned if she was going to bid at a higher price now.

'Seventy offer,' came the reply.

Time for a show of force. 'Mine. I'll cover your size.' She was putting her cards on the table now, revealing that she'd buy as much as they would sell.

'Sixty-four million,' said Graham.

Eva felt a malevolent smile creep across her face. That was a bad move on the part of the seller. An unrounded number meant the other side was genuinely telling her their total size. If she bought it all, the counterparty would be wiped out and wouldn't be showing any more offers in the market.

'Done, I pay on,' said Eva, making it clear to the market that she'd buy more at that price. Ten minutes left and she still had some size to buy. Before anybody else had a chance to put an offer in, effectively capping the market, she made her play.

'97 bid.' Several minutes passed in tense silence. '98 bid.' Still nothing. Time to go in for the kill with a big increase in price, an insanely aggressive move, but without an offer in the market it was worth a try. 'A hundred bid, Graham.'

'A hundred? Are you sure?'

'Like I said, par bid.'

'Yours, I've got two different sellers.'

'Graham, tell them their size is my size and I'm going to be bid over. I'm keeping this market here till the close. I'll take them both out.'

'That should be enough to scare off your sellers.' Big Paul rolled over to her desk in his chair. 'Where are we at?'

'Two counterparties have sold me fifty million each and gone away to look at doing more. I've got five hundred and fifty, so I only want fifty more, max,' she told him tersely, glancing at her screen. 'Still, only a few minutes till close.'

Big Paul was rigid at her shoulder as Graham came back on the line.

'Par ten on offer.'

'Mine, do twenty million.'

'He'll do fifty.'

'No, twenty's fine,' she said, and the power was back with the seller. Another twenty seconds dragged past.

'Yours at a hundred.'

'How many?'

'Twenty.'

'Done.'

'Second seller giving you.'

'Okay, how many?'

'A hundred.'

Shit. She couldn't take a hundred, but there was under half a minute to go till four o'clock.

'Is that his full size? I want his total size.'

If she could just drag this out until the market level was taken at four o'clock, the last trading price would be her trade at 100.00. She switched screens and tapped this number into her pricing spreadsheet. If the market closed at this level she'd be making thirty million euros. Thirty million euros in a day's trading! There were one, maybe two other traders on the floor who could say they'd had a day like that in their whole career.

'Two-fifty is his full size.'

She watched in silence as the seconds to four o'clock ticked away.

'I'll take ten million,' she shouted down the line as the clock turned four, collapsing back into her chair laughing as the market closed. She was still three hundred million short, and without her bidding the price would collapse tomorrow on the open as these big sellers came in. She would make a killing.

Big Paul hauled himself out of his creaking chair and onto his feet. 'Right then. Time for some PR. Follow me.'

Eva trailed after him across the trading floor, unsure where he was headed until he marched straight through Brad Whitman's office door without even knocking, causing him to look up with a half-annoyed, half-expectant expression on his face.

'Brad, you know Eva, right? I heard we're scrabbling around for money to make target in time to get the comp ratio up for a decent bonus pool, so I thought we'd come and share a bit of good news.' Big Paul grabbed Eva's arm and thrust her forward. 'What's the P'n'L going to be on the Bellwether BTPs, Eva?'

'Um, should be about thirty million euros. So about thirty-five million in dollars.'

The smile that spread across Brad Whitman's face was far less vacant than the one he'd given her earlier, and he seemed to be looking directly at her for the first time. 'Good work,

Eva. That's what I need to hear. Did you hear the Exotics desk posted a ten-million-dollar loss yesterday? Those useless fucks. Thank God I've got some traders who actually make money, eh?'

Eva and Paul backed out of the office nodding and smiling and headed back towards their desks.

'Right, I need a drink,' announced Paul once they were out of earshot. 'And if I do, you definitely do.'

'*You* need a drink?' squeaked Eva. 'You were the one telling *me* to relax. I thought you were confident it would all pan out.'

'Yeah, well, you've got to front it out but nothing's done till it's done, right? Four mil down's not a comfortable place for the guy with the biggest balls in the world let alone a whippersnapper like you.' He pulled his jacket off the back of his chair. 'Come on. You need to get me to the boozer sharpish for a medicinal libation to help me recover from the heart attack you've nearly given me today.'

'It's only four o'clock,' she protested. 'We can't leave now.'

'*Au contraire*, my little friend. Today, we can do whatever the fuck we want. We just made the best part of full-year budget on a single deal. Robert'll forgive us anything once he sees the P'n'L. Angela, if anyone asks we're with Market Risk,' he called across to the team secretary, as he headed for the door with Eva trailing in his wake.

19

Docklands, November 2005

'Not drinking? You're kidding, right?' Eva looked up at her friend incredulously. She'd been in the pub for several hours by the time Sylvie arrived, and had expected her to be delighted that she was up for making a night of it. Sylvie, though, seemed unwilling to stay for the one-for-the-road that Big Paul was insisting they have before heading off to somewhere they could talk properly.

'Well . . .' said Sylvie. 'I'm sort of on the wagon right now. And I thought we were going to, you know, go somewhere to do a bit of catching up?'

Robert, who had joined Eva and Big Paul in the bar and was unashamedly eavesdropping on the conversation, gave them a beseeching look.

'Ladies, you're not going to make us finish this bottle of champagne alone, are you now? What does it take to make you let your hair down? Thirty million of P'n'L has to be worth a celebration. And, anyway, you can't leave me alone with this fat fuck. He tried to follow me home and climb into bed with me the last time we had a night out together.'

'You know you love it,' shouted Big Paul, rubbing his fingers in a circular motion over his nipples and then grabbing

Robert's face in both hands and planting an extravagant kiss on his forehead.

Eva squeezed Sylvie's hand. 'Do you mind staying just for one? We've had an incredible day.' She lowered her voice and added, 'Then we can go somewhere else and talk properly. Robert's my boss, so I can't really say no. Plus, it's no bad thing to celebrate getting your best friend back with a glass of champagne, right?'

Sylvie didn't look convinced but, sensing an opening, Big Paul insistently pressed a glass into her hand. 'Here's to big P'n'L and commensurately large Edward de Bonos. Ladies, they don't call me The Whale for nothing!'

'If you think your P'n'L is the reason they call you The Whale, I've got some bad news for you,' Robert told him, causing Eva to snort the mouthful of champagne she had just taken down her nose and cast around for a napkin.

'Laugh it up, bossman. But money talks, and our P'n'L is telling you that come bonus time, you gots to make it RAIN.' He broke into song, tunelessly shouting, 'Ooh, yeah, I wish it would rain down, down on me,' before gyrating rhythmlessly around the table in an approximation of a rain dance.

Sylvie laughed and sipped cautiously at her drink, not wanting Eva to think that she was unwilling to celebrate her success. That would look like sour grapes of the sort that had caused them to fall out in the first place and in any case, half a glass wouldn't hurt. They'd stay for one, and then she and Eva could go on to another bar where there would be enough privacy to explain why she was having a break from drinking, which she could hardly do with Eva's workmates earwigging. It was strange and nice to have a little bit of a drink after so long, anyway. She'd never said that she would never touch another drop. Now that she had her life on an even keel maybe she could do this once in a while, have just the one and then stop.

Robert slid along the bench towards them with his best charming face on until he was inches away from Sylvie, and Eva groaned inwardly at his blatant lechery. Tall and well built with close-cropped dark hair and slightly crooked front teeth, she had to admit he was good-looking enough in a certain light, but she almost felt sorry for him, given the certainty of the impending rebuff.

'So, how come Eva never told us she had such a beautiful friend?' Robert was saying. 'Is she ashamed of us? Or of you?'

Eva cringed at his smarminess and prayed that Sylvie wouldn't cut him down too ruthlessly; after all, she was the one who still had to get up and work for the guy tomorrow. Eva watched as Sylvie broke into a faintly evil smile and parted her lips to speak, but she never actually caught her reply because the raucous group at the table behind them spilled a tray of drinks, drenching the back of Eva's shirt with red wine and sending her rushing to the bathroom to wash it out. On the other side of the table, Big Paul was already topping up the glasses and signalling to the waiter to bring another bottle.

★

From: eva.andrews21@hotmail.com
To: sylvie_marchant_artist@yahoo.com
Date: Friday 3rd November 2005 08:04
Subject: Please tell me you didn't

A question. What the TWATTING TWAT do you think you're doing? We were supposed to be meeting up last night so that we could bury the hatchet, not so you could get pissed and insist we stay out half the night. I'm sorry I ditched you but it was one in the morning and I had to be up for work in five hours. As did Robert. You know, my boss. Who, incidentally, is still not on the desk despite the fact the markets opened more than an hour ago.

Now, I apologize in advance if it turns out that the reason you're not answering your phone is because you have in fact been dismembered by a serial killer. However, the evidence is all pointing to a far more sinister possibility: that you've shagged my boss.

I can think of at least five reasons why you'd better bloody not have:

He's got a girlfriend (or more likely three or four at any given moment).

He constantly tries to take the credit for my work and thinks it's amusing to tell me to fetch him coffee.

He will try to get you to tell him things about me to undermine my professionalism.

He's a complete and utter tool. Trust me on this.

HE'S MY BOSS. Of all the people in the world, only one of them is my boss. Let's have a rule whereby you're allowed to shag any one of the three billion men on the planet except for the one that's MY BOSS.

NOW PICK UP THE DAMN PHONE.

Sylvie's phone was still going straight through to voicemail at 9 a.m. when Robert swaggered in across the trading floor.

Even without his dishevelled and triumphant appearance, Eva already knew what had happened. By the time she'd got the wine out of her shirt in the bathroom the night before, Robert and Paul seemed to have persuaded Sylvie to stay for another drink, so they did, and then that had sort of segued into the next one because the glasses just kept being topped up and Eva hadn't been as careful as she usually was, what with having started drinking at 4.30 p.m. and skipping dinner. Sylvie had seemed to get plastered unusually quickly too, and then suddenly it was midnight and they were all still in the bar. There had been no chance to catch up properly with Sylvie because she'd been pinned in the corner by Robert for most of the evening, while Big Paul had monopolized Eva with an endless series of compliments about how gutsy she'd been that day, interspersed with hilarious tales of buccaneering in the markets of yore. She felt both annoyed and guilty. Sylvie had clearly wanted to leave when she'd arrived, but what could Eva do when her boss was virtually ordering her to stay?

In hindsight, it was obvious how it had all come about. Robert had taken one look at Sylvie and got a big toothy smile on his face, and Big Paul was his practised wingman, clearly figuring that getting your boss laid could only improve your bonus prospects. She'd watched them in action enough times but had never been close to the receiving end, so she simply hadn't realized that she and Sylvie were being played. She felt bad about having led Sylvie into the shark pool, especially after what she'd said on the phone about hating herself for sleeping with random guys. But after a couple of drinks Sylvie had acquired her old sheen of drunken recklessness, and then she had been the one resisting Eva's suggestions that they head off. Eva had spent at least an hour trying to persuade her to come home with her and sleep in the spare room until, exhausted and nauseous, she had eventually given up and left, having extracted a promise from Sylvie that she would get a taxi home when the bar closed.

What had happened was doubly galling, because she'd always been so careful not to let the different parts of her life collide, keeping her carefully constructed professional persona well clear of the incompatible elements. Early on in her career she'd studied the bomb-proof veneers of her most successful colleagues, noting the relaxed, confident chumminess which spoke of an upbringing that had revolved more around ski trips to Verbier than sitting in the corner at SWP meetings with a packet of Quavers, and concluded that it was best to keep her life firmly compartmentalized. This had been a generally successful strategy, though there had been that one rather excruciating time her father insisted on meeting her at her office on a trip to London, no doubt thinking an incursion into the citadels of capitalism would be a good opportunity to size up the enemy. Quite by chance, Robert had chosen the same moment to leave for the evening as Eva met her father in reception, giving her no choice but to introduce them. She'd been distracted for a few minutes by a work call and had been mortified to turn round when she finished to find Keith lecturing a smirking Robert on the finer points of socialism.

She should have learned her lesson then, she thought, remembering how, cheeks burning, she'd had to practically drag her father out of the building. She'd thought taking him out for a nice meal would temper some of his criticisms of her work and lifestyle but there had followed an awkward dinner during which Keith had managed to make her feel horribly guilty for being part of a financial system that stripped workers of their protections and in which the benefits mostly accrued to a few winners like her. At the end, instead of thanking her for picking up the tab, he snatched the bill from her hands and calculated how many Bolivian peasants could live for a month on the cost of this single meal.

Of course he had a point, she thought, but it wasn't a straightforward one, and it also wasn't as if she was single-handedly responsible for global inequality. Keith had at least perked up later that evening after she'd handed over a five-grand cheque for cleft palate operations for African orphans, but the next day she had walked onto the trading floor to find a picture of a hammer and sickle stuck to the back of her chair and everyone calling her Red Eva.

It was clear that there was nothing to be gained from allowing the different parts of her world to collide. Why on earth had she told Sylvie to meet her at the bar? It had seemed like a good way to make a polite escape from an evening of work drinks, and the thought that Sylvie and Robert would look twice at each other hadn't even crossed her mind, since they had nothing in common and each held everything the other stood for in contempt. Ah well, she thought, that was the upside: it wasn't as if anything would come of it. She would put her life back into separate boxes and not make the same mistake again.

Besides, she had other things to worry about. A nagging feeling had been bothering her since she dragged herself out of bed that morning, and it wasn't just a function of her ferocious hangover. As the morning passed and she spoke to

brokers and other people on the trading floor, she was starting to realize that what she'd done yesterday was being
talked about all over the market. With hindsight, she thought,
it might have been a little on the aggressive side of things.
The line between pre-hedging a client trade by buying what
you needed in advance to fill their order, and using your
buying power to move prices in the market was a hazy one.
On one side of that line was what they did every day, and on
the other the murky area of market manipulation, an offence
technically punishable with jail. There was nothing glaringly
wrong with what she'd done, she reflected uneasily, except
maybe that bit right at the end where she'd ramped the price
and left it there to force the market to close on a high. It
would have left a funny-looking spike in the data, now she
thought about it. At that moment one of the sales guys wandered over to her desk and leant against it.

'You must have made a fair whack on that Bellwether
Trust trade yesterday,' he remarked casually.

Eva avoided looking up. 'Yeah, we did.'

'I mean, that would have been some serious P'n'L, right?'
he persevered.

She frowned and put down the pen she was fiddling
with. 'Yes, Toby. We're a trading desk. We make money from
trading. That's what we do.'

'Ooh, touchy.' He laughed. 'It's just that it was a bit ballsy,
that's all I was going to say.'

Calm, she told herself. It wasn't smart to let people see
that she was feeling nervous about it. It was only natural that
people were going to make comments on a trade of that size,
and she was going to have to brazen it out with a bit more
composure.

'Sorry, look, I'm just a bit busy right now. And maybe one too many drinks last night, you know how it is.'

Mollified, Toby wandered away, but Eva's heightened sense of anxiety lingered.

20

South Kensington, July 2006

One fine morning in an office at Imperial College London, Benedict Waverley could be found upending the contents of a small cardboard box onto his new desk and propping a photo of Lydia and the boys against his new computer monitor. He was very happy about the desk, the first he'd ever had that was next to a window. From where he sat he could see an actual living tree and a patch of blue sky. The office would be shared with two other people, one of whom, it turned out, he'd already met and got on well with at various conferences. He felt that this was a good sign, a sign that coming back to London had been the right decision. Of course, regardless of whether the signs were good or bad it wasn't as if he had much choice in the matter, at least not if he wanted to keep his family together. He would be sad not to be around when the Large Hadron Collider went live but at least he would still be involved in analysing the data from it, and he recognized he was lucky to have landed such a plum research and supervisory role when competition for these posts was so stiff.

Yes, he told himself, there was every reason to feel optimistic about the future. Lydia would surely be a lot happier back in London. It hadn't been a great life for her with him working all hours at CERN, and lately she'd been spending huge swathes of time back in England with her parents. He'd missed them terribly, the kids anyway, though in fact it had been a bit of a relief to have a break from Lydia. It had been a long time since he'd felt as though he could do anything right as far as she was concerned.

It had been a couple of years since their marriage had started to fray around the edges. With hindsight they had rushed into things, but Lydia getting pregnant so quickly had rather clinched matters, and it had been easy to get swept along on a tide of doing the right thing. When he'd voiced his doubts to his mother shortly before the wedding, she'd marched him off for a walk on the Heath and talked to him in a new way, a grown-up way in which she'd never spoken to him before, or indeed since.

'Your marriage will work if you make it work,' she told him. 'That's something that your generation seems to have lost sight of. A good marriage is not one where both people have spent a decade or more sampling all the delights that the opposite sex has to offer and then suddenly stumble across another person whom they immediately recognize as the missing part of their soul. It's simply one in which you make a choice and then bloody well stick to it. You get up every morning and renew your decision to be the best husband or wife you can be, and you forgive each other when you fall short, which of course you often will.'

'That doesn't sound much like you and Dad,' he'd responded doubtfully. 'He's always telling people how he fell in love the first time he saw you across a crowded room and decided then and there that he would marry you.'

'Oh, darling. Don't you know by now that that's all just

so much hyperbole? Daddy and I have had as many ups and downs as anyone else, and God knows there's been plenty to forgive. You can hardly have failed to notice your father's roving eye. I was pregnant when we married too, you know. Who knows whether we'd have ended up together other-wise?'

Benedict digested this as they strolled through the grounds of Kenwood House, genuinely surprised. He'd always unthinkingly accepted his father's fairy-tale version of events, in which the prince swept the princess off her feet and they lived happily ever after. No one had ever sug-gested that there had been any falling short or forgiving to be done. And what on earth did she mean by his father's roving eye? Christ, he didn't want to know. He had enough problems of his own without having to process a bunch of new and unpalatable facts about his parents. Benedict took his mother's arm and steered her towards the Brew House coffee shop, changing the subject back to his own situation.

'But what if . . . there's someone else that I have feelings for?'

His mother fixed a beady eye on him. 'Then you'll just have to be mature enough to recognize that in time they will pass. Daddy and I like Eva too, darling, she's very charming.'

Benedict blanched at the mention of Eva. He hadn't done a terribly good job of hiding his feelings, he realized now, but it was startling and unsettling to hear his mother speak so matter-of-factly about what he thought was his secret tor-ment.

'I remember when you brought her out to Corfu,' Marina continued, oblivious to his discomfort. 'She was such a sweet little thing, so awkward and gauche. I just wanted to take her under my wing. And that awful tattered bright yellow sundress she wore all week. I was itching to lend her something but didn't dare offer in case she felt criticized. One could tell how badly she would have felt if she'd thought she wasn't fitting in.' She drew to a halt in front of the cafe entrance. 'But darling, if things were going to work out between the two of you they would have done so a long time ago. Lydia's a splendid girl and she's absolutely dying to marry you. You don't get a better foundation for a marriage than that. And you're having a baby together. A baby! You don't know yet what an incredible thing that is, but you'll love that baby more than you ever thought possible. You're going to have a wonderful life together, I just know it.'

Benedict had felt much better after this conversation, and as the wedding got closer he had grown more and more certain that his mother was right. And there had been so much to do, what with the move to Switzerland and Josh's arrival and starting work at CERN, that he hadn't had time to dwell too much on things as the days sped past in a blur. Between the baby and his job he barely had a second to spare, but he found he was ecstatically happy despite surviving on sometimes as little as five hours' sleep a night. He came to feel everything his mother had said he would about his son and more. And being at CERN was something else, working with some of the most brilliant minds in physics to get these huge, groundbreaking experiments up and running, and everyone feeling as if they were truly on the brink of something momentous, a new era in understanding the universe.

And then there was Lydia. At first she'd seemed as happy as he was. They'd rented a beautiful old apartment on Rue Pécolat, close to Lake Geneva, and had been surprised and relieved at how the sky didn't fall when the baby arrived. During the pregnancy there seemed to be a queue of people lining up to issue warnings about how difficult having a baby was, how dreadful giving birth would be, how much life would change, how likely it was that Lydia would miss the intellectual stimulation of her work, and how hard it would be to live in another country away from friends and family. By the time the baby was due they had been so petrified by all the well-meant warnings that the reality turned out to be far less apocalyptic than they'd been led to expect, and a haze of contentment had descended. When, a year after Josh had popped into their world, Lydia had announced that she was pregnant again, Benedict had taken it in his stride.

As it turned out, the reality failed to match his expectations once again, this time for very different reasons. The second pregnancy was much harder than the first, with Lydia suffering terrible morning sickness for most of the nine months, and by the time Will arrived she was already resentful of Benedict, how much time he spent working and how little he helped at home. Unlike Josh, who had emerged with a sort of serenity about him, Will was a colicky baby and would scream for hours on end, defiant in the face of all attempts to soothe him. Benedict would start each day with the best of intentions about getting home early and giving Lydia a break, but by the time he finished his work he would be so exhausted that the prospect of returning to a tearful and angry Lydia and a screaming Will was enough to have him finding reasons to stay even later.

He'd suggested a nanny; he couldn't have afforded it on his salary but there was no question that his parents would be willing to help out, and besides, if they had a nanny perhaps Lydia would be able to work too. But Lydia wouldn't hear of it, saying that she wanted the boys to be cared for by their parents. That might be how certain sorts of people do things, she'd said pointedly, but she wasn't about to palm her children off on some stranger and then pack them off to boarding school in short trousers only to retrieve them ten years later physically grown but emotionally stunted. Benedict resented the implicit criticism of his family. If she wouldn't accept the solutions that he offered he could hardly be to blame if she was unhappy. Still, he could perhaps have been a better husband, and that was before one even mentioned the incident in the stationery cupboard.

The incident in the stationery cupboard, as he now thought of it, had been an act of utter insanity at the CERN Christmas party. He'd asked Lydia whether she wanted to come with him and even offered to arrange a babysitter, but in a masterstroke of passive aggression she had insisted that Will's colic was too bad to leave him, and that in any case she was simply too exhausted for parties and he should go along on his own. He'd taken her at face value, knowing full well that face value was the exact opposite of how these statements were intended but not feeling like spending an hour jollying her into coming only to have her monitor his every drink and insist they get a taxi home by ten because she'd have to be up for the 4 a.m. feed.

By then it had been many months since he'd been out socializing, or had a drink, or, for that matter, had sex. Since the baby had arrived he'd tried very hard to make Lydia happy, but nothing seemed to work. When he stayed out late she got angry, but his presence at home seemed to annoy her too. If he came home after a long day and sat down with the newspaper for even fifteen minutes she would ostentatiously tidy up around him with the baby on one hip, silently making the point that she had no such luxury. But if he attempted to help with the housework, or with the kids, he invariably did it wrong: the washing needed to be split into whites and coloureds or things would run, the nappies needed the frills pulled out properly around the legs or they would leak and just make more work for her than if she'd changed them herself in the first place. Attempts at love-making were coldly rebuffed and sometimes even met with a stern talk on how tired she was and how insensitive it was of him not to realize that it was normal for women not to feel like sex for months after giving birth, though he recalled sadly how they'd been back in the saddle within weeks of Josh's arrival.

The Christmas party had felt like a much-needed opportunity to let off some steam, a release valve, as he saw it. He hadn't intended to get legless, just to have a couple of beers, but there had only been wine on offer and after the first few glasses a few more had seemed like a marvellous idea. The other thing that had seemed like a marvellous idea after those additional few glasses of wine had been allowing himself to be tugged into the stationery cupboard by a young colleague named Stephanie, who had cornered him in the corridor and quizzed him on the finer points of lepton production, hanging on to his every word as though he was some sort of rock star, which in a funny way of course he was, a rock star of the world of particle physics, if you will. Then she'd made a rather outré joke about confusing hadrons and hard-ons, and things had gone from there. It had stopped seeming like such a good idea when another giggling couple had stumbled into the same cupboard and discovered him on top of Stephanie with his trousers down, illuminated from the doorway in what must have been a profoundly undignified tableau.

The following day, in the wretchedness of the early morning light, he'd reasoned that he would have to tell Lydia. CERN was such a small community that it could easily get back to her, and besides, he wasn't sure he could live with the self-loathing. It transpired too late that his discoverers had been models of discretion; he'd already told Lydia by the time he realized that he could have got away with it, and even though the aftermath had been too dreadful for words, he still felt that it had been the right thing to do. A painful but cleansing period of honesty had followed. Lydia's recriminations had been bitter and, he could see now, largely justified. Benedict hadn't been a good husband. He had avoided his responsibilities as a father and his infidelity was merely a manifestation of a deficit of the respect he should have accorded her. He had failed to fully commit to the partnership in a spirit of love and generosity. It had been brutal, yes, but at the end of it he felt as though they understood each other much better, and they eventually resolved to work on their marriage in a new spirit of honesty and reconciliation. It did mean that he had to give in to Lydia's demands to return to London when a suitable position could be found, since she could hardly be expected to move on knowing that he still regularly ran into the person with whom he had been caught in flagrante delicto, and in any case Benedict couldn't bear the knowing, flirtatious glances Stephanie still gave him, and had taken to darting into the loos whenever she passed.

It surprised Benedict as much as anyone that he had turned out to be a cheat, a man who had committed adultery, twice if you counted kissing Eva, which he supposed Lydia would had she known about it. (He hadn't confessed to that one. It had only been a kiss, after all, and it would have been unforgivably cruel to tell her when she'd been pregnant and about to marry him.) He'd always assumed that cheats were despicable people, but it turned out that it was easy to condemn adulterers if you were a person for whom the opportunity had never arisen. Having never anticipated that the opportunity to be unfaithful would materialize, he had never steeled himself against it, and therein lay the problem. He had been, if not defenceless exactly, then unready, lacking the wit to take good decisions quickly when circumstances called for it. Now that he knew such things could happen, he would take precautions and that in turn would make him a better husband. Simple, really.

One other good thing had come out of the whole mess: he was feeling more understanding towards his father again. Since the day his mother had hinted at his father's infidelities he hadn't been able to help but view him in a different light. A distance had opened up between them and was, if not so marked as to be a source of sadness for both men, at least the cause of a niggling sense of perplexed discomfort that some of the ease had gone out of their relationship.

Benedict had avoided examining any of this too closely, but in his newfound spirit of honesty he thought about it all now, and felt that he had perhaps judged his father too harshly. If a good and well-intentioned man like Benedict could end up in such a situation, perhaps something similar had happened to his father. Perhaps he had made a mistake or two, and was as sorry as Benedict was. Perhaps he had even spent many years devoting himself to his family to try to make up for it, as Benedict intended to. After all, he concluded, who can ever understand the intricacies of any marriage except for the two people in it?

Benedict's reverie was broken by the ping of an email arriving. That was good news, confirmation that he'd at least managed to redirect his messages to the Imperial server. He'd spent most of the morning simply trying to connect to a printer. If it took a particle physicist several hours to get a printer to work he could only wonder how the rest of the world coped. How many physicists does it take to port to a printer? There was a joke in there somewhere.

From: eva.andrews21@hotmail.com
To: benedict.waverley@cern.ch
Date: Monday 24th July 2006 16:32
Subject: Hi

Dearest Benedict,

It's about time one of us sent a proper email, so here goes . . .

Hope Lydia and the rugrats are fine and everything's tickety-boo at CERN.

There's plenty to catch up on this end, since it seems like you haven't been in touch with anyone for a while? Anyway, Julian has moved in to my place, so that's all very grown-up and not at all commitment-phobic of me. It's really nice, better than I thought it would be. I know I was wondering about whether moving in together was the right thing to do when we last met up but it's actually completely fine. You never know, one day maybe we'll be in marital bliss à la Benedict and Lydia!

Speaking of which, here's the other big news: Sylvie boinked my boss, got pregnant, and married him a few months ago in a flurry of confetti and insincerity. I feel you doing a double-take – yes, you did read that right. All of this happened in the space of the last eight months and I guess you've been busy with work and kids. Have you changed your number? We've all tried to phone you with no luck. Anyway, the wedding was a small and hurriedly-put-together affair at Marylebone registry office followed by the groom and the witnesses (me and Lucien) getting plastered at the Marylebone Tap while Sylvie looked on, pregnant, sober and fuming. They've bought a house in Hampstead, your old stomping ground, and the baby's due soon.

It's starting to feel like shotgun weddings are quite the thing, what with you and Lydia and now Sylvie and Robert. I used to think they only happened in Victorian novels and that these were the days of happy promiscuity but apparently you lot are more traditional than I ever realized. Hopefully they'll be as good together as you two are, but knowing Robert as I do after five years working with him I have to admit I have my doubts, as the man's a total dick.

We can at least still count on Lucien not to get hitched during a bout of chivalry. He's the same as ever, brought his latest squeeze to the wedding – some species of model apparently. I suspect glamour rather than catwalk, but didn't get a chance to ask as she spent most of the night in the loo, emerging only occasionally to down another vodka and slimline tonic while sniffing furiously.

Are you in London any time soon? Meet me for lunch?

Eva

Benedict sighed. He'd have loved to meet up with Eva and confide in her about everything that had happened, but he didn't think that would go down well with Lydia, who, with the impeccable radar women seemed to have about such things, had always sensed a threat. After that excruciating lunch at Giraffe he'd tried to smooth things over but just made it worse. She had ended up accusing him of siding with Eva and made it clear that if he was any sort of a husband he wouldn't consort with people who belittled his wife. Matters hadn't been helped by Josh wandering around singing *forfucksake, forfucksake* in a cheery little voice for weeks afterwards. He knew he should explain but he needed some time to work out how to phrase it, and so he'd avoided Eva's calls and that had made it impossible to take Sylvie and Lucien's calls too. Still, there was always email; he felt hurt that they hadn't at least emailed him to ask him to the wedding when they couldn't get through to his phone, even if it had been a rush job. Now he thought about it, though, the truth was that they'd all been going their separate ways for a long time, and this just confirmed it.

Anyway, the most important thing was keeping his family together. If he was honest with himself, which of course he must be now because that was the new way of doing things, somewhere deep inside he had never really let go of the fantasy of one day being with Eva. But that wasn't real life. He had Lydia and the kids, and Eva was living with that prettified personal trainer of hers. She had evidently long since moved on, and it was time that he did the same. And Sylvie and Lucien had barely made any effort to stay in touch since he'd had kids, instead conducting the friendship by proxy through Eva. He just wasn't fun enough for them anymore, he supposed; their eyes glazed over at the slightest mention of his family or his work, which was basically the whole of his life now. That hurt, of course it did, but there was no point in dwelling on it. Times changed, people moved on. He nudged the mouse so that the pointer was no longer hovering above the Reply button, and went back to unpacking his box.

21

Hampstead, July 2006

Several miles across the city, another box was being unpacked. Sylvie unwrapped the tissue paper from around a small sculpture of a hippopotamus and placed it on the shelf next to the dancer already positioned there. The contrast between the slender ballerina and the bulbous open-mouthed hippo was pleasing. It almost looked as if the figurine was serenading him, a gracious hand outstretched towards the toothy gaping maw. Sylvie had made these little statues years ago at school, and while they weren't going to win any prizes they had a certain childish joy to them, making them well suited to the nursery.

This must be the nesting phase, Sylvie thought to herself. The wretched tiredness had finally been lifting over the last week and she'd decided with a sudden sense of urgency that it was time to get the house ready. After much nagging Lucien had agreed to hire a van to collect her belongings from the various different addresses where they had accrued over the years and bring them to the new home that she now shared with her husband, and, in a few weeks' time, their daughter. She turned the words over in her mind. Husband. Daughter. They seemed alien to her, not words that could really apply to her life. How had she wound up here?

The answer was of course prosaic: she'd got knocked up by accident. She didn't really know why she'd refused to even consider an abortion. It wasn't as if her circumstances were ideal for raising a child on her own, which is the way things had initially looked like being. Perhaps it was partly that she hadn't realized until she was so far along, when she was already sixteen weeks pregnant. What she had thought was her period had arrived only a few days late, and she'd been on the Pill, so when she missed the next period she figured it was just a hormonal blip. When the following one also didn't arrive she went to the GP, who seemed astonished by her obtuseness. Lots of women have some bleeding in pregnancy around the time of their first missed period, he told her. About a third of them, to be precise. And no form of contraception was a hundred per cent reliable, not even the contraceptive pill. Had she had a tummy bug a few months ago?

That was the moment she finally believed she was pregnant, because suddenly she knew exactly how it had happened. That first night she'd spent with Robert, the night she went to meet Eva after work and ended up falling off the wagon, she'd drunk so much that she had thrown up several times the next day. And then the day after that she'd felt better, and that evening Robert had paid her a follow-up booty call. It was hardly the most auspicious start to a life. If she'd realized when she'd been four or five weeks along maybe things would have been different, but the GP had sent her to the hospital for a scan the very next day and there was the baby, waggling its arms and legs, and she had known immediately that, despite never having particularly liked children and regularly thinking that if she heard Tony Blair or Gordon Brown say 'hardworking families' one more time she might actually puke, despite all of this, she was going to be a mother.

'Looks like a girl to me,' the sonographer had told her, taking her hand and adding, 'Want a tissue, love?' when he noticed her eyes reddening.

Of course, this wasn't exactly what she'd planned, she thought as she walked out of the antenatal clinic, but then, what in life actually *had* turned out as planned? She hadn't made much of a success of anything else so far, but Sylvie found herself suffused with a weird hopefulness that she was going to make a success of this one thing. She would be a good mother, bohemian enough not to be hidebound by convention but caring and attentive enough to raise a daughter who didn't pass through the world slashing and burning all before her as she went. Sylvie could teach her all the things she'd learned the hard way so that her daughter wouldn't have to learn them the hard way too: how important it was to have the humility to work hard and value the things you achieved for yourself, but also the confidence and breadth of perspective not to look for happiness in the wrong places, like the bottoms of wine bottles and wraps of coke and the beds of people who couldn't care less about you. The baby hadn't been planned but Sylvie felt . . . what was this unfamiliar sensation? That was it: she felt ready.

*

Once Robert had accepted she wouldn't change her mind about keeping the baby, they had fallen back into the habit of tumbling into bed together several times a week. Sylvie suspected he would simply fade away to a name against an incoming amount on her bank statement each month once the baby arrived, but she was making the most of the sex and the feeling of intimacy while it lasted; it was probably going to be a long time before there was much of either of those things in her life again. Because of this, it came as a shock when, lying together in his bed one night, naked and satiated, covers tangled around their legs and both looking down at her swollen belly, he said, 'Do you think we should just get married and have done with it?

'No, hear me out,' Robert continued when she snorted with laughter and whacked him with a pillow. 'You're having this baby and I'm on the hook for it financially whether I like it or not. I've always half fancied the idea of having a mini-me eventually, and it's going to look a whole lot better at work if we go down the marriage route. You'd be surprised at how conservative some of the management are at American banks. I don't think they actually mind that much if you're going to strip clubs and banging some twenty-year-old, but a veneer of respectability at least is smiled upon. Christ, it would be worth it just to put an end to the evils I'm getting from Eva when I arrive at work every morning. She's like Medusa, that one; her glare could turn a lesser man to stone.'

Warming to the idea, he went on, 'Now, from your point of view there's plenty of upside. There'd be a prenup of course, but I'd buy a nice house for us in some expensive spawning ground and pay for the kid to go to a decent school and all that. You wouldn't have to live in a broom cupboard in the Outer Hebrides and shine shoes anymore or whatever the fuck it is you do for money.' He wrinkled his nose at the thought of her living and working arrangements. 'I can't guarantee that I'm *not* going to bang the odd twenty-year-old, obviously. And you'd have to do the corporate wife bit, throw the occasional dinner party and get your nails done with the other wives or whatever the job description says. But basically it makes good sense all round, given where we are. What do you say?'

Sylvie grinned. 'That I've been waiting for this moment ever since I was a little girl and it's everything I dreamt of?'

He rolled over onto his side towards her and brushed a few strands of hair away from her face, then dropped his hand down to her stomach in a gesture that could almost be described as tender.

'Yeah, well, we're not really the hearts-and-flowers type, are we, you and I? No point in pretending we haven't both been around the block a few times but maybe that's the beauty of the thing. It might not be Romeo and Juliet, but look where that got those buggers anyway.'

And he wasn't entirely wrong, when she thought about it. You had to admire his straightforwardness, his complete lack of guile. Robert was a shagger, but a lot of his charm lay in his unwillingness to dissemble about it, and once she'd agreed he'd been as good as his word. They'd done the deed swiftly and then bought a house in Hampstead, an area which appealed to her because of its artistic and literary associations and to him because, despite its pretentious lefty reputation, it was these days being colonized by wealthy bankers much like all the other desirable parts of London.

So that was how Sylvie had found herself in her beautiful house and enviable life, reeling from the suddenness of it all.

She nudged the dancer a little closer to the hippo, picked up the now empty cardboard box, and closed the door of the nursery behind her.

*

Perhaps a townhouse hadn't been the wisest choice, Sylvie reflected, as she hefted her ever-expanding bulk down the last flight of steps into the kitchen. Sometimes she felt that she would never get back upstairs again and would have to ask Robert to haul a mattress down to the ground floor so that she could sleep there until the baby came. She'd been intending to make a sandwich but the armchair in the corner of the room was too inviting, and with a sigh she lowered herself into it. It was impossible to get into a comfortable position to sleep at night when you were the size of a cruise liner. Outside the window, the early afternoon sunlight filtered through the leaves of the oak tree in the garden, casting a shifting filigree of shadow across the kitchen wall. How peaceful it is here, she thought, allowing her eyes to close.

Sylvie didn't know whether she had been asleep for two minutes or an hour when she was jolted awake by a loud ringing. Heart thudding, she heaved herself out of the chair and over to the kitchen table where she had left her phone.

'Hello?'

'Will you accept a call from HMP Brixton?' came an unfamiliar voice on the line.

'Sorry, what?'

'You have a call coming through from Her Majesty's Prison Brixton,' came the voice again, with an edge of impatience this time. 'Will you take the call?'

'I'm not sure you've got the right number. But okay, yes, put it through.'

'Sylvie? It's me. Can you hear me?'

It took her a moment or two to realize that the panicky voice was her brother's. Her knees felt weak and she had to lean forward against the edge of the table.

'Yes, I can hear you. Lucien, are you really calling from prison? What the hell's going on?'

'Sylvie, things have gone really wrong here. I've fucked up big time.'

'What's happened? How can you be in prison?'

'God, Sylvie, I'm sorry. I didn't want to call you, what with the baby about to arrive and everything, but I tried Mum and the old bitch didn't want to know. It's just . . . things have gone really wrong at my end.'

Sylvie steadied herself to reply with a confidence that she didn't feel.

'Calm down. It's fine. Just tell me what's happened.'

'I'm on remand. I got caught with a couple of keys of coke.'

'Shit, don't say that on the phone. If you're calling from prison they're probably listening in.'

'Doesn't matter. They caught me red-handed. I'm going to have to plead guilty, try to get a reduced sentence. I thought they'd let me out on bail but they've remanded me in custody. I need someone I can trust to help me. I know you're due any day and there's no way I'm going to ask you to come and visit me here but I need some help. Can you get Eva to come if I put her name on my visitor's ticket?'

'Yes. Yes, of course, don't worry. We're going to sort this out. I can send Eva, no problem. Put her name down and I'll call her right now and get her there as soon as possible, today if we can work out the logistics. Lucien, don't worry, we're going to fix this, I promise you.'

'Listen, don't worry, sis, I'm a big boy, I can look after myself. I'm just going to need a bit of help sorting things on the outside, my flat and all that,' he was saying, and her heart started really pounding then, because she could hear how frightened he was and she hadn't heard Lucien actually scared and trying to be brave since he was ten years old and about to get a beating from one of their mother's boyfriends for some act of insurgence or another. 'Listen, I'm going to get cut off in a minute. You will send Eva, won't you?'

And then the line went dead and she was standing in the kitchen listening to just a crackle and he was gone and she was married to Robert and about to have a baby and her brother was in prison and she wasn't sure how they'd got here but she had better phone Eva right now, Eva would help, Eva would know what to do, so she dialled her number but there was no answer so she hung up and dialled again.

22

London, July 2006

Eva, as it happened, was at that moment otherwise engaged. She and Julian were spending the day together, as was their routine on Saturdays. They rose at nine for coffee and news-papers on the terrace, then strolled along to the gym where they each spent ninety minutes working out before recon-vening in the spa for a lengthy wallow. After that there was the walk along to the bagel stand, where she would have rocket and tomato on toasted onion-seed and he would have cheese and pickle on sesame. The day was so predict-able, and yet so utterly satisfying. There was a quiet bliss in mornings like this, she felt. Life was good. They had been living together for more than a year now, and after a certain amount of turbulence as they worked out exactly who was expected to load the dishwasher, things had settled down and their home and relationship had become a haven from the pressures of her job. It all just worked.

Julian must have been thinking something similar as they wandered along the river, because he reached down to grab her hand. Noticing this, she deftly slipped her arm through his and squeezed it, thus avoiding the ickiness of public handholding without causing any upset. This, she thought, was just one example of how good she'd got at successfully navigating the pitfalls of the relationship. He'd almost completely stopped calling her a minky, too, she noted with satisfaction.

'Shall we go across to Greenwich and take a walk in the park?' he asked, breaking her train of thought.

'What for?'

'I don't know, whatever people take walks in parks on sunny days for,' he teased. 'We are allowed to deviate from the routine and do something spontaneous, just for the fun of it.'

Eva grinned. 'Why not?'

Squeaky-clean and damp-haired from the spa, they caught the DLR across the river and wandered through Greenwich Market and up past the Maritime Museum into the park. They sat down in the grass near to the old observatory, where years ago, she remembered, her father had taken her to the Planetarium and shown her the night sky projected onto the inside of the dome. Her eight-year-old self had been awestruck, stunned by the realization of the hugeness of it all.

'How do you get to be someone who knows about planets and stars?' she'd asked Keith on the Tube on the way home.

'I think you'd need to be a physicist for that,' he'd told her. It had felt like a momentous day to her, the day she had decided what to be, and she'd thought about it all the way home on the train sitting beside an oblivious Keith, who would no doubt have been astounded to know the extent to which his casual answer was going to affect the course of his daughter's life.

★

Eva and Julian gazed out at the endless vista stretching down the hill, taking in the classical grandeur of the Queen's House before sweeping on past the English Baroque of Wren's Old Royal Naval College and across the Thames towards Docklands, the City and St Paul's beyond. The sun burned down, making Eva's hair feel slightly itchy as it dried. Her skin gave off a faint smell of chlorine that mingled with the scent of recently cut grass. The air was almost still, the breeze only just perceptible as it trickled past her ears.

'This view is to die for, isn't it?' said Eva. 'I defy anyone to look out at all this and not fall in love with the city. I don't think I've ever told you this,' she continued, 'but with hindsight I think that one of the really important events of my life took place here.'

'You hadn't ever told me that,' he said when she finished telling him about the trip to the Planetarium. 'But what changed? How come you ended up in banking instead of being a physicist like that mate of yours at CERN?'

She shrugged. 'I didn't fancy another five years doing a PhD, piling up a load more loans and never getting out into the real world. It's all very well looking up at the stars when you're eight, but the real world's not quite like that, is it?'

'I suppose not. But in any case, your story makes this the perfect place.'

'What do you mean? Perfect how?'

'Well, I'm hoping it's not the only life-changing event that you're going to have here. The thing is, I brought you here to ask you something.'

Julian shifted around until he was kneeling in front of her, down the hill slightly so that even though Eva was still seated on the grass he was just about looking up at her. For a few seconds she wondered idly what he was doing and allowed her face to arrange itself into an expression of mild enquiry, before a sudden cold certainty snapped into place in her mind as he carefully arranged himself on one knee.

He gazed up at her with shining eyes. 'I know this is cheesy but I wanted to do it properly. Eva, you know how I feel about you. Will you marry me?'

Eva stared at him open-mouthed. She knew she needed to formulate a response but her mind seemed to have frozen. The harder she pushed herself to think, the more her mental gears refused to shift, as though an iron rod had been thrust into the cogs of her thinking machinery. She registered an elderly couple and their basset hound standing a short distance away smiling encouragingly at them, having stopped to watch the heart-warming scene unfold. Eva tried her hardest to force the wheels to turn but when they finally creaked into action they accelerated out of control, producing not some sensible response to the question of whether she wanted to marry the man down on one knee in front of her, but instead a series of increasingly fantastical imaginings in which the basset hound suddenly ran over and savaged Julian, or she herself levitated into a nearby tree, or a bomb went off, hurling them down the hill, or a meteorite fell from the sky, obliterating them and everything around them so that only a smoking crater was left.

Her mind was still spooling through this series of unlikely events that would prevent her from having to answer the question when the silence was finally broken by the tinny and unmistakable sound of the Crazy Frog song. The noise offered a momentary relief, an external distraction and an excuse to look away from Julian, still waiting on bended knee, and glance around, until after a few seconds it became apparent that the sound was coming from her own pocket. She realized with an inward groan that she must have left her phone unlocked on her desk yesterday while Big Paul was around and he'd changed her ringtone to the most annoying tune yet produced by the twenty-first century.

'Don't answer that!' Julian yelped as she stood up and reached into her jeans pocket.

'I'm not, I'm just stopping it ringing.' She glanced at the number. Sylvie. Eva hit the Reject Call button and stuffed it back in her pocket. Julian remained looking up at her expectantly. The phone resumed ringing again almost immediately. Sylvie again. She silenced it and crammed it back into her pocket.

'This isn't exactly going to plan,' Julian said. 'But just so you know, this is the bit where you fall into my arms and tell me that you'd love to marry me.'

'Julian, get up. I'm really sorry, but . . . just get up.'

She looked down at her feet as Julian's face slackened and paled and he clambered upright and brushed the dirt off his legs. The elderly couple hurried off towards the observatory followed by the basset hound, which turned away slowly with a mournful parting look.

'So that's a no then,' said Julian quietly. 'You don't want to marry me.'

'Julian, it's not that I don't want to, it's not a yes or a no. It's just that I didn't see this coming. I haven't had a chance to think it through. I know this is awful but I can't just say yes on the spot if I'm not totally sure. Changing my mind later would be even worse.'

'We've been together for two years. I'd say that's plenty of time to think about it. Where did you think our relationship was going? Oh, that's right, you haven't thought about it. You think about where your career is going, you have time to think about that, but not about where we're going.'

The phone started ringing again.

'Julian, I'm really sorry but I'm going to have to answer this. It's Sylvie and she wouldn't keep calling if it wasn't urgent. She could have gone into labour early and Robert's in New York this week. I'm going to have to take this, okay?'

But he was already striding away from her down the hill and she had a sudden overpowering sense of déjà vu, remembering a time when five years earlier another man had strode away from her down a hill, and in the same moment realized that it didn't feel as bad this time, and wondered whether that was because it got easier the more times it happened or whether it was simply because she had wanted Benedict to stay so much more than she wanted Julian to.

She hit the Accept Call button on her phone. 'Sylvie? What is it? Is the baby coming?'

'No, it's not that. It's Lucien. Eva, he's in prison.'

23

HMP Brixton, July 2006

Eva spotted him as soon as she entered the visiting room, slouched on a plastic chair at a melamine table of the sort she remembered from her school canteen. He was wearing his own clothes, jeans and a hoodie, and looked skinnier than when she'd last seen him at Sylvie's wedding a few months earlier. At the table to his left, a weaselly-looking hard-nut with full-sleeve tattoos was growling at a lank-haired sobbing woman. To his right, a boy with a crew cut and a shell-shocked expression on his face, who couldn't have been much older than eighteen, sat with what must have been his mum, trying not to look as petrified as he obviously felt.

It seemed incredible to her that Lucien could be forcibly held in this place. She hated herself for thinking it, knew that Keith would despise her for voicing such a thing, but most of the other men in that room at least looked like they belonged there. But Lucien? Sure, he was a rogue but he'd always been easy to forgive; his penchant for mischief and his unreliability were inextricable from his sheer appetite for life, encompassing whatever passed before him: people, sex, drugs, alcohol, adventure, it almost didn't matter what, so long as it wasn't boring. Over the years she'd never quite managed to shake off the slight hunger he provoked in her with his reckless smile, full of mingled awareness and disregard for the spark that crackled between them, which had never burst into flame since that one time, years ago, but had still prevented them from ever quite settling into the comfort of friendship. But Lucien wasn't laughing now, and he wasn't a lovable rogue to the police and the courts; he was just another bloke who'd been caught with a lot of class A drugs. He hadn't seen her as she entered the room and she watched him for a few moments, overwhelmed by a rush of something softer yet fiercer than what she usually felt for him.

He stood up from his seat as Eva approached and for a moment they hovered, unsure how to greet each other in this unfamiliar setting, before settling for a tentative hug. He smelled of stale sweat with a sharp chemical undertone.

'Are we allowed to do this?' she mumbled into his ear.

'What, hug? Yeah. I think so. I'm only on remand so things aren't all that strict. You get to wear your own clothes, that sort of thing.'

Lucien withdrew awkwardly from Eva's embrace and they sat down on the plastic chairs on either side of the table and for a moment neither of them knew what to say. He ran his fingers through his greasy hair, and then drummed them on the tabletop.

'So, have you bent over to pick up the soap yet?' Eva tried a joke, suddenly desperate for reassurance that he would laugh this off like he did everything else.

Instead he glared at her. 'That's not as funny as you think it is. You've been watching too much *Law and Order*.'

They sat in silence for another moment or two until Lucien's frown softened.

'Listen, thanks for coming. I didn't want to ask Sylvie, what with the pregnancy and everything,'

'I doubt she'd have managed it to be honest. I don't know if you've seen her lately but she's the size of a house. I'm constantly on alert for a phone call saying the baby's on the way. I thought that was what she was calling about, actually, when she rang to tell me what had happened with you. It came at a bit of an awkward moment.'

Lucien grimaced. 'If you were in bed with Mr Pecs I don't want to hear about it. I've got enough to worry about without that image in my head.'

'Worse, actually. Or better, depending on how you look at it. He'd just asked me to marry him.'

'Jeez. You're not going to are you?'

'Why'd you say it like that? What do you have against Julian?'

'Well, you don't love him, for starters. And you're not going to thank me for saying this, but he's a bit of a plank. You know, no personality.'

His casual dismissal sparked a flare of annoyance in her. 'Lucien, you've met him all of twice. How can you possibly pronounce on his personality? Anyway, you barely even know me these days, let alone who I do or don't love.'

'Okay, well, you asked and I told you,' said Lucien, unruffled. 'Maybe I'm wrong, but I reckon I know you well enough to tell how you feel about someone. We may not have seen all that much of each other lately, but we've got enough history for that.'

'God, you're arrogant. You always bloody were.'

'Well, you tell me. Do you love him? Are you going to marry him?'

Eva sighed and looked away towards the rows of tense or sad conversations playing out all around them.

'I don't know,' she admitted. 'How do you even decide something like that? I've told him I want some more time to think about it. He's not exactly delighted, but what can I do? I mean, there are so many reasons to say yes. He's got a good heart and we have a good life together. But when I think about spending the next thirty or forty or fifty years together I'm not . . . I suppose I'm just not excited. It feels like settling. Which of course is what people do, isn't it? They settle. Everything in life's a compromise and you're better off just accepting that.' She rubbed her eyes. 'But the thing is, I can reason around it all I like but when I think about going home and telling him I'll marry him I feel like there's an enormous wall in front of me blocking my path. I can't even imagine saying it, let alone actually doing it.' She stopped. 'Anyway, why on earth are we talking about my love life? Lucien, I'm so sorry. How are *you* doing?'

'Okay. Kind of.' He looked down at his hands and picked at a fingernail. 'Actually, not really, to be honest. I'm shitting myself.'

Eva lowered her voice. 'What happened? Sylvie filled me in but she didn't seem to know very much. You got caught with a load of coke?'

'Yeah. Two kilos, to be precise. No chance of claiming possession instead of dealing, if that's what you're thinking. I'm going to plead guilty and hope I get a short sentence for a first offence, but it's definitely going to be jail time.'

'God. What were you doing with two *kilos* of coke? I thought you were focusing on the promoting thing? I mean,

I know you've always done a bit of dealing on the side but two kilos? What's that even worth?'

'Thirty-five grand wholesale, maybe a hundred retail. Yeah, I know,' he said, catching the horrified look on her face. 'I don't need you to tell me I've screwed up.'

'But why would you even take such a big risk? I mean, it's not like you need the money, is it, what with all the club nights?'

Lucien looked away with an unusually sheepish air about him. 'Well, obviously I gave that impression. Particularly to you, seeing as you have this stellar career and everything. But the thing is, my promotions company never really took off. I never made what you could actually call a living from it. There's too much competition, every ageing raver calls himself a promoter, and the clubs cream off most of the money anyway. Whereas I've made a decent wedge selling drugs over the years. Blown most of it too, unfortunately. Anyway, I wouldn't usually have handled that much coke but I owed someone a favour. It was only supposed to be at my flat for one night. I don't know how but the police knew exactly what they were looking for, they kicked the door in less than twenty minutes after it had arrived.'

'Do you know what sort of sentence you're looking at?'

'Maybe five years, if I'm lucky. I'd do half of it in jail and half on licence. So thirty months, minus the time I spend in here on remand. It's doable. I'll be somewhere low security, there'll be a library and a gym so I can spend my time reading and exercising. It won't be so bad.' His voice sounded strained and raspy.

'No, of course it won't.' Eva tried to force her own voice

to sound upbeat. 'We'll visit you all the time, and it's not even that long till you'll be out.'

'To be honest, I'm almost as worried about getting out as I am about being in here. What am I going to do then? Not sell drugs, that's for sure. You'd have to be a mug to land yourself in here twice, and I'll have a record for dealing so if I ever got caught again I'd end up doing serious time. And it's been feeling like the party's over for quite a while now, anyway. I just didn't know what to do next and it's going to be even harder when I get out, because well-paid, life-enhancing careers for ex-cons aren't exactly in abundance, are they?'

'Oh, Lucien. You can't worry about that now. We'll think of something, you've got us on your side.' Eva felt desperate for him to believe it, but in all honesty she wasn't sure what life would hold for him at the other end of a prison sentence. For a moment she thought that he might actually be about to cry, but with a visible effort he pulled himself together.

'Listen, you're not here to be my agony aunt. There's a few things I need help with. Sylvie's not much use right now and I need someone I can trust.'

'Of course. Tell me what I can do.'

'Well, first up I'm going to need someone to sort out my flat and put my stuff into storage. It's rented and the landlord doesn't know about this yet. But the most immediate issue is Herbert.'

'Sorry, Herbert?'

'Yeah. My guinea pig. My next-door neighbour's got him, the cops let me take him round there after they arrested me. She's not willing to look after him for long, and anyway, she's keeping him in a cage and he's going to hate that. He's usually free range around the flat, you see.'

'You have a guinea pig? You're a drug dealer with a pet guinea pig? Called Herbert?'

'Yeah, well. I wouldn't have got him myself, it was Bianca. You know, that girl I was seeing? You met her at Sylvie's wedding? Anyway, she's too irresponsible to look after a pet properly. She went away for the weekend without getting anyone to feed him so I sort of confiscated him. I was going to find him a home but no one wanted him and he kept sidling up to me and giving me this really sad look and in the end it got to me and I decided he could stay. So now I need you to take care of him. Sylvie won't do it, she says she has a phobia of rodents, which is ridiculous because Herbert's a guinea pig and they're only rodents on a technicality.'

'I'm not sure my life's that pet-friendly either, you know.'

Lucien's features darkened. 'Eva, I'm asking you to do one thing for me in really desperate circumstances. You don't have to, but if you don't then you'll have to take him to the vet and have him put down, because we can't leave him to die slowly in a cage with someone who doesn't want him and won't look after him. If you can live with that on your conscience, so be it.'

Eva held up her hands in surrender. 'Okay, okay, I'll take Herbert. But I live in a flat and he should have a garden to run around in and maybe some guinea pig friends, so I'm going to have to try to find a better home for him when I can. You might not be able to get him back when you get out but I think guinea pigs have a pretty short lifespan so he may well not be around by then anyway.'

Lucien looked away, and Eva realized too late how tact-less she'd been. She wasn't sure whether it was the prospect of never being reunited with his guinea pig or the realiza-tion that the world would keep turning as he sat in a cell day after day but she noticed his hand, the smallest two fingers gnarled with old scar tissue, trembling where it rested on the table before he saw her looking and stuffed it into his pocket.

*

Short of time, the remainder of the visit had been business-like. Lucien had given her the phone numbers of his landlord and his neighbour and a list of things he needed her to do, and then a bell had rung and they'd briefly embraced before being herded towards their respective doors at opposite ends of the visiting room, one leading into the bowels of the prison, the other to light and freedom. Outside the gate she'd found herself gulping the treacly London air into her lungs as though the odour of cheap disinfectant and desperation that hung heavy inside the prison had slowly been suffocat-ing her. She couldn't imagine breathing that air for another hour, let alone weeks and months and years.

24

London, August 2006

And then, a descent into darkness. It began with Sylvie's voice on the phone, crying and afraid, *something's wrong, please come.* Then the rush to the hospital in the middle of the night, Julian's hands taut on the wheel as they ran red lights. The nervous wait outside the doors of the maternity unit, an hour of agonized not-knowing until they were taken through to a cubicle, where Sylvie, face white and pinched, ramblingly told them how the baby had been distressed so they'd done a caesarean, lifting the limp creature from her belly as she watched and immediately rushing her away to the ICU, that Robert had gone with her, and that she'd heard someone say something about oxygen deprivation and, oh God, is the baby okay, is the baby okay, won't someone please tell me that the baby's going to be okay?

The maternity unit seemed in chaos. Eva sat with Sylvie while Julian went to find a doctor, eventually returning with an exhausted-looking consultant in scrubs who quietly explained that the baby was being cared for on the neonatal unit, that she was stable and the father was with her, and they would take Sylvie there in a few hours, once she'd had a chance to recover from the operation and could get into a wheelchair. Would the baby be okay? When the consultant had left they still didn't know.

Sylvie was sinking in and out of consciousness, and eventually Eva sent Julian home and got into bed beside her for the several hours it took Robert to return, pale and shaking. A midwife followed and removed Sylvie's catheter before loading her into a wheelchair and pushing her through the strip-lit corridors, Eva beside her, to the neonatal ICU and up to the incubator where a tiny baby lay on her front wearing just a nappy, bent legs tucked up beneath her, body covered in leads and monitor pads, a breathing mask over her face.

There in the early morning light, in the antiseptic- and plastic-scented hospital unit, Sylvie's world stopped turning and for an incalculable moment, the beeping monitors and whooshing breathing apparatus fell still. The universe shrank to a single point, a bright speck of life within the incubator in front of her, and when the world started up again it was the same and yet completely and irrevocably changed.

*

Later Sylvie would tell Eva that it had been like looking up and seeing the sky for the first time, something vast and silent that had been there all along, like noticing a truth so huge that it was almost impossible to widen your perspective enough to actually see it.

'And what *was* it, this truth?' asked Eva in frustration, but all Sylvie could say was, 'Love', and though she tried she wasn't able to explain any better.

*

A moment of brightness, and then the plummet into night. Sylvie chose a name, Allegra, and sat beside the incubator for all her waking hours, often singing, occasionally crying, but as quietly as possible so as not to distress the baby. Sometimes Allegra was well enough to be held, sometimes not.

Would the baby be okay? That depended on what you meant by okay, because being okay was now a much more elastic concept than it had previously been.

The baby in the next incubator died suddenly in the night two weeks after Allegra had arrived. Sylvie and Eva held each other and wept silently as his parents, their previously shining, hopeful faces now collapsing in on themselves like dying stars, had returned to the unit in the morning to collect their son's belongings: a tiny hat, the paper teddy with his name, Miles, and birthweight that had been stuck to the end of his incubator.

Robert told Eva to take as much time off as she needed; he'd hold the fort. Of course, this meant that he'd be in the office all hours covering her work as well as his own while she was with Sylvie in the hospital, but that was probably best for everyone anyway.

Every evening Julian collected Eva and Sylvie and drove them home, arriving each time with snacks, magazines, bags of baby clothes and nappies. Sylvie had been kicked off the maternity ward after a few days; they needed the bed and couldn't house every parent with a baby in the hospital. Didn't she know that London maternity wards were overcrowded and in crisis? She'd been lucky to be allowed to stay as long as she had.

Julian picked up Sylvie's washing as they dropped her off at home at night and brought it back cleaned and ironed, smilingly waving away her tearful thanks. Eva watched him, touching her ring finger with the thumb and forefinger of her right hand. She couldn't hope to meet a man with a better heart beating in his chest, she thought to herself. Next time he asked, she'd say yes.

*

Slowly, slowly, over the weeks, Allegra's monitors were removed until finally, three months after she'd been born, she was ready to go home. It was such a relief to leave the hospital with her, even with a feeding tube and oxygen canister, away from the horror and tragedy and the inhuman need to inure yourself to it just to survive. Yet the future was uncertain and full of its own terrors.

Cerebral palsy, the doctors said, but they were reluctant to make too many predictions. She'd definitely have some cognitive impairment, and some loss of control over one side of her body. Beyond that it was hard to say, though when Sylvie asked straight out whether she'd ever live independently the neonatal doctor said gently that it was unlikely.

*

When a few weeks later Robert had to go to New York, Eva stayed over, ending up in the double bed with Sylvie, who lay rigid and sleepless, checking the cot beside her every few minutes to make sure Allegra was still breathing. Late in the night she heard Sylvie whisper something into the darkness so quietly that Eva, who was half asleep, wondered if she had dreamt it.

'Don't leave me, will you?'

Eva rolled over. 'What are you talking about? It's bloody 2 a.m. I'm not going anywhere till morning.'

'That's not what I meant. Please don't leave me to cope with this alone. I love her so much, but I don't know if I can do this on my own.'

Eva was properly awake now. 'I'll never leave you, you idiot,' she promised in a fierce whisper. 'I swear you won't have to do this on your own, whatever happens.'

'Robert's not going to last much longer. We both know it. He won't even look at her, hardly touches her. It's like she disgusts him. We both do. Even when he's here, he comes in at ten at night, sleeps in the other room, leaves again at six.'

'Fuck him. He'll be here or he won't. We'll do it without him. Between the two of us we'll love her as much as any child was ever loved. Twice as much.'

A silence.

'You'll think I'm a monster, but sometimes I think . . . I think about getting up and walking out the door. Just keeping on going. Starting a new life somewhere else. Or just walking until I reach the sea. And then carrying on walking.'

Eva sighed and rested a hand on Sylvie's arm. 'Of course you do. You wouldn't be human if you didn't. It's okay to have those thoughts. But here's a thing my father used to say to me: you are what you do. Not what you think, not even what you say you'll do, but what you actually do. So every mother of a disabled baby who plunges into despair in the middle of the night and thinks about walking away, or even darker thoughts, *if only my child had died instead of this*, and then gets up in the morning and loves and cares for that child, that's who she is. She's a mother who gets up in the morning and loves and cares for her child. The rest means nothing, nothing at all.' Allegra stirred in her cot and Eva lowered her voice back to a whisper. 'Go to sleep now. I'll be here in the morning, and every other morning that you and Allegra need me, I promise.'

25

Docklands, April 2007

It had been a strange meeting and Eva wasn't entirely sure what to make of it. Brad Whitman had called her into a side room at the end of the day, and Eva had approached with a feeling of trepidation. It was unlikely to be good news; though it had been a relief when Robert had taken a job in the States – since it had been all Eva could do to remain coldly civil to him after he'd left Sylvie and Allegra – he hadn't yet been replaced. That had meant she couldn't be cut any more slack at work, and balancing the long hours with the need to support Sylvie, let alone spend time with Julian, had left her exhausted and stretched to the limit. As she entered the meeting room she saw that Brad was already sitting there with a man and a woman, whom she vaguely recognized as being from HR. They talked briefly about a compliance audit of old trades and produced some printouts from the booking system.

Her stomach sank when she realized they were from the Bellwether Trust trade from a couple of years back. At the time she had been nervous that she'd ramped the market a bit too conspicuously, but as the months passed it had seemed as though nothing would come of it and she'd eventually stopped looking over her shoulder. Could it really come back to bite her after all this time? Apparently the answer was yes. The HR man had used words like 'market manipulation' and 'internal review' and 'formal warning'. None of them would meet her eye, and after he had finished speaking Brad stood up and held the door open, leaving her in no doubt that the meeting was over.

As she walked back to her desk with her heart pounding, her phone started to ring in her pocket. Julian. He'd rung several times today and each time she'd put him straight through to voicemail. She just didn't have time for it.

Alert as ever to anything out of the ordinary, Big Paul turned round as she sat down.

'What's up?' he asked.

'I've just been given a warning,' she said slowly.

'How do you mean, a warning?'

'A formal warning from HR over a trade. Do you remember that Bellwether Trust one I made all that money on a couple of years back? The one I pre-hedged by buying all those bonds in the market? They're saying what I did was market manipulation, that I deliberately ramped the market. I mean, you could argue it either way, you always can. But apparently there's a regulatory review going on.' She spoke the words as if feeling her way through a fog.

Big Paul swivelled his chair so that he was facing away from her and looked at his bank of screens as he spoke.

'Listen. Meet me downstairs in five. Not in reception. In the coffee shop by the dock.'

'What? Why? I need to start closing the curves. I guess I could come out for ten minutes if it's important. But why don't we just walk down together now?'

'Christ, you really don't get it, do you? Seriously, wait five minutes, and then come and meet me, understand?' He stood up and pulled his jacket off the back of his chair, walking away towards the lift before she had a chance to say anything more.

*

When she reached the cafe he already had two cups of coffee on the table in front of him and he pushed one towards her as she sat down.

'Here you go. I'm doing you a favour by being here and I don't want to stay long enough to risk being seen by anyone, so sit down and listen up. I'm about to explain a few things that you clearly haven't been around long enough to work out for yourself. That HR meeting you just had? That's the start of the dismissal process. You're out.'

'Out? What do you mean, I'm out?'

'You're out of a job, one way or another. They're going to take whatever they've got on you, and believe me they've got stuff on you the same as they have on all of us, and they're going to use it to force you out of the bank. How you handle the next few weeks will determine how nasty this gets for you. Worst-case scenario, they fire you and you leave with no pay-off and a revoked FSA authorization so that you'll never work in the City again. But if you play it right you should be able to swing it so that they make you redundant with a severance pay-off, or at least let you leave by mutual agreement with all your deferred stock from your previous bonuses.'

She stared at him. 'What? But why would they want to get rid of me? For fuck's sake, look at my P'n'L, it's as good as anyone else's.'

He leant back in his chair. 'Shit, I can't believe you're still this wet behind the ears. This is just the game, Eva. It's a regulatory review and you got caught in the net. They've got to throw someone to the wolves and this time it's you. You're a dead man walking. I can't be seen to be associated with that, but you're a good kid and I don't want to see you get screwed over too badly. Don't take it personally, it happens to everyone sooner or later.'

'It hasn't happened to you.'

'Yeah, well, I'm different. I'm a lot better connected than you are, and I know where more than a few bodies are buried.' He sat back in his chair. 'Anyway, it *has* happened to me. At a different bank, a long time ago, and the reason I've still got a career is that I handled it right. That's not common knowledge, so don't go shouting it about.'

She rubbed her temples with her fingertips. 'What am I going to do if they fire me? This is the only thing I've ever done. It's who I am.'

'Yeah, well. You need to hold your shit together. Here's what you're going to do. Don't talk to anyone about this, you don't want to taint yourself. You got that? You don't want anyone to know this is happening. You come into the office every day and you act exactly the same as you always do, but every free minute you have, you call all the contacts and headhunters you know and try to wangle another job offer pronto. That way you can just resign with your reputation intact and everybody's happy. Apart from that, you need to position yourself internally so that HR and Brad know they can't just sack you without a fight. They don't like unfair dismissal lawsuits, especially from minorities and women, so you need to hire yourself an absolute fucking hellbeast of a lawyer and take him along to the rest of your HR meetings so they know you won't just roll over. That won't be cheap, but it will be worth every penny.' He stood up to leave. 'That's about as much as I can tell you. Good luck.'

As he turned to go, she asked, 'Paul? Why me? Do you know why this is happening to me?'

He paused, one hand on the back of the chair. 'Shit, it's not personal. They get rid of ten per cent of the front office headcount every year, so the chances are this will happen sooner or later in a trader's career. Why do you think there are no old traders? Sure, the successful ones sometimes bail out once they've got enough to retire on, but where do you think the rest of 'em go? I better get back to the desk now. Wait at least five minutes before you follow me, understand?'

*

Eva sat and finished her coffee, giving Big Paul the five minutes he'd requested before returning to the office. There was no sign of anyone on the desk, so she closed the curves and then picked up her bag and left. As she walked out of the building her mobile started ringing. It was Julian again, but she didn't answer it. She'd be home in a few minutes and she didn't want to tell him about this on the phone. Besides, she needed to think things through on the walk back. She was certain that she was freaking out underneath it all, but her thoughts were oozing through her mind like mud. She was being fired. In a matter of weeks she would be out of a job. After all the long hours and late nights, the endless, relentless, grinding sacrifice of everything else in her life, everything she had worked for was about to disappear. Eva turned to look back at the office, the windows glowing orange in the fading light. Why would this happen now, when she had finally got to a point in her career where she had felt if not exactly indispensable, then at least as if she belonged? An insider, almost. She had experience, she knew her job, and she was good at it. How could this be happening?

Outside in the open air, she suddenly found herself struggling to breathe, inhaling and exhaling suddenly an effortful process that her body actually needed to be instructed to perform. She started to walk, one foot in front of the other until she reached a nearby park. The sky felt low and ominous. Was it possible to feel claustrophobic outdoors? In a tree above her, a crow shifted its feet and then dropped off its branch like a stone, startling her before it turned and swooped upwards. She stopped and watched until it was a vanishing speck against the grey clouds, trying to shake off the feeling of the sky closing in on her.

*

As she reached her front door and turned the key in the lock, a spurt of stomach acid rose into her mouth, and she had to swallow hard to force it back down. The door swung open but instead of the empty hallway that she was expecting, Julian was standing there. A strange energy buzzed in the air as they looked at each other, both of them surprised. He had a weird expression on his face, and for a split second she thought that somehow he already knew. For a moment her muscles slackened in relief and she leant forward, about to take a step towards him and fall into his arms, when something at the edge of her vision stopped her. There was a row of suitcases and bags lined up along the wall by his feet. Her mind tried to process the scene but she didn't seem able to gain purchase on the facts; they darted or slithered out of her grasp as she reached for them. But something old and instinctive, deep within the lizard-brain, stopped her moving forward to embrace him. Eva let her arms drop to her sides and they stood and stared at each other.

'You haven't been answering your phone,' Julian said.

'No.'

'I needed to talk to you. I didn't want you to come home to this.'

'What have I come home to, Julian? I'm going to need you to explain it to me.'

He paused. 'It is what it looks like. I'm leaving.'

Eva felt as though she was encased in a bubble. His words bounced off its surface. She opened her mouth, but only a strange bark of laughter emerged.

'I'm sorry,' he said. 'I've met someone else.'

At last. Something she could understand.

'You've been cheating on me?'

'Not really. Not exactly. Would it even matter to you if I had? You've known for a long time that I haven't been happy and you haven't cared enough to do anything about it. You didn't want to marry me. Now I've met someone who actively wants a future with me instead of reluctantly defaulting to it.'

'Let me guess. A personal training client? Tammy? Candida?'

'So what if it is a client?' The plea for forgiveness in his eyes flattened into something more defensive. 'That's mostly how I meet people. I'm not ashamed of it. It's how I met you, remember?'

Eva groped around for a reaction, but she couldn't work out what she felt. Pain? Anger? Relief? All she could think about was how she wanted to sit down on her own in a quiet room with a drink. She just didn't have the emotional resources to deal with this, on top of everything else. If this was going to happen no matter what she said or did, it was best for it to happen fast.

'Right,' she said. 'I'll let you get on and move your stuff then. Put your key on the table as you leave. I'll give you an hour, will that be enough?'

'That's it?' he demanded. 'That's all you have to say to me after nearly three years together? My God, you really never gave a shit about me, did you?'

'You're lucky I'm making this so easy on you, Julian. And you aren't really the one in a position to get angry here, so spare me the histrionics.' The barb flew out, a tiny poisonous dart precisely aimed to exact a sliver of revenge, and she saw that it had reached its intended target.

His expression darkened and closed and when he spoke his voice was flat. 'You always were cold-blooded, Eva, but this is incredible. It just proves I'm making the right decision. I don't even know why I was so worried about upsetting you. Have a nice—'

She presumed the last word was 'life', but the end of the sentence was lost in the sound of the door that she slammed shut behind her. Eva walked away down the corridor towards the lift.

26

London and Sussex, November 2008

In the year since she'd lost her job and Julian had left, Eva had barely been back to her own place. She had her own bedroom at Sylvie's and spent most of her time there helping with Allegra, which was a lifeline for Sylvie but also for Eva since the alternative was aimless, miserable days alone in the empty rooms of the apartment she had once loved but which had long since become a part of a life she could no longer occupy. Allegra was two years old now, and a new kind of normal was establishing itself. The oxygen tank and the feeding tube were gone, but managing her fits and feeding her could still be difficult.

The weeks between Eva's first HR warning and the final termination of her contract had been agony, filled with hours spent pacing around outside her office on the phone to head-hunters and contacts in other banks, trying to scope out the territory without betraying her desperation. Whether word had got around the markets or whether people just weren't hiring she had no idea, but in any case it had all been to no avail. The wind had already been starting to blow in a different direction and as the days and weeks passed, unprecedented upheavals were taking place in the global economy.

Tectonic plates had begun to shift, slowly at first as the US data had begun to turn bad, with housing numbers and non-farm payrolls sliding, and then more quickly, as Northern Rock experienced the first UK bank run in a century as the extent of its liabilities became apparent. The bad news snow-balled into an unstoppable avalanche as Lehman Brothers filed for bankruptcy and governments scrambled to bail out their financial institutions. Eva followed the stories obses-sively and impotently, as events that weren't ever supposed to happen started occurring one after the other with frighten-ing regularity. Mingled with the horror was fascination at watching these economic, political, and maybe even histor-ical, forces ripple through the stratosphere.

Trying to steer a derivatives book through this perfect storm would have been nightmarish, and she felt a certain schadenfreude at the thought of Brad Whitman working hundred-hour weeks trying to stem haemorrhaging losses while watching his bonus and probably his career evaporate before his eyes. When she tried to calculate the impact of these market moves on some of the positions she'd left behind in her trading book her eyes watered. But, oh, to be an outsider at such a time was maddening too. No Bloom-berg, no market gossip or inside info, just another civilian standing by. The bit of her that wasn't appalled by the thought of all the people losing jobs and pensions and sav-ings was frustrated at being sidelined in such remarkable times, a mere onlooker to the sort of turbulence that traders see once in a lifetime, if that. She'd come into the market at the beginning of her career at just the time of the Russian default and subsequent failure of Long Term Capital Man-agement, and had been able to do nothing but stand and watch open-mouthed as the real players made and lost fortunes on the back of unprecedented volatility. Now it was happening again, only worse.

Like everyone else, she was kicking herself for not paying attention. The signs had been there all along for those who had been able and willing to break away from the groupthink and look on with disinterested eyes. She'd always thought she was one of those people, but now she could see how much she'd bought into the crowd mentality, virtually ignoring the housing bubble inflating and the massive increases in consumer and government borrowing around the globe. Of course, she'd known that these things couldn't go on forever but for a trader it wasn't enough to be able to say that; when your time horizons were only ever as far ahead as your next bonus it wasn't in your interest to constantly focus on the long-term macroeconomic picture. Beneath all the shock and panic on the surface, she thought that if you sat quietly you could hear other rumbles running through the deeper tributaries of social consciousness, as people began to question the very foundations of Western civilization.

*

In the light of all this, Eva had mixed feelings about going back home. On the one hand a bit of familial support wouldn't go amiss; on the other, she was far from certain that support was what she would be met with. Her arguments with Keith were usually good-natured, but she was feeling more in need of comfort than ideological debate, and she was aware that spending a decade watching the rise of what he viewed as a capitalist kleptocracy had not been easy for her father. Eva eventually took a gloomy train ride down to Sussex and arrived to find him clearly feeling vindicated. She had been there only ten minutes when he rather pointedly turned the volume up several notches for a Robert Peston special on the radio.

'You're actually enjoying all this, aren't you?' she demanded. 'My losing my job, the credit crisis? Go on then, just say it. You think I brought down the economy, but it's bullshit.'

'Yes, well,' he said in measured tones that made clear the 'well' neutralized any agreement implied by the 'yes'. 'I'm not saying that you caused the crisis, of course, but you were a small cog in a big machine that enabled it to happen. The derivatives you traded were so complex that almost no one understands them, so the few people who did could use them to make the numbers look any old way in the short term. Then by the time it all comes out they're sitting in the Cayman Islands in a Jacuzzi full of dollar bills.'

Eva stared at him across the kitchen. 'It's all so simple in your head, isn't it? Good people are socialists, and capitalists are greedy and evil. Except the world is more complicated than that. Here's what I really did: I provided liquidity to markets and facilitated the efficient allocation of risk. I helped people to hedge their exposure to inflation and interest rates on things like railways and infrastructure projects, real social goods that simply wouldn't have gone ahead otherwise.'

'Well, now. The Victorians managed to build the railways without CDOs.'

Eva rolled her eyes. 'You're nostalgic for the days of chimney sweeps and Gin Alley? Give me a break. If you want to bring history into it, you barely need to glance at a textbook to see that markets are what make people free and affluent.'

Keith delivered what he clearly felt was the killer blow in an infuriatingly complacent tone. 'I don't even know why you're defending a system that chewed you up and spat you out.'

'Because I actually believe in what I'm saying!' Eva banged her hands against the sides of her head. 'I don't think you've ever really got that. I know you've always thought I was a victim of false consciousness, or else just bending my ideals to fit my self-interest, but I'm an intelligent adult, and I believe in liberal democracy and capitalism and well-run markets. I find you just as incomprehensible as you find me, clinging to ideals that have been shown to cause massive harm every time they've been implemented.'

Unused to the argument veering into personal territory, Keith chose to focus on the political. 'I'm not saying social ism's perfect, but you of all people should know there's no such thing as a free market. It's a Platonic form, an unreachable ideal. Here in the real world, markets aren't free. There are natural monopolies, geographical constraints, regulatory barriers to entry, cartels as far as the eye can see.'

'Jesus. If you want to talk about utopian ideals, take a look at your precious communism. It runs completely counter to human nature. No one is going to work harder than the guy next to him with his feet up if they get paid the same regardless. It's a race to the bottom, or even worse, if you look at history, it spawns dictatorships under which millions of people die in gulags, as much as your lot like to gloss over those inconvenient truths.'

Eva was infuriated to find herself growing tearful as she

spoke, and Keith was clearly taken aback by her display of emotion.

'I don't want to argue with you, Eva. We simply disagree on this.'

'Yeah, but it's not just a disagreement about whether cats are better than dogs, is it? Underlying it is the fact that you've never approved of anything about the way I've lived my life. To most people I was a success, and I worked so hard. But you, you never once told me you were proud of me, do you know that? And now, when I could really do with some support, all I get is a bunch of Trotskyite self-righteousness. All you care about is your precious ideological purity. It's more important to you than your own daughter.' Even as she said the words she knew she wasn't being entirely fair, but she was too upset to care.

'I don't have to always agree with your values to be proud of what you've achieved, Eva,' he said slowly, reaching around for a type of language he was unaccustomed to using. 'And I know your mother would have been too.'

But Eva wasn't listening. She upended the cold remainder of her coffee into the sink and walked out of the door to head back to London.

*

Her flat was on the market but things weren't looking good; the torrent of money that had been pouring into bricks and mortar during the early part of the decade had suddenly dried to a trickle, and words like *asset bubble* and *negative equity* were increasingly being bandied around. The estate agent had advised her to 'price it realistically for a quick sale', which apparently translated into an asking price that would mean taking a substantial loss on what she'd paid for it. Even so, there had only been a handful of viewings.

Every time she thought about what she was going to do next, she came up against the immovable wall of uncertainty. If the flat sold quickly and for a reasonable price, she could buy something smaller closer to Sylvie and Allegra and somehow start again. But if not . . . well, it didn't bear thinking about. She'd be stuck in this limbo or forced to absorb the sort of loss that would leave her if not completely destitute then jobless and without any of the financial security she'd thought she'd achieved in a decade of hard toil. Thinking about the future was like staring into a void: the job had consumed everything, all of the time and energy that other people had spent on husbands, children, hobbies, creative fulfilment. There had been no Plan B.

27

Hampstead, November 2008

Another day, another trudge around the leaf-carpeted streets of Hampstead. The daily walks with Allegra weren't really a chore, more a way to pass the time. The front wheel of the buggy was clogging up with sodden leaves, forcing Eva to stop on the footpath in Flask Walk and kick at it to try and dislodge them. She glanced at her watch. It was an hour before Allegra's teatime and she knew that Sylvie would appreciate the break if she kept her out till then.

Eva pushed the buggy out on to New End and down through the back streets in the direction of South End Green. The thing she liked most about this part of London was the way the houses all seemed to have little individual touches, bird-boxes or shutters with heart shapes cut out, or panels of elaborate plasterwork above the windows. She tried to remember to look up when she was walking, because that's when you saw the things no one else noticed: an ornate chimney pot here, a pre-war advertising sign there. Of course, not watching where you were going came with its own hazards, and only the day before an elderly woman had whacked her in the shins with her umbrella after she'd almost mown down her gaggle of chihuahuas with the buggy. The streets of Hampstead teemed with belligerent old ladies and their posses of tiny canines, and they weren't to be trifled with.

The whole texture of the place was so different to her Docklands home. In some ways one was a monument to the past and the other to the future, the power of the class system and hereditary privilege versus the sheer unanswerable force of money. Undoubtedly both had their winners and losers, but Eva had always felt that the latter was at least open to anyone and was transparent about its true nature, whereas class was exclusive and all the more pernicious for hiding its true nature under cover of notions of gentility and noblesse oblige. Even the windowpanes had a different quality to them here, a sort of rippled, watery imperfection that contrasted with the invisible smoothness of the sliding doors to her own apartment terrace.

The day was starting to fade to dusk. Eva liked this time of evening, when lights were beginning to be switched on but before curtains had been drawn, so that she could peer through the windows to catch snippets of activity, a mother ushering her overexcited children to the dinner table, an old man sitting on the sofa with a Jack Russell and a book in his lap. They were quietly idyllic, these scenes, and spoke to her of a sort of domesticity that had never really featured in her own life. This thought reminded her that now she had fallen out with Keith she had no real home to go back to, and gave her an ache deep inside her ribcage. A ridiculous response to these glimpses of other people's lives playing out, she chided herself, because if life had taught her one thing it was that appearances rarely tell the real story. She'd spent long enough tending to her own carefully cultivated work persona to know that apparently calm exteriors could have all sorts of things seething underneath. You could look through the windows at any one of these people, but you would only ever see what was there, not what wasn't. The losses and absences didn't show, despite so often being the immovable facts around which a life orbited.

That woman, laughing as she herded her protesting children to the table, she might have a story you wouldn't see at a glance. You wouldn't be able to see the miscarriages she had before those children came along, or the brother who'd died, or the father she'd had to put into a home because his dementia had become too much to handle. All you saw was the bright flash of happiness, and it wasn't anything close to the whole truth.

Even so, looking in from the outside, these rooms full of books and cats, rocking horses and pianos, seemed infused by the lives richly lived within them. They weren't particularly ostentatious in any modern way, though there were endless understated touches of period grandeur played down or gently mocked by flourishes of eccentricity: a mermaid figurehead from a ship's bow on the front of a house on Pilgrims Lane, and around the corner, a plaster bust with a jaunty hat surveying the world from an upstairs window. Benedict had grown up around here, though she didn't know exactly where. It had been two years since he'd stopped answering her emails and phone calls, and after a while she'd given up trying. On one level it made sense; how long could you keep a friendship going when it so often felt strained? Ever since that row with Lydia their meetings had become more infrequent, and when they did meet up the conversation had been much harder going than it used to be. The problem was the accumulation of subjects that they couldn't talk about. Lydia and the kids seemed to be off limits – since their disastrous lunch it had sounded insincere or even sarcastic whenever she'd asked after them, even to her own ears. And any mention of Julian seemed to render Benedict stiff and unresponsive, and of course they could never speak of the kiss they'd shared on Hampstead Heath. That left their jobs and maybe Sylvie and Lucien to chat about but it wasn't enough, really. There was too much of a sense of dancing around the subjects that they couldn't talk about, now that those subjects had expanded to cover most of their separate lives. And Benedict had drifted apart from Sylvie and Lucien by mutual consent since he'd married and had kids, so it had been strangely easy to simply disappear from each other's lives.

And yet Eva would never have been the one to allow the friendship to just wither and die. She'd assumed they would soldier on through the awkward patches and out the other side, just like they always had. But, evidently, dissolving the friendship hadn't been unthinkable to Benedict. *What's the point in flogging a dead horse when our lives have so clearly and permanently diverged?* he must have asked himself. And what *was* the point? After all, one of the things she'd always felt about Benedict was that she knew him, really understood what went on inside his head and heart. He'd never been very good at hiding how he felt. Even after he got together with Lydia, she'd been sure that he still cared about her. It was one of those things that in her more naive days she had just assumed was a constant.

These were the streets and houses of his childhood landscape, the environment that had shaped him. It couldn't be more different to her own. Was that why she'd been so easy for him to cast off? Had there always been an undercurrent that she'd failed to notice, an innate sense that they were simply cut from a different cloth?

Her own childhood had been spent in a house unbowed by aesthetic considerations. Once in a while her father had rolled up his sleeves and given the place a perfunctory clean, but the two of them had generally lived perfectly happily among the old tins of paint, broken vases and suppurating coffee mugs. It hadn't seemed all that much like her friends' homes but there had been plenty to like about growing up with a parent who absent-mindedly treated you like a miniature adult. Keith would rarely remember to usher her to bed at a sensible hour, so during her formative years Eva had been able to enjoy plenty of boisterous dinners punctuated by drunken arguments about Hegelian dialectics, one of which, she vividly recalled, had descended into a punch-up that had left a media studies lecturer named Geoffrey with a bloody nose. She hadn't often dwelt on the fact that it was just the two of them. One parent seemed fine, plenty even. Anyone else would surely have felt like an intruder. And yet she could see now that something had been missing. Keith had never seen her point of view or understood her decisions, and they never really talked about their lives or how they felt about anything. She'd always seen it as a strength that they were the sort of people who didn't need big soppy heart-to-hearts, that they cared about loftier, more important things, but his political beliefs seemed to her now suspiciously like something to hide behind to avoid any emotional connection; now that her world, not some abstract ideology but her real, actual life, had fallen apart around her, all he wanted to do was score political points. And when she looked at her own life now, it too seemed defined by the things that were missing: a mother, a career, a home. Benedict. A cluster of black holes exerting their irresistible gravitational pulls, warping and distorting all that remained.

And then, of course, there was the other loss, not even really her own but nevertheless the one in front of her every day. Eva had fallen in love with Allegra right alongside Sylvie, and the baby had seemed to blossom with their love, making progress even as the doctors warned them not to expect too much, slowly but surely learning to eat and take a few steps and say a few words. But even as they celebrated each milestone, they both knew that the loss was profound. At the moment of Allegra's birth, they had lost a part of her that would prevent her from ever growing into the person she should have been, and in private they each grieved for the Allegra who would one day have reached her full potential without the agonies of learning difficulties and cerebral palsy, the Allegra who should have been looking forward to a life of first kisses and first days at university instead of leg braces and Statements of Educational Need.

*

The sky darkened and the rain began to fall, softly at first and then harder as Eva turned and headed for home along the edge of the Heath. She paused to fix the rain cover over the buggy, ensconcing Allegra in a warm, dry bubble. The raindrops hit the ground as she walked, splashing into puddles and rustling into piles of leaves and sliding onto the tarmac under the roaring wheels of the cars that were making their way up East Heath Road in ever-increasing numbers as rush hour took hold. The watery symphony prevented Allegra from hearing Eva crying quietly, the sound instead floating up into the sky unheard and out into a universe in which babies were born disabled and mothers died and people were deserted by those they loved.

28

Hampstead, Winter 2008–Spring 2009

Eva opened unenthusiastic eyes and peered out into another new day. What to do with it? On balance, she thought, she would spend it in bed just like she had the day before, and if she was honest, like quite a few more days over the last month.

It had started with a cold, a bad one with burning eyes and a hacking cough and a throat so sore she could barely speak.

'We'd better quarantine you,' Sylvie said after taking a look at her. 'There's no way you're giving that to Allegra, she'd be back in hospital in an instant.'

So Eva had gathered some supplies and stayed in her room. After a few days, the bug had subsided but the days were getting short and cold and every morning it was harder to motivate herself to get out of bed. The world outside was full of noise and friction and the streets were crowded with people smiling and talking on phones, people with things to do and places to go. Eva, by contrast, walked through the streets like a ghost. Whenever she went out, she wanted nothing more than to be back in her room where there was no reminder of what she was or what she should be. She never felt hungry, so she was shrinking and that felt right too, that she was occupying less space. The layer of residual fat from her trading years had melted away. Sometimes she fantasized that the process would continue until she disappeared altogether.

*

'That's enough now,' Sylvie said from the foot of the bed the next morning. 'You're going to have to pull yourself together, because if I have to look at your miserable face any longer I'll jump off a fucking bridge.' She paused then continued when no reaction was forthcoming from Eva. 'You've lost your job and a boyfriend you didn't particularly like, not the use of your legs. It's only a job. And a boyfriend. You can get another one of each. You just need to get out of bed and pull yourself together.'

Eva stared up at the ceiling. 'I can't get another job, not in the City, anyway. And what the hell else can I do? Go off and become a yoga teacher?'

'I don't know,' snapped Sylvie. 'But you'll get another job eventually and everything will be fine. So what if Julian left you? He should have done it ages ago, you never loved him and frankly it showed.' She sat down heavily on the edge of the bed and rubbed her eyes. 'Look, I'm sorry if this sounds harsh but, to be honest, it's quite hard to stomach when all of your problems are temporary. In a year's time they will probably all have disappeared. I face far bigger challenges than you every single day, and do you know what I do? I get on with it.'

'I know you do. You've been really brave,' conceded Eva.

Sylvie shrugged. 'Brave? Everyone loves going on about how brave I am and isn't it great that I'm coping so well, because they need a narrative that tells them everything's okay. And guess what? Everything's not okay, and it's not going to be okay, and I still get out of bed every morning and stick a smile on my face even if I feel like my heart is breaking, because what's the alternative? That's life. You play the hand you're dealt.' Sylvie stood up and moved over to the door, adding as she left the room, 'There used to be more fight in you than this. Pull it back, Eva, because we still need you.'

The irritation Eva felt at Sylvie's lecture was the strongest sensation to pierce her listlessness in weeks. Sure, Sylvie had problems, but she didn't have a monopoly on them. One person having a very bad time didn't nullify everyone else's troubles. And hadn't Eva been right there beside her every single step of the way? Yes, Allegra was Sylvie's daughter and it was hardest for her, but she wasn't the only one who loved her, had been devastated for her, fretted about the future.

But it was indignation rather than anger, and it dissipated quickly, leaving in its wake an acceptance that everything Sylvie had said to her was basically fair enough. Later that day she got out of bed and took Allegra for a walk for the first time in weeks, and when she woke early the next morning, her torpor had lifted a little. She noticed the birds singing outside and their tones sounded clearer, sharper. Eva dressed and went down to the kitchen and made coffee, taking satisfaction as the beans in the grinder moved from an agitated rattle to a smooth whirr. She poured a mug and took it upstairs.

Sylvie looked thin and tired, Eva noted as she watched her friend sit up in bed and take the drink from her hands. Her eyes were puffy and her arms protruded stick-like from her nightie, and her hair was a two-tone tangle of light brown roots and copper ends.

'I'll get Allegra up and do breakfast this morning,' Eva told her.

'Are you sure you're okay on your own?' Sylvie raised a sceptical eyebrow. 'You've got to be really careful to make sure she doesn't choke. And she's getting so uncooperative about having her nappy changed, she had a tantrum and nearly fell off the changing table yesterday.'

Eva held up a reassuring hand to halt her. 'I know I've not exactly been showcasing my resourcefulness lately, but I can handle this. Have a lie-in and I'll call you if we run into any trouble.'

*

As the days slowly grew longer, a tide was turning. Despite keeping her feelers out no job offers had materialized, and after almost a year on the market the flat still hadn't sold, but with the lighter days came a sense of optimism so pervasive that Eva decided to take the plunge and try to raise capital for the business idea that had been niggling at her for years. She quietly worked up a business plan, but the trouble was that there couldn't have been a worse time because the banks weren't lending. The credit crunch had made capital scarce and there weren't exactly millions of investors out there looking to put their cash into risky start-ups, as Eva explained to Sylvie over breakfast one morning.

Sylvie looked up from spooning porridge into the mouth of an uncooperative Allegra, who was using her good hand to smear the lumpy gruel across the table. 'Well,' she said, 'there's always me.'

Eva blinked. 'What? When you say "me", you mean "you" as in you? Like, you personally?'

'Yes, me. Don't sound so surprised. This comes at a good time, actually, because the NHS Litigation Authority is about to pay out the first tranche of Allegra's compensation and I need to invest it.'

'Well, I can help you do that. But I can't let you invest in the business. It's too risky. You're going to need that money and there's no way I would risk losing it.'

'It's okay, I trust you,' Sylvie reassured her. 'If anyone can make it work it's you and I'd rather invest in somebody I know and have faith in, than some company I know nothing about. I wouldn't recognize an Enron if it bit me on the backside.'

Eva smiled and shook her head. 'It's really lovely of you to offer, but look, half of all new businesses fail in the first year. I believe in my idea, I really do, but start-ups are risky for all sorts of reasons. God knows the middle of a global recession isn't the time I'd have chosen to start a business if it didn't happen to be when I was out of a job. Obviously I wouldn't be doing this if I didn't think it was going to work, but there's no way I could take responsibility for the money that Allegra needs for her future. I can help you decide where to invest but you need to be really conservative, gilts, inflation-linked bonds, that sort of thing.'

Sylvie looked crestfallen and returned to mopping up the tabletop porridge swamp. 'Are you sure? Because I was thinking that maybe it would be good for me to come in on the business. I'm going to need to make some money sooner or later, and it's going to be tough to find a job that I can fit around Allegra.'

'Well,' said Eva slowly, 'this doesn't mean that you can't come in on the business. I'm going to need an extra pair of hands, and it would be great for that to be someone I trust. Why don't you come in as a partner?'

'What, without investing any money? That's not fair though, is it? What with its being your idea and all the work you've done on it.'

'Well, consider it payment in lieu of rent for squatting in your spare room. For that, I am going to give you half of the business. Since at present the business is worth the princely sum of zero pounds sterling, I actually feel like I'm getting a pretty good deal.'

'You really mean it? I'm going to be a partner?' Sylvie leant across the table and took Eva's face in her hands, depositing a kiss on her forehead. 'That's amazing. Thank you. You won't be sorry, I promise.' She sat back down and frowned. 'But that doesn't solve the money problem. If you won't take our money, you're going to have to get it from somewhere else. Maybe you could hit up some of your old City contacts?'

Eva took a long swig from her coffee mug. 'Yeah, that's exactly what I was thinking.'

*

'Hello there, Fatboy. How's it going?'

'Eva, old girl,' Big Paul's voice boomed from the phone. 'Long time no see. How are things with you?'

Eva moved over to the window, took a deep breath and launched into her sales pitch. 'What matters, my friend, is not how things are with me, but how they are with you. And I'm going to answer that question: things are great with you, because it's your lucky day. I'm calling to make you an offer you can't refuse.'

'I always knew you'd succumb to my animal magnetism eventually. Tell me, it was the rippling abs, wasn't it?'

'Well, there's that, obviously, but I also have a business proposition for you.'

'Proposition away.'

'I'm looking for an angel.'

'Baby, I can be your angel. Assuming you happen to be into big fat hairy unkempt angels.'

She grinned at the mental image. 'Thanks, but for this particular initiative I won't need you in wings and a loincloth. I have this amazing business idea, and you are one of a select few lucky investors chosen to share in my inevitable success.'

'Thanks. I love investing in start-ups, something about the tinkling sound of dreams shattering as they go to the wall.'

Eva continued, undeterred. 'Very tax efficient, this sort of investment. Did you know that you can do it as an Enterprise Initiative Scheme and claim thirty per cent of your investment back from the taxman on day one?'

'Keep talking.'

'Come over for dinner and I'll pitch it to you properly. It'll be at Sylvie's place in Hampstead, she's my business partner. It saves us having to sort out a babysitter for Allegra.'

'Ah yes, Robert's sprog. How's she doing? What with the, um, retardation, or whatever the politically correct term for it is these days.'

'Allegra's doing pretty well actually. She's two and a half now, and she's saying a few words and almost walking. All stuff they'd normally do earlier, obviously, but given how uncertain the prognosis was in the beginning we're over the moon. Do you see much of the lovely Robert these days?'

'Not a lot, no,' Big Paul told her. 'I get the odd Bloomberg but we were never exactly besties, more workmates and drinking buddies. I wouldn't be too hard on him though, he was in bits after the little one was born. I took him for a drink and I swear the poor bloke nearly cried.'

'Yes, well. Sadly that didn't translate into sticking around and actually taking care of her.'

'Yeah, I hear you. How's the mum, your friend Sylvie? Am I safe to come to this meeting or is she gonna hold it against me that the only time we met I was Rob's wingman? And thus could be unjustly construed as bearing some responsibility for her having got up the duff in the first place? Robert reckoned it happened that night we were all out together.'

'I doubt that's top of the list of things she thinks about, but if anything she'd probably thank you. Not everyone understands this but Allegra's a blessing, not a curse. You don't have kids, do you?'

'Nope. Not the daddy type. Couldn't if I wanted to, in any case.'

'How'd you mean?'

'I shoot blanks, not to put too fine a point on it. I was married once, a long time ago. We were only youngsters, childhood sweethearts you could call it. I wasn't too bothered about having kids, I was only about twenty, but after a couple of years she marched me along to the clinic to get tested and it turned out my boys were swimming backwards or something. It wasn't long after that she ran off with a bloke who packed a bigger punch in the fertility stakes. Last I heard she was living in Hereford with a plumber and three or four of the little blighters.'

'Wow, I'm sorry. I had no idea.'

'Well, you wouldn't, would you. It was a long time ago and it's not on my CV. I was just Paul in those days, not Big Paul, before all the Dom P and lunches at Le Gavroche went to my waistline.' He sighed nostalgically. 'Still, it was probably for the best. Who'd keep the strip clubs of Soho in business if I turned into a family man? The fabric of this fine city would have been the poorer for it.'

'Indeed it would.'

'Anyway. Enough about my stunning physique. When do you want to pitch Eva's Widgits to me?'

*

'. . . and that's why we feel justified in projecting that we'll break even at the end of year two and go significantly into profit by the end of year three.'

It was Friday night and Big Paul was sitting at Sylvie's kitchen table, his fingers laced behind his head and an implacable expression on his face. In front of him were an empty dinner plate and an almost empty wine glass.

'It's not a terrible idea,' he said slowly. 'There are some obvious obstacles, but it's not utterly shit.'

Eva leant forward. 'High praise indeed, and wholly justified. Think about it. How many times have you tried to order things over the internet only to find that it takes so long to retrieve the damn things from the sorting office that you may as well have gone and bought it on the high street? Internet shopping has vast potential but it's being hobbled by twentieth-century delivery systems unable to cope with the notion that people go out to work and don't have a spouse sitting at home. The Plop-Box will solve all that. The basic design will be classic, like those old red post-boxes, and it will come in different shapes and sizes to fit the dimensions and style of your porch or garden. You leave it unlocked and empty, the delivery man puts the parcel inside and closes it, it locks automatically and gives him a receipt, then you open it with a key or code when you come home. Simple, yet exquisitely practical.'

Big Paul looked thoughtful. 'Well, first off, I'm assuming Plop-Box is a working title, because it sounds like a mobile khazi. Second, the distributors are your biggest challenge. They have to agree to accept a receipt from this thing instead of a signature from a person. Have you spoken to anyone yet? Royal Mail? DHL? The Post Office is pretty monolithic and hardly well adapted to change.'

'We've had initial talks and they made promising noises, but we need to have a prototype in place to get them to commit, and that's why we need capital now. I really don't think it's going to be that hard a sell once we have proof of concept. Think about it. Every time they fail to deliver a parcel, they have to take it back to a sorting office and then attempt to redeliver it. That adds costs for them. If the house-holder buys a Plop-Box, they're spending money that will not only save them inconvenience, but will save the distributors money too. Everyone's a winner.'

There was a few seconds' pause and then Big Paul said, 'Okay. Done.'

'Done?' asked Eva.

'Done,' he confirmed. 'Two hundred.'

Sylvie's face dropped. 'Oh. Two hundred quid won't go far.'

But Eva was smiling broadly. 'Not quid, Sylvie. Grand.'

Eva and Big Paul watched in amusement as she processed the information, furrowed brow giving way to widening eyes. 'As in, thousand pounds? Two hundred thousand pounds?' she squeaked. 'Just like that?'

'Yeah, just like that,' said Big Paul. 'With one caveat. You have to change the name. Now, do you know why I'm doing this? I'm doing it because I know you, Eva. I trust and believe in you, but more than that, I know that you are so anally retentive that you would walk over hot coals before you let this business fail and lose a penny of my money. And just to give you some added motivation, let's be clear that if you prove me wrong, I will hunt you down and destroy all that you love.'

Still smiling, Eva fetched the bottle of champagne she'd bought that day in the hope there would be a reason to celebrate, and Big Paul, satisfied that it was of a suitable calibre to pass his lips after scrutinising the label, uncorked the bottle and handed the first glass to Sylvie.

She waved it away. 'I'll stick with juice, thanks.'

'AA, is it?' He peered at her suspiciously.

Sylvie looked taken aback. 'Not exactly. I never made it quite that far. But some people are better off not drinking, and I'm definitely one of them. We all know what happened the last time you handed me a drink,' she added, gesturing upwards towards Allegra's bedroom. This was the first time that their previous meeting had been alluded to, and an uncomfortable hush descended upon the table.

'Yeah.' Paul shifted in his chair. 'I suppose now's a good

time to say that I'm sorry about that. We may not have behaved in an entirely gentlemanly fashion on that occasion. I was sorry about the baby and Robert and everything.'

Eva shot him a glare across the table, causing him to backtrack.

'Shit, I don't mean I'm sorry about the baby. Probably you're really happy about the baby. Actually, I've got no idea how you feel about the baby and I'm just trying to make the right noises but digging a hole so big I'll probably emerge in Azerbaijan—'

'Relax.' Sylvie stopped him with a smile. 'I've got a thick skin and I know people don't always know what to say. I'd honestly prefer that they give it a shot, even one as incompetent as that, than ignore Allegra completely. For the record, I'm delighted about my daughter. She's beautiful and I love her. Sometimes it's tough and I worry about the future, but mostly she's a huge source of joy in my life.'

Big Paul leant back in his chair. 'Good. Great. I was really sorry to hear about what happened, that's all. Really bad luck.'

'Look,' said Sylvie, 'in my situation you rethink your ideas about what constitutes bad luck. Spend half an hour in the waiting room at Great Ormond Street and you'll see children with feeding tubes, oxygen canisters, tracheostomies, colostomy bags. We don't have any of that anymore. The kids themselves, they don't sit around measuring themselves against other people or railing against the injustice of their circumstances, so unless their condition is really painful, and Allegra's isn't, most of the bad stuff is to do with worrying about the future. For the first year I did nothing else. I'd wake up in the middle of the night and lie there for hours thinking about what will happen to Allegra when I die. It blunts itself after a while. I mean, say I live to seventy-five, that's more than another thirty-five years from now.'

Big Paul nodded thoughtfully. 'True. And who knows what will have happened in thirty-five years' time? What with global warming, probably all that'll be left will be Keith Richards and a bunch of cockroaches sitting around on a rock. Maybe we should *all* be running through the streets screaming.'

'Exactly,' said Sylvie. 'But you're not, are you? Because no one can live like that. I've given up stressing about it. I'm going to do what's in my power to make each day a good one, and beyond that everything will just have to take care of itself.'

'I'll drink to that,' said Paul, and raised his glass.

29

London, Spring 2009

Lucien shifted uncomfortably and looked out of the window of the bus. The suit he'd been given by the woman at the Dress for Success charity was digging into his crotch and armpits. He hated the thought that he was going to have to put this suit on again tomorrow morning, and the next day, and the next. Still, at least he'd got the job. It wasn't much of a job but it was a start. Sylvie and his parole officer would be pleased.

He thought back to when the manager had asked at the end of the interview whether he had any questions and, realizing he was expected to come up with something, he'd asked what it was like working there.

The manager had smirked. 'What do you think? It's a bloody call centre. No one wants to be here. It's the seventh circle of hell. Everyone you speak to hates you and it pays tuppence more than the minimum wage. Only people who are desperate do it, people like you. We've taken on a few ex-cons under the reintegration scheme, and they actually tend to stick around longer than most because they have the least choice about it. You're going to hate every second of it, but if you turn up every day for a year, then suddenly HMP Hellhole isn't the last thing on your CV and you're back in the game. A rehabilitated member of society, so to speak.'

This probably wasn't a totally unfair summary of the situation, but the bastard could have at least tried to put a gloss on it, Lucien thought grimly. Still, he could manage anything for a year, right? For a moment he half wished that tomorrow morning he'd be waking up back in Spring Hill. The open prison where he'd spent most of his sentence wasn't all that bad in many ways, it had lovely grounds and he'd even had a PlayStation. Moving to a jail out in Buckinghamshire had meant fewer visits, but that hadn't been such a bad thing. The first handful of visits from Eva had left him feeling so low that he'd had to put a stop to them; after a few sessions of listening to her bang on about her high-flying job and her plank of a boyfriend and their latest weekend mini-break in Rome, he'd known he couldn't tolerate years of the same, so he'd put her off by saying he was using his slots for other mates, even though precious few of the people he used to call his mates had actually ever bothered to visit or write. It had taken a while but she'd got the message eventually, though she'd still been good enough to top up his prison bank account regularly and send frequent care parcels and the occasional picture of Herbert before she found him a new home.

It would have been nice if Sylvie had been able to come more often, but she had more than enough on her plate, what with the baby and everything, so once a month had been okay. The thing about visits was that you got so ravenous for proper human contact that you'd be bouncing off the walls for twenty-four hours beforehand, but then you'd have your visit and it would remind you of everything you were missing and how badly you'd screwed up your own life and the lives of the people around you, and then you spent the next twenty-four hours cycling through anger and shame until you finally just felt numb and deflated. It was worse for the men with partners and kids. They would work themselves up into a welter of misty-eyed sentimentality between visits, and spruce themselves up as much as possible in anticipation of an emotional and affectionate catch-up, only to be met by a tired and angry woman who'd had to take three trains to get there and was more worried about how she was going to pay the latest electricity bill than how much her good-for-nothing jailbird boyfriend was missing her cooking.

At least he didn't have that to worry about. But what it also meant was that he didn't have much of a life waiting for him on the outside. He was going to have to start from scratch, and it wasn't going to be easy. Sylvie had said he could stay with her as long as he got a job, but it was funny how hard he found it living under her roof. You'd have thought that living by somebody else's rules and having no privacy would be second nature to him now, but in the three weeks he'd just felt prickly all the time, and very much in the way. It would get easier once Eva had sold her flat, he consoled himself. As soon as she found a place of her own he would get the spare room instead of the sofa, and wouldn't be woken up at 7 a.m. every morning by Sylvie bringing Allegra down for breakfast.

Still, it was pointless focusing on the bad stuff. There was plenty of upside in being out of prison, including hot baths, decent food, and not least being in proximity to women again. There were two girls a few rows ahead of him right now on the half-empty bus, sitting facing each other across the aisle and swapping gossip in excited voices. They were like birds, he thought, brightly coloured chattering birds of paradise, light and skittish and exquisitely free of the sort of baggage that was weighing him down. That was just what he needed to make him feel light again. They were the usual princess/best friend combo, a willowy blonde wearing far too much make-up but pulling it off in the way that only really young, really pretty girls can, and a shorter, stouter friend in a green jumper loose enough to reveal a flesh-coloured bra strap biting into a plump shoulder. He leant forward and rested his arms on the back of the seat in front.

'Excuse me, ladies.' The stream of chatter halted abruptly and two enquiring faces turned towards him. He grinned and ratcheted an eyebrow up a notch to maximize the impact of his rakish good looks. 'Do you have the time?'

The best friend looked at him accusingly. 'You've got a watch on,' she said.

Lucien glanced down at his wrist resting on the seat-back, protruding from the too-short sleeve of his suit jacket. Shit. She was right. He really was out of practice. Lucien felt the eyebrow drop back down a fraction involuntarily.

'So I have. But that doesn't matter, because what I actually wanted to know was,' and here he turned his best thousand-watt smile on the princess, 'do you have the time for me to buy you a coffee?'

The princess looked back at him suspiciously. That was okay, with the pretty ones there was always a split second when they sized you up, made you sweat for it. He could feel it all coming back to him, the old magic flowing into his bloodstream. You could get a bit rusty, but the deep memory, the muscle memory, never left you, and by God he had a muscle with a memory that he'd like to show this girl. Maybe he'd say that to her later on. Or was that too creepy? Okay, maybe too creepy, he decided, and sex puns were never a good idea, but whatever, her glossed lips were parting to speak now. He hadn't watched lips part like that in a long time, and in some ways it was those little details he missed the most; he was a connoisseur, an appreciator of the seemingly minor details, parting lips and parting thighs . . .

'But you're . . . like . . .' she said, and then stopped.

What? What was he? Like, just so handsome? Maybe not that, since the expression that was now coalescing on her face wasn't that of someone being bowled over by his good looks. Was something going wrong here? Did he have food in his teeth?

She finally found the right word to finish her sentence. '. . . old,' she ended. 'You're properly old.'

The friend's face was creasing up now, and a gale of laughter burst forth. Both girls clutched at each other, pulling themselves to their feet and staggering away towards the front of the bus, which was by now slowing to a stop. As they reached the open door, the princess skipped straight through it still hooting with laughter, but the friend turned back to shout a parting shot over her shoulder for the whole bus to hear.

'Dirty old man!'

Now a range of faces were turned towards him: the ruddy moonface of the driver, the shocked pale visage of a prim-looking librarian type, the crepey mask of an old dowager, and on the seat beside her, the wrinkled snouts of two pugs. Even the dogs looked appalled.

'Any more funny business and you're off, mate,' shouted

the driver, jabbing a thumb towards the door and then finishing off with an audibly muttered, 'Bloody pervert,' as he turned back to the wheel.

Lucien scuttled off the bus at the next stop, which happened to be on the Finchley Road. He was still a twenty-minute walk away from Sylvie's, but the humiliation was more than he could bear. Old? Lucien? He was thirty-bloody-five. When did mid-thirties become old? Middle age didn't even start till fifty these days, so thirty-five wasn't old by anybody's standards. Well, maybe a teenager would think that was old, but nobody else. He stopped suddenly and stood still on the pavement. They weren't, were they? Sixteen or something? He supposed they could have been. They didn't look it, but you could never really say.

Doing a quick calculation in his head he realized that, yes, he could technically be old enough to be their father. Technically. Was that a bad thing? He'd been thirty-two when he went inside, and he'd never had problems like this back then. True, he'd sometimes knocked a few years off his age for the really young-looking ones at his club nights, just to put him in his twenties. But that was because being thirty-something didn't seem so cool amongst clubbers, even if you were the promoter, there because your job demanded it. Or had, he thought dolorously. Past tense. As of an hour ago, his job was call-centre worker.

Suddenly he wanted, no, needed, fiercely needed and richly deserved, a very large drink. He had twenty quid in his pocket that Sylvie had given him for emergencies. Could you get really pissed these days on twenty quid? He was going to give it his best shot. Lucien gazed up and down the Finchley Road until he spotted the nearest pub, the North

Star, and limped towards it in second-hand grey slip-on shoes that were starting to rub.

*

Ensconced on the threadbare upholstery of a corner bench with a pint of beer and a whisky chaser on the sticky table-top in front of him, he reflected on what had just happened. They weren't even proper women anyway, he decided, no experience of life and nothing much to say for themselves beyond shrieking and giggling. Now he thought about it, they'd been shrieking and giggling about some friend's fingernails when he'd first noticed them, and who needed that? He might be down on his luck right now, but he could still do better.

Besides, he admitted to himself ruefully, he *wasn't* as young as he used to be. Did he even have the energy and enthusiasm for the game anymore? It was like anything else in life, you had to be hungry for it to do it properly and succeed. And what he needed was a real woman, not some, some . . . flibbertigibbet. Christ, he was starting to sound like one of the Victorian novels he'd read in the prison library. He thought about how hard Eva had laughed when she'd found him on the sofa with the copy of *Pride and Prejudice* that he'd smuggled out with him because he was only halfway through it when his release date came around.

Now Eva, there was a real woman. Like him, she was down on her luck right now, but she'd always had substance, which was exactly what those stupid girls today didn't have. And she was loyal and faithful and that was what a man needed, he reflected sentimentally over another drink. Not the sort to embarrass a man on a bus, to kick a man when he was down. She'd waited all these years for him, after all. Well, she hadn't exactly been waiting for him, he corrected himself, but she'd always wanted him and they'd both always known it. He'd taken advantage of that somewhat in the past, he'd be the first to admit it, but with the older, wiser head he had on him now he could see she would be good for him.

'She's always needed me,' he told the new friend he'd got talking to at the next table, an oldish bloke named Derek with glasses and a bibulous nose. 'Cheers for this, mate, much appreciated,' he added, raising another pint to his lips.

'Bitches, they're all bitches,' muttered Derek. 'Let me tell you about my ex-wife.' He proceeded to do so at length, but Lucien didn't mind as long as he continued to punctuate his story with rounds of drinks. It was midnight and the pub was closing when the tales of recrimination drew to a close.

'Back to mine, mate?' asked Derek, but Lucien had formulated a plan that he was raring to put into action. He needed to see Eva, to tell her what he'd decided about their being together, and he needed to do it tonight.

'Sorry, mate. I've got to go and see this girl. The one I was telling you about.'

'I wouldn't bother, mate. She's bound to be a bitch.'

But of course Eva wasn't a bitch, whatever Derek said. It was still a good fifteen-minute walk, but Lucien didn't feel the cold. The stars swirled above him and he felt as though he was floating. It was an epiphany, that's what he was having. Eva would make him happy, and of course he would make her happy too. She hadn't been doing too well lately according to Sylvie, who'd told him a while back that she seemed so depressed for so long after losing her job and being dumped by The Plank that she'd been quite worried about her.

Eva didn't seem all that depressed to him, though. She was taking herself off to the library every day to work on this big business idea of hers. She seemed quiet and thoughtful, but not about to jump off Beachy Head. She was just like him in many ways. They had both been hit by adverse circumstances, but they were both going to pull themselves back up again. More than that, they could pull each other back up again. Down the line they could get a place together, once she managed to sell her flat. He didn't know how much equity she had in it, but it was surely quite a bit, what with how much she used to earn, and they could both get jobs. Maybe even have a couple of kids, seeing as everyone said it was so great.

Hell, he was getting ahead of himself now, but when you thought about it, it all made perfect sense. He was at the front door now, struggling to get his key into any one of the locks hovering in front of him. The house was dark and quiet. Everyone would be in bed and Sylvie would be angry if he rang the bell. After several abortive stabs into the wood of the doorjamb, he hit gold and slid the key home with a satisfying scrape of metal on metal. He staggered into the hallway and instead of turning left into the sitting room towards his makeshift bed on the sofa Lucien mounted the stairs, weaving unsteadily up to the first-floor landing.

He stopped outside Eva's door, foggily working out his next move. There was really only one way to make an announcement of this magnitude, and that was naked. After all, she would be in bed, naked or nearly naked, and she'd surely want him to join her after he'd said his piece. No point ruining the moment by forcing her to wait while he wrestled his socks off, he always hated that bit. Lucien dropped his clothes onto the landing carpet and opened the door. It was completely dark inside the room and he suddenly realized there was something he ought to have done beforehand, which was to relieve his aching bladder. No matter; here was the door to the en suite. Ahh, that was better. Suddenly the whole room glowed and for a moment he thought maybe this was part of the thing, the epiphany, but then a voice behind him spoke and he realized that someone had turned the light on.

'What the fuck are you doing?' said Eva.

'Shh,' he told her, lurching backwards and putting his hands out to stop himself falling onto the bed, so that the warm stream of urine ran down his legs. Suddenly the whole thing seemed really funny, this situation, and even life itself, and his effervescent happiness burst forth. 'I've got something important to tell you,' he gasped, struggling to get the words out through bursts of laughter.

'Lucien, you're drunk. And naked. And . . . oh my God, were you taking a piss in my wardrobe?'

Eva didn't sound as happy as he was, but she would do in a minute because he was about to make her the happiest woman alive.

'I know, I know, that'sh all true but none of it matters because I love you.'

'You what?'

'I love you and I think we should be together. Eva Andrewsh, I fucking love you!'

'Oh my God, you're actually pissing on my bed!'

★

Lucien wasn't feeling as good as he'd expected. He'd made his announcement but was hazily aware that it wasn't being as well received as it ought to have been, and in addition the room was spinning and there was a sort of slithery feeling in his stomach. He leant back heavily on the bed just as his oesophagus contracted, forcing the contents of his booze-filled stomach to leap up into his throat and be expelled through his mouth with considerable force. For a moment he felt terribly relieved, and then Eva, the bed, the wall, the lamp and everything else receded into darkness.

★

Consciousness returned in brutal phases. The room was dim, but even the watery light pouring through the curtains slammed into his eyes like a wall of pain. His skull contained a curdled egg. That thought aroused the ire of his stomach, which threatened to crawl out through his parched mouth. The air was heavy with the stench of urine and vomit. He became aware of a figure standing above him silhouetted against the light, soothingly blocking the source of anguish and giving off the glow of a celestial being.

'Here,' said Eva. 'I brought you a cup of tea.'

'You're an angel,' croaked Lucien. 'A ministering angel.'

'Well, it's more than you deserve. Do you remember what you did last night?'

He gave it some thought. At first his memory was an empty void, but then dreadful snippets started to flow back to him.

'I may have . . . declared my love to you?'

'Yes. Naked. While simultaneously urinating on yourself. And on my bed. And then you . . .'

'Oh, Christ.' Suddenly it was all there, clear as day. 'I told you that we were meant to be together, then I threw up and passed out?'

'That's about the size of it. And now for the good news. Your new boss phoned and he says that even though you're late for your first day of work, if you're there within the next hour he won't fire you. I've booked you a taxi. You have ten minutes to shower and dress.'

Lucien catapulted out of bed and was halfway out the door when he stopped and turned back.

'Eva?'

'Yes?'

'You were tempted, right?' He smiled his wickedest grin and stood there, unashamedly naked, his tall, naturally slender body sculpted by all the hours he'd spent in the prison gym. Eva ran her gaze across him. Even now, she felt a pang of longing to touch him that was so deeply written into the fabric of her being that she doubted it would ever disappear altogether. Could you ever completely shake off those teenage loves or did they stay with you forever, no matter how ludicrous they became?

'You've made me some pretty bad offers in your time, Lucien Marchant, but that was undoubtedly the worst,' she told him, and smiled as he ran for the shower.

30

London, February 2010

From: benedict.waverley@cern.ch
To: eva.andrews21@hotmail.com
Date: Saturday 8th February 2010 18:04
Subject: It's been a while . . .

Hey Eva,

Sorry it's been a while. I tried your Morton Brothers email but it bounced back so I guess you've moved on to bigger and better things. Or who knows, maybe you've renounced worldly gain and gone off with Julian to live in an organic yurt commune or something.

I know I didn't reply to the last few emails you sent a couple of years ago. I suppose you gave up on me and I don't blame you. I can't imagine you want to listen to me moaning on, but I do finally want to explain why I've been AWOL.

Gulp. Here goes. A while back I did something I'm not very proud of. I cheated on Lydia. It wasn't that long after that disastrous lunch we had together in London, when you and she had a bit of a set-to. Anyway, you might have noticed at the time that we weren't doing very well together, and then I totally screwed things up by getting drunk and having sex with another CERNite at the Christmas party, and after that the only way I could make amends and save my marriage was by doing whatever Lydia wanted, and one of those things was for me to stay away from you.

Eva, please understand that I was desperate to keep my family together and petrified of losing my kids. Obviously I realize now that I should have at least explained, but I couldn't face telling you that I was a spineless sexual incontinent who had to allow my wife to decide who I could be friends with. So I bottled it. Or rather, kept kicking the can down the road thinking I'd get round to sorting it all out at a better time, except a better time never materialized and the longer I left it the harder it was to get in touch and explain.

Needless to say, things didn't work out with Lydia. We limped on together for a while, and then finally divorced about eighteen months ago. I've thought about getting in touch with you a lot since then, but to be honest I've been a bit of a wreck, because even when your marriage is categorically unsalvageable, it turns out that divorce is really, really painful. It physically hurts the heart. Anyway, I'm back in London working at Imperial College – I'm still on the team looking for the Higgs but it's mostly analysing data for me now. I have the boys every other weekend and Wednesday nights and Lydia and I are on relatively civil terms, so I think we're going to be okay but my God, it's been a rough ride to get here.

If you can forgive me enough to write back, I'd love to know how you're doing, where the road has taken you.

I know things have sometimes been complicated between us, but aren't they always, one way or another? Hasn't life just turned out to be like that?

Benedict

From: eva.andrews21@hotmail.com
To: benedict.waverley@cern.ch
Date: Sunday 9th February 2010 11:36
Subject: RE: It's been a while . . .

'a couple of years'

That would be what, FOUR of them?

Honestly, I'm glad you've been having a really bad time, because frankly you deserve it. So you dropped off the edge of the planet because you couldn't face making yourself look bad? Guess what? It's not all about you. Did it ever occur to you that maybe there would have been times when I needed a friend, even a feeble-minded, sexually incontinent one? You think you're the only one who's had a difficult few years?

From: benedict.waverley@cern.ch
To: eva.andrews21@hotmail.com
Date: Sunday 9th February 2010 17:15
Subject: RE: It's been a while . . .

I'm so sorry. You're right. I've been utterly self-obsessed, and a terrible friend. This is going to sound awful, but it honestly hadn't occurred to me that you might be having tough times too. Everything was going so well last time

I heard from you. I have no defence. I'd like to try to make it up to you if you'll let me, with a butt-clenchingly earnest apology and pretty much anything else you ask for.

What's been happening? I really hope things haven't been too bad for you, but you're making me worry . . .

From: eva.andrews21@hotmail.com
To: benedict.waverley@cern.ch
Date: Tuesday 11th February 2010 19:32
Subject: RE: It's been a while . . .

It's taken me a couple of days to answer because I've really had to think hard about how to respond. Even though that last message was half-joking, the truth is that it *has* been a really tough few years. I know it's never been the done thing to say how we really feel but I'm getting too old to beat around the bush, so here it is. You really hurt me, Benedict. I know things were never straightforward between us, but to just ditch me like that without an explanation? That was pretty low and I've spent the last couple of days thinking about whether I want someone who could do that back in my life. I'm only giving you the benefit of the doubt because it sounds like you've been having a bad time too, but don't kid yourself that I forgive you because I don't.

Here's what's been happening. I can't remember whether you knew that Sylvie was pregnant (I have a feeling I told you in one of the emails you never replied to) but she had a baby, a beautiful little girl named Allegra who is now nearly four. There's no easy way of explaining this so I'll just come out and say it: the hospital didn't monitor her properly and as a result she was starved of oxygen at birth and has some brain damage. She spent months in hospital before she could come home and it's still not totally clear what the prognosis is for her in the long term. She definitely has some developmental delay and a bit of cerebral palsy, mainly down one side. The doctors didn't seem terribly hopeful at the beginning but she's outstripped our expectations. And, oh Benedict, you should see her. She's all enormous eyes and perfect little fingers and toes. I was never too keen on kids before, but I suppose now I do understand a tiny bit of why it was so important to you to keep your family together.

Anyway, Sylvie's marriage to Robert (my old boss) didn't last long – no surprises there. Being a father, let alone to a disabled child with everything that entails, wasn't a part of his life plan and he decamped pretty soon after the birth, though he did at least have the decency to give Sylvie the house, and I'm living there with her now.

What else? You may or may not be surprised to hear that Lucien got caught with a load of coke and sent to prison just before Allegra arrived (that's a whole other story, he's out now), so there's really been no one else and I've helped out with the baby as much as I can. In the early days I worried that Sylvie would just fall apart but after the initial shock wore off she's sort of grown into her new life and seems a lot stronger now. It's weird, throughout our twenties she seemed lost and the spark just went out of her, but even though life's not exactly easy for her now, it feels like she's got the fight back in her. She's started painting again too, and recently managed to get a few of her pieces into the Affordable Art Fair and they actually sold, so it seems as though things are finally starting to happen for her.

Oh, and while all of this was going on, I got fired and Julian broke up with me and I couldn't sell my flat and I fell out with my father, who blamed me for the global economic collapse and thinks I'll be first up against the wall when the revolution comes. So, yeah, not a good few years.

I'm tempted to leave it there so that you wallow in maximum guilt, but I suppose I should be honest and say that things have at least been looking up lately. I've finally sold my flat and patched things up with Keith, and Sylvie and I have started a business. We've been working ourselves into the ground this last year, but it's up and running and starting to do really well.

So. That's pretty much everything that's been going on at this end. Got to go now.

From: benedict.waverley@cern.ch
To: eva.andrews21@hotmail.com
Date: Tuesday 11th February 2010 23:48
Subject: RE: It's been a while . . .

I've been sitting here for almost two hours trying to reply to your message but I can't seem to get the words out right. I think maybe that's because what I'm trying to say is simple but email's not really conducive to communicating how much I mean it. What I want to say is this: I'm so very, desperately sorry you've had to go through so much without my being there to support you, and Sylvie and Lucien too. I wish I'd been a better friend to you all.

Would you be willing to meet up with me? Please, Eva? I'd really like the chance to say that in person. Just name a time and a place. I'll be there, any time, any place. (Except for Wednesday nights and next weekend and alternate weekends thereafter. But any other time.)

*

Benedict sipped at the rather chichi little cup of coffee he had inexplicably ordered, reflecting that caffeine so late in the day wouldn't help him to sleep that night. When he'd finally reached the front of the melee at the bar he suddenly realized he didn't know what he wanted, but the barman hadn't seemed inclined to indulge him and, reasoning it would be better not to get drunk and maudlin, he'd blurted out his order almost at random. Eva was going to think he was mad when she arrived to a cold espresso instead of a nice glass of wine.

He didn't know why he'd suggested they meet at the Southbank either, except that they'd once come here for what had turned out to be a very pleasant lunch on one of his trips back from Switzerland. They'd agreed on a bar by the river that neither of them had been to in years, and now he was there he found that he was at least ten years older than most of the other patrons, who at seven thirty on a Saturday evening were already drinking and flirting with reckless abandon. How young and absurd they appeared to his jaded eyes, the boys with their tight jeans strutting like peacocks and the girls who looked barely more than children, flicking their hair and squawking with laughter at the boys' tepid witticisms. *Laugh it up, kids,* he thought, *you don't know what life's got in store for you.* And then, hearing how old and bitter his interior voice had become, *For God's sake, Benedict, you're thirty-five, not fifty-five.*

He wasn't looking forward to watching Eva's expression when she saw him. When people meet after a length of time measured in years they assess one another for damage, and he knew that on him the damage was profound. His eyes had bagged and his hair was greying along with the stubble on his chin that he now rather fervently wished he'd taken the time to shave.

The fact that he was in love with Eva had taken varying degrees of prominence in his life at different times, but had nonetheless been a constant for more than fifteen years. Could it really be that long? His feelings had waxed and waned, burning brightest in the years after they'd met and then going almost into abeyance when he and Lydia had first been married and his love for the boys and their life together had eclipsed almost everything. In that period they had been relegated to the status of inconvenient truth and shoved into the background, and he wondered whether it was really wise to reopen that wound now. Still, perhaps he was getting this meeting all out of proportion considering how long it had been since they'd seen each other. Perhaps it would be awkward, or they'd have nothing to say to each other, or she'd have changed so much they'd have no connection anymore.

That train of thought juddered to a halt the moment he

saw her. As soon as his gaze met hers, it was clear that it was too late. She was standing in the doorway scanning the room and as her eyes came to rest on him she smiled and in that moment he remembered what an effervescent smile like that could do to you, and he realized too how very long it had been since anyone had smiled at him like that. She was slimmer than when he'd last seen her, and her hair was longer and kind of messy around her face. She was wearing jeans, slightly flared at the bottom, with plimsolls and a blue corduroy jacket, nothing special but somehow she made it look so right. At least he was old enough not to bother trying to pretend to himself anymore. You couldn't talk yourself into or out of loving someone. God knows he'd given falling out of love with Eva and falling in love with Lydia his best shot.

*

It took her a moment to recognize him, hunched over a cup of coffee in the corner, surrounded by bright young things banging up against him and sloshing their drinks onto his table. Perhaps not the best choice of venue, Eva thought. She stood by the door for a few seconds and took him in. He looked older, not in a bad way exactly, but greying around the temples and where he'd always been a bit gangly, he seemed more solid now. He looked sort of . . . grown up.

At that moment he looked up and spotted her and broke into a smile, and the years seemed to drop away from him. A picture popped into her mind unbidden, a much younger Benedict silhouetted against a bright summer sky at the top of Brandon Hill. She walked towards him, reflecting self-consciously that the passage of time since they last saw each other had been kinder to him than it had been to her. The years of working long hours, the shock of losing her job, the anxiety over Allegra, the weight of supporting Sylvie, had all etched themselves onto her face, she knew.

'You look amazing,' exclaimed Benedict, standing and moving around the table to hug her as she reached him.

'Ha, sure,' she said, waving off the compliment and stepping back when he finally released her from the embrace. 'It's been a long decade,' she added by way of explanation.

'Are you mad? You look . . .' he paused, evidently casting around for the right word.

'Old?'

'No. Well, actually, yes. Old-er. But in a good way. Not bland like the kids in this bar. You've gained . . . poise.'

'I've gained laughter lines and crow's feet, is what you mean. Still, what can you do? I guess we're not kids anymore.'

Benedict gestured at the table without sitting down. 'I got you a coffee. I have no idea why.'

She raised an eyebrow. 'I think I'm going to need something harder.'

'It's at least a ten-minute wait at the bar. This place is a lot more crowded than it used to be. Also, it's full of all these hideous *young* people. Shall we go somewhere else?'

As they pushed their way through the crowd and towards the door of the bar Eva could feel Benedict close behind her, and when they made it out into the open air she hesitated only a moment before taking his proffered arm.

Once they were safely seated in a pub a few minutes' walk away from the river, they found themselves looking across the table at each other tongue-tied. Where could they possibly begin?

Eva was the first to break the silence. 'Well. This is nice. And by nice, what I mean is, very, very weird.'

Benedict grinned. 'It is, isn't it? Seeing you takes me back to a time before our adult lives had really begun. It makes me think how shocked the old Benedict and Eva would have been if they'd known everything that was going to happen to them.'

'God, I know just what you mean. When I spotted you in the other bar, I had a sudden flashback to an afternoon we spent lying out on Brandon Hill. It might even have been our last day in Bristol, come to think of it, and I think we were having one of those ridiculous conversations about the meaning of life or something. We really didn't have a clue, did we?'

'Don't say that. It makes me feel like I should warn the poor, unsuspecting bastard.' Benedict cupped his hands around his mouth and mock-shouted through them into the past: 'Do everything differently! Every decision you're going to make over the next ten years, do the total opposite!'

Eva laughed. 'It's not been that bad, has it?'

'No, I suppose not. I'll never be sorry I had my kids, and it's been a great time to be working in my field. So that's two things I got right. What about you? What would you tell the old Eva?'

'That patchwork skirts are not a good look?'

'I thought you carried them off with panache.'

They smiled at each other across the table, the gap bridged, before Benedict's expression became serious. 'Listen, tell me about Sylvie. I'm really, really sorry I wasn't around when she was going through the mill. I suppose after you guys left Bristol we mostly conducted our friendship through you, but

I always considered her a friend. I doubt she feels the same now, though. I haven't been there for anyone, have I?'

Eva shrugged, unwilling to contradict him on that point. 'Sylvie's doing okay. She's so different now you'd hardly recognize her. I mean, she's the same old Sylvie, but she's grown up so much. I don't know what I would have done without her over the last few years. She's had so much to cope with herself, and still managed to kick me into shape when I was wallowing in self-pity after I lost my job. And don't hate me for saying this, but I wondered after I read your message whether you couldn't do with a dose of that yourself, to be honest.'

'I can see how it could have sounded like that. But, actually, I'm feeling pretty positive about things these days. The boys seem happy again now that everything's settled between me and Lydia, and work's picking up. We had a lot of setbacks, not least because a passing bird dropped a baguette down a vent into the particle accelerator last year, but things are really starting to move forward now. It's only a matter of time before we find the Higgs. We only moved back to London because Lydia insisted after . . . after I . . .' Benedict looked down at the table.

'Shagged a colleague?'

He held up his hands. 'Fine, I'll bloody say it if you're going to make me. It's no more than I deserve. We only moved back after I shagged a colleague, but actually it's turned out fine. Most of the interesting work now is analysing the data from the experiments and I can just as easily do that from London. I'm happy at Imperial. I've even got my own office, with a spectacular view of the car park. Obviously, it's a struggle not to let the prestige go to my head.'

He ran his fingers through his hair. 'So I've nothing to complain about. It's just that . . . God, you know how you said that we're old enough to speak openly? It's just that this is so bittersweet. Seeing you, I mean. Have you ever had a moment when you look back over your life and see really clearly all the moments when you could have done something differently and then your life might have taken a whole other direction?'

Eva took a sip of her drink. 'We did miss a few opportunities, didn't we? Somehow we never quite got into sync.'

Benedict's eyes bored into hers, and his voice was urgent. 'Is that it then? We missed our moment?'

She smiled. 'Well, we definitely missed one or two. But who's to say how many you get in a lifetime?'

Benedict stood up and moved around the table towards her. 'Right now it feels like all the chances I ever missed are laid out in front of me. I'm not going to miss another one.'

He took her wrist and pulled her up to standing in front of him. As he reached out and put his arms around her and drew her body close to his and lowered his mouth to hers for their second kiss, almost a decade after the first, Eva had a sensation of shedding a skin, as if the past was sliding away from her.

*

Several hours later, Eva bent a bare arm behind her head, looked up at the ceiling above Benedict's bed and let out a long sigh.

'Really? That bad? Not worth the wait?' laughed Benedict.

'Ha. Hardly. It's just . . . why haven't we been doing that for the last fifteen years?'

'Well, that would mostly be down to all the time you spent ignoring my soulful stares.'

'If I recall correctly, the initial barrier was your having a girlfriend, a fact that you kept remarkably quiet about when we first met.'

'Well, all the time you subsequently spent mooning about over Lucifer wasn't exactly conducive to romance, even when I'd ditched said girlfriend in the hope of getting it on with you.'

'Fair point. But of course, your impregnating and marrying someone else was also a bit of a stumbling block. Not to mention the emigrating. Oh, and the four-year hiatus in replying to emails.'

Benedict rolled onto his side to face her. 'How is this all so easy to say to each other now, when it was impossible back then?'

'I know. How is it possible for two people to arse around for fifteen years, only for it to just fall into place one day?'

'It does seem crazy, doesn't it? But, well . . . maybe it wouldn't have worked out back then. Maybe we didn't miss our moment at all. Maybe this is it, this is the only moment we ever could have had.' His voice brightened. 'And what's a piffling fifteen years compared to the fifty we've got left, anyway?'

Eva smiled at the implication that the remainder of their lives might be spent together, a ridiculous suggestion after a single shag, and yet at the same time one that seemed as natural as rolling over naked to the other side of the bed and climbing on top of Benedict, a man she knew so well and yet so little that she could indeed imagine spending a lifetime getting to know him.

31

Hampstead, April 2012

The alarm went off at 7 a.m., just as it did every Monday morning. Without opening her eyes Eva shoved the clock off the bedside table, and then rolled over with the aim of stretching herself out against Benedict for a last blissful five minutes of slumber. Encountering only a cool expanse of sheet, she extended an arm and felt around for him, then raised a reluctant eyelid. Big mistake. The sunshine streaming in around the curtains might as well have been airborne caffeine for all the chance she now had of getting back to sleep. The other eyelid begrudgingly followed suit, and she lay there adjusting to the daylight and listening to Benedict banging around in the kitchen of the flat they had been renting in a Hampstead mansion block for the last eighteen months. With a bit of luck he was making an early start on restoring the place to some semblance of order. By the time they'd finally decanted the boys into Lydia's car last night they were both so exhausted that they'd collapsed onto the sofa, lacking the will to repair the wreckage that their home was reduced to every other weekend. Eva didn't really resent the socks and comic books and half-eaten apples that lay strewn over every available surface, but she did wish that she had a bit more time to recuperate before launching herself into another week.

Still, it had been a good visit. Yesterday they had taken Josh and Will to Kew Gardens, followed by lunch at the Angel Inn and the Sunday afternoon kids' showing of the latest Star Wars movie at the Everyman. She had initially approached her new role of de facto stepmother with a high degree of trepidation, but the boys had quickly shown her what to do. They could be a handful at times, but they were quite straightforward once you grasped that if you made sure that they had sufficient food, sleep and exercise the rest would follow. And it had turned out that kids were a lot more fun than she'd realized, or at least Benedict's were. They were as messy and noisy as she'd expected they would be, but they also found uncomplicated joy in everything around them and they were entertainingly like their father, giving her strange glimpses of what Benedict must have been like growing up. Heredity was a fascinating thing when you observed it close up to see the ways in which a child resembled and differed from someone you loved. They'd certainly inherited his scientific bent, she thought grumpily as she stepped out of bed and onto the sharp corner of a solar-powered rocket lying on the floor. Eva limped into the kitchen where Benedict was standing at the sink and slid her arms around his waist from behind, savouring the solidity and warmth of his body.

'Got to run,' he said, turning round and kissing her on the mouth. He tasted of toast and coffee. 'Busy day.' He brushed her hair off her face and kissed her again.

'Aren't they all?'

'Listen, thanks for being so great with Josh and Will this

weekend,' he told her. 'I know we could do with some more time to ourselves.'

'One of these days,' she said. 'We've got the next fifty years, remember?'

Benedict stroked her cheek and smiled, before reluctantly peeling her arms from around him and slinging his bag over his shoulder. 'Right, I've got to get going. Oh, and by the way, there's a gift for you on the coffee table. It's not a big thing so don't get excited, just a little something I picked up when I took the boys to the Science Museum on Saturday.'

'Yeah, well, I think I've got a little something from the Science Museum embedded in the bottom of my foot. Not to mention scattered across our bedroom floor.'

'I know, I'm sorry. Leave it and I'll clear it up when I get home tonight, promise.' He dropped a last kiss onto her face and headed for the door.

The cafetière was still warm, so she poured herself a mug of coffee and took a swig from it as she padded through to the sitting room to find out what Benedict had left her. There was a plastic bag in the middle of the coffee table and she picked it up and slid out what at first glance appeared to be just a picture frame, but on closer examination was actually a framed Carl Sagan quote printed on a page of a calculus book, so that a graph and a series of formulae were visible in the background. It read: *For small creatures such as we, the vastness is bearable only through love.*

How very Benedict, she thought. One of these days she would teach him how to get extra Brownie points by actually wrapping a gift, but she didn't really mind. It was strange how good, how loved and inspired, something like this made her feel, when a similar sort of gesture from Julian would have made her queasy. Though she did feel a bit nauseous, now she came to think of it. The feeling had been coming and going over the last couple of days but she'd been trying to ignore it, partly because she was rushed off her feet and partly because lately she'd learned the hard way that it was easy to imagine things and there was no point in continually getting your hopes up.

She didn't feel like she was imagining it now, though. Did she have time to pop out to the shops? As ParcelBox had taken off, her working day had grown longer and Benedict had been under pressure too, with frequent trips to Switzerland and the ever-pressing need to analyse the vast amounts of data being spewed out by the Large Hadron Collider for telltale traces of a Higgs-like particle. They were barely managing to keep on top of their workloads let alone spend a decent amount of time together, but it was a crucial time for both of them. The ParcelBox London presence was gathering momentum with thousands already installed, and it felt like they were close to reaching a tipping point in the capital, when they would stop being a novelty product for early-adopters and start to establish themselves as a standard accessory for working households. Then they would begin the planned big push into Birmingham and Bristol. Sylvie was doing a brilliant job on product development; her retro design based on the old red post boxes had been by far the most popular of the range. Eva had had her doubts about taking on Lucien as a full-time salesman but he'd worn her down using every tactic he'd learned in his year of telesales, as well as offering to work on commission and promising not to seduce clients on visits. He seemed to be enjoying the job so much that she occasionally wondered whether he stuck to the letter of this agreement, but since his skills as a salesman were indisputable she avoided probing too deeply.

Eva glanced at the clock on the mantelpiece and made a swift decision. She would nip out to the chemist while her laptop was booting. There was a faint chill in the air outside, but she could feel it dissipating even as she walked. The air was soft with morning haze and laden with a summery feeling of abundance. A little way along the street she startled a squirrel on the ground, sending it scurrying up the trunk of a nearby cherry tree, where it knocked off a blossom that fluttered down to the pavement in front of her. It was an almost laughably idyllic morning, she thought, feeling rather as though she ought to be clicking her heels together as she went. Even the irritable traffic queue and barging pedestrians on the High Street couldn't puncture her mood; it just reminded her how lucky she was to be out of the rat-race and not having to battle her way across London to an office each morning.

In the chemist, a bored-looking assistant was positioned beside the aisle wielding a fragrance bottle. It was the only route to the counter and Eva readied herself to fend her off, but before she had a chance to protest the trigger-happy perfumier engulfed her in a cloud of something strongly reminiscent of Toilet Duck. Her body's response was instantaneous and unstoppable: the coffee she'd drunk shot up from her gullet without warning, forcing her to bend forward and deposit it noisily on the mat in front of the make-up counter. The physical relief was immediate but as she straightened up she was confronted with the face of the assistant, whose complacent expression had given way to barely concealed revulsion.

'I'm so sorry, I don't know what came over me,' Eva gasped. 'Can I help to clean it up?'

They both looked down at the mess and the assistant shook her head. 'Do you know, I think I'm just going to put that whole mat into a bin bag and chuck it out.'

For a moment Eva considered bolting but she knew there was no other chemist open nearby, so she staggered to the front, grabbed a pink box from a display next to the checkout and threw it onto the counter. The young woman on the till looked down at the box and then back up at Eva, the distaste on her face slowly being replaced with a look of dawning comprehension. She winked as she ran it under the scanner, whispering, 'I think we both know what that's going to say!'

*

Ten minutes later Eva was sitting in her bathroom watching a single blue line stubbornly refuse to turn to a cross. Three minutes, then four, then five ticked past until it was clear that the pregnancy test was not going to change from negative to positive. But what about her churning stomach? Could the test be wrong? Could it just be too soon? Her phone started to ring in the sitting room and Eva went to answer it, still holding the stubbornly unchanging test.

'Eva? It's Sylvie. There's no way you could look after Allegra today, is there? I've got a stomach bug, been up half the night vomiting.'

Eva groaned. 'I think I've got it too. But I could come over and help if you're completely out of action. Give me a few minutes to pack up my laptop and paperwork and I'll bring it over and we can do some combination of work, throwing up and looking after Allegra together.'

She hung up and carried the pregnancy test into the kitchen to bury it at the bottom of the bin where Benedict wouldn't see it. She wouldn't bring it up; if anything, the continual focus on it was making it less likely to happen. Sex could almost be a chore when you had to do it to schedule. It was becoming a lonely journey for this sort of reason, both of them leaving things unvoiced because they feared that talking about them would only make it harder. It was a horrible feeling after the closeness that had enveloped them for most of the two years they'd been a couple, and an unwelcome reminder of the time there had been too many things they couldn't talk about and their friendship had faltered.

Being together was so overwhelmingly right that it seemed impossible they could ever return to such a state, but now a distance was starting to open up between them, no one's fault, but a function of a situation that neither of them could fix. Eva couldn't count the number of times she'd imagined telling him, saying the words, *I'm pregnant*, and watching his face as he realized that in her belly was a baby that was theirs, that belonged to them both. Now the fantasy brought tears to her eyes and she pushed it roughly from her mind. She closed the bin lid and was just about to go and pack a bag to take to Sylvie's when her phone rang again. It was still in her hand and she looked down at the screen, noting before answering that this time the call came from an unfamiliar number.

*

Benedict was strolling along the Brompton Road towards Imperial College when his phone started to ring. He tugged it out of his pocket and saw that it was Eva, which was strange because he'd seen her only half an hour ago. It couldn't mean . . . could it? Benedict was painfully aware that her period was due; he didn't mention it, tried to keep the pressure off, but each month he was on tenterhooks. He was starting to worry that it would never happen for them. It had been well over a year since they'd ditched the condoms, and as the months rolled by it was getting harder and harder for them both to act nonchalant each time her period arrived.

He'd known what she was thinking: that Lydia had got pregnant at the drop of a hat, so there was nothing wrong with him and it must be her. You couldn't open a newspaper these days for articles about how female fertility drops off a cliff after the age of thirty-five. Rationally, they both knew that what the GP said was true, that it could take a while to happen for some people, but there had been that nagging voice in his head saying, it's all too good to be true, nothing's ever perfect, you can't have it all.

He so desperately wanted for Eva to experience what he had with his kids, the love, the enchantment, the sheer wonder. He still regularly burned with a mixture of adoration and shame when he saw them. He'd been such an imperfect father, and watching the pain and confusion that the divorce had caused Josh and Will had been agonizing. In the dark of night a small voice whispered to him that this was the reason that he and Eva couldn't conceive, that he was being punished for not being a good enough father to his existing children.

Still, the boys seemed happy enough these days, in fact once everything had been settled they had seemed to take the new arrangements in their stride almost better than he had. After he and Eva had got together she'd insisted he read a book on helping children to cope with divorce and step-parents, and try to follow the advice in it. It hadn't always gone to plan, he remembered, thinking back to the last time he'd attempted to give them the recommended 'safe space in which to express their emotions'.

'Boys,' he'd said, clearing his throat. 'I thought this might be a good time for a bit of a chat. Obviously there has been a lot going on, and Mum and I both know you've had to cope with a lot of uncertainty. I know that my moving in with Eva is a big change for you. Is there anything you want to talk about?'

'Oh, Dad,' grumbled Josh. 'Do we have to talk about the divorce again?'

'Well, no, we don't have to,' said Benedict, taken aback. 'Not if you'd rather not. It's just that it's better to talk about things that are upsetting you and not keep them bottled up inside.'

Will and Josh looked at each other.

'The thing is,' Will piped up, 'we're not really that upset about it anymore. Loads of kids at school have divorced parents, and step-parents too. In my class there's James, and Tom and Rufus, and probably a bunch more.'

'Oh. Ah. Right.' Benedict rubbed his chin. 'So you're okay with it all, then? We don't have to talk about it if you don't want to.'

Josh sighed and then said patiently, as if explaining to somebody very slow on the uptake, 'We can talk about it if you want, Dad. It's just that we've talked about it quite a lot already, and we don't really have anything else to say. We'd rather watch *Finding Nemo*. You did say we could see a film today, remember.'

★

So apparently the children didn't feel that their lives had been totally ruined by what he'd done. Was it too much to hope that he and Eva could have a child too, that their life together could contain the richness and joy that he got from Josh and Will? The night they'd got together they had talked about whether they'd missed their moment, and he'd said that perhaps this was the only moment they could ever have had. But what if this moment was too late for them to have a baby? That was the fear that kept him awake at night, listening to Eva's breathing to try to ascertain whether she was already asleep or lying awake worrying beside him. And now, the phone was ringing and Benedict had a sudden bolt of certainty that it was finally going to happen for them, that she was ringing to tell him she was pregnant, and he couldn't keep the smile out of his voice as he flipped open the phone and said, 'Hi, Eva?'

32

Hampstead, August 2012

The daylight filtered through the stained glass, casting a blue glow across Eva's cheek as she sat in a pew near the front of the church watching the candle she'd lit flicker in the shadowy corner. She'd been coming here most days in the four months since Keith had died; barely able to concentrate on work, she found being alone in the empty flat intolerable. It didn't seem fair to spend too much time at Sylvie's, alternating between sitting frozen and crying as Sylvie tried to usher a curious Allegra away from her. In the weeks since the call from the hospital Eva had wept everywhere, in the street, on the Tube, in Starbucks, amid stares and glares from the people around her. Then, on one of the endless walks that she took to get out of the flat and tire out her body, she'd come past St John-at-Hampstead and realized the doors were open.

There was a sign up saying visitors were welcome to come in, sit quietly, light a candle, and so this was what Eva had done nearly every day since. Usually she had the place to herself; a few times a churchwarden had cautiously approached offering a listening ear, but each time she'd waved them away and soon they left her alone. This was where she felt most calm. Alone at home her grief felt like fear, like staring into an abyss that threatened to engulf her, but here in the muffled almost-silence beneath the soaring ceilings, and surrounded by the engraved memorial stones, it felt less frightening, like something natural and part of the greater mass of human experience.

The church was a place that didn't recoil from sorrow; its business went on around her with quiet acceptance of her private loss. Each of these carved stones would have been laid by someone feeling something akin to what she now felt. That one there, for a boy of only eighteen killed at Flanders: what devastation must his parents have felt as they stood in this place a century earlier, as the memorial to their son was pushed into place? Eva knew that losing a child must be worse than losing a father, and yet she didn't see how it was possible to feel more pain than she did now.

It was supposed to get easier. That was what everyone kept telling her: it gets easier. But it didn't feel like it was getting easier, in fact some days she was so exhausted she almost wanted to let go of the life-raft and drown. The passing of weeks and months somehow didn't seem to be taking her any further away from the day that she'd stood in the kitchen with her hand still on the rubbish bin in which she'd just buried her dashed hopes of a baby, and learned that she would also be burying her father. *Was she the next of kin to Keith Andrews?* the nurse on the other end of the phone had asked. *There was some bad news, did she have someone with her? A massive coronary,* she'd said, *I'm so sorry,* and just like that her father, the last of her flesh and blood, who'd raised and fed and taught and encouraged and been proud of and disapproved of her in almost equal measure, was gone.

⋆

Behind her, Eva heard the church door open and then close with a soft thud, and she lowered her head as if in prayer to hide her blotchy face and deter anyone from attempting to talk to her. She glared at her knees, wishing the interloper away as the footsteps progressed down the aisle and then stopped a few feet away from her.

'Eva?' came a familiar voice, and she jerked round to see Benedict standing there. For a moment they gaped at each other before he slipped into the row behind her.

'What are you doing here?' he asked, resting his arms on the back of her pew.

Eva turned back to face the altar. 'I could ask you the same question.'

'I took the afternoon off. I thought I'd come home and spend it with you but you weren't answering your phone so I walked around a bit and ended up here. For a chat, you know.' He gestured vaguely upwards. 'We used to come here when I was a kid. Christmas and Easter, mainly. I pop in every now and again when I'm passing. Not that often and usually when things aren't going brilliantly, I have to admit.' A wry smile crossed his face and faded again. 'I didn't know you came here though. You hadn't mentioned it.'

Eva sighed. 'No. Bit embarrassed, I suppose. What with the way I usually dismiss religion as being for nutters. But, well, they leave the doors open and let me sit here as long as I want. I don't know what else to do all day. I can't seem to concentrate on work anymore.' She paused and they sat in silence for a few seconds before she spoke again. 'It's just . . . Benedict, I just can't seem to find a way to make sense of it all. I mean, I know there's not much to make sense of. He wasn't that old, but he wasn't that young either. People die, of course they do, and at our age it's normal for people's parents to die.

'But . . . I just can't seem to process it. And people seem to expect me to get on with things like it's nothing. Even Sylvie seems a bit uncomprehending, though obviously she's being amazing, shouldering most of the workload for the business. And to be honest, *I* would have expected me to be getting on with it by now. When other people lost parents, you know, colleagues at work or whatever, I sort of expected them to be over it pretty quickly. It's just the natural order, isn't it? But sometimes I feel like I can hardly breathe. Maybe it's worse because he was both parents to me. I feel like I've just lost both my parents at once.' Her voice was gravelly. 'I feel like I'm grieving for my mother too, and for the life we never got to have together. Does that sound crazy?'

'Of course it doesn't. And you don't need to rush to get over it. Honestly, I still feel quite shocked and heartbroken that I'm never going to see him again, and that must be nothing compared to what you're feeling.'

'It's just that . . . I can't really believe he's gone. And . . . oh, Benedict,' Eva's voice cracked, 'maybe if we'd managed to have a baby, maybe it would be easier, but the reality is that I have no family left now.'

Benedict reached out a hand and tangled his fingers in her hair. 'I'm here. I'm your family. And Sylvie and Allegra and Josh and Will. And Lucien, too.' He sighed. 'Eva, I'm sorry. About all of it, all of the disappointments. We can still try IVF. It could still happen for us, we just have to keep the faith.'

Eva rubbed her eyes. 'Some days it's almost too painful to

keep hoping. And now it's even worse, because if I could have a baby, he'd be in that baby, his genes. Maybe it would even look like him. But now all that's left of him is in me, and yet there's nothing inside me that I can find any comfort in. I'm full of broken glass.' She put her head down on her hands. 'And this, this should be your moment of glory, right when the Higgs discovery has just been announced, and instead you're left sitting here with me like this. You must wish you weren't here, how could you not.'

Benedict took her by the shoulders and turned her to face him. 'Don't ever say that again,' he said fiercely. 'Eva, you're not spoiling anything for me. This is all that matters, this, here, us. It's the only place in the world I'd want to be. And of course I'm excited that we found the Higgs but it's not as if we haven't known we were closing in on it for a long time.' He ran his fingers through his hair. 'Let's face it, even the media seemed to think that the most surprising thing about it was that the world's most brilliant physicists considered Comic Sans an appropriate font in which to announce their historic findings.' He pulled her back against his shoulder and she managed a weak smile. 'Eva, I'm right here with you, not just for the good times, but for the bad times too. We're all going to have pain in our lives, sooner or later. Sometimes it can even be a gift.'

Eva snorted wetly. 'How can pain be a gift? That would be a worse present than the bloody bath salts your aunt gave us at Christmas. If this is a gift, I want the receipt so I can take it back and exchange it for a nice scarf or some attractive stationery.'

Benedict laughed. 'Look, I know the religious stuff all seems crazy to you. Some days it seems crazy to me too, but other days it seems to make perfect sense. Is it really so mad to look for something bigger than ourselves?'

'Well, I don't know about mad. The thing that really matters is whether it's true, whether there's any evidence for it. Otherwise it just seems a bit cynical, like Pascal's wager that you might as well believe in God because if he doesn't exist you haven't lost anything, and if he does you win the bet.'

'Ah, but there's a less cynical formulation of the same argument. Camus, I think: "I would rather live my life as if there is a God and die to find out there isn't, than live my life as if there isn't and die to find out there is."

'The thing is, no one really knows anything, not you, not me, not even the bloody Pope. And I know you can argue that if you start to believe things without evidence you might as well believe any old arbitrary thing, and yes, we could be just a bunch of mammals floating through infinite space on a rock, scrabbling around in the dirt until the lights go out, but in that case nothing really matters, does it, not your father's death, not factory farms or Houla or Beslan, not Auschwitz, not anything. And yet deep down we know that these things do matter. So is it really such an arbitrary thing to hope for? That suffering matters, that love survives?'

Eva leant her head back and rested it against his hand. 'No. Right now that doesn't seem like such an arbitrary thing to hope for. Some days I can almost believe it myself.' She straightened up. 'Not that Keith wouldn't be laughing if he could hear this. Not really his bag, religion. But I think he knew a bit about love. He and my mother weren't married, you know, because they didn't believe in such bourgeois constructs, but I'm certain she was the love of his life. It's strange to think of them feeling about each other the way we do.' She pushed a wet strand of hair back from her cheek.

'Well, yes,' said Benedict. 'You're lucky if you find that sort of love once in a lifetime. Not to mention how he felt about you. I know you sometimes thought he could be a bit too wrapped up in his politics, but it was always obvious to me how proud he was of you.'

In front of them on the stand, the tea-light Eva had lit was guttering. They sat quietly watching it for a few minutes, and then Benedict stood and took her hand.

'Come home with me now,' he told her. 'You're not alone.'

His hand was warm against the small of her back as they walked back along the aisle beneath the glowing gaze of stained-glass saints and through the heavy doors into the daylight beyond.

33

Dorset, August 2015

'What was the spirit of our age, do you think?' said Eva to no one in particular.

She was lying on the shingly sand of a Dorset beach watching Allegra blundering around excitedly in the shallows with Josh and Will, overseen by Benedict. In her bathing suit the stiffness of Allegra's left side was pronounced, her arm curled and her leg inflexible, but the boys, now aged eleven and thirteen and strong and tanned from a holiday in Greece, were used to playing with her much less roughly than they did with each other. Eva watched as Allegra splashed them and in mock fury they lifted her up by her shoulders and legs and threatened to dunk her, before depositing her very gently in the inch or two of water at the sea's edge. It was an idyllic English summer's afternoon: azure sky, gentle breeze flicking the corner of an unopened paperback, the faint tinny beat of a pop song drifting across from the radio of a group of teenagers further up the beach.

Lucien, who was lying on his back beside her wearing a pointy cardboard party hat, shielded his eyes with a hand and looked up. 'Oh, we're having one of those conversations? It's been a while. What brought this on?'

'The music, I think,' said Eva, who was also thinking

about the fact that she would turn forty this year. 'That song, "Another Girl", it's by the Beatles, isn't it? It made me think about how the Sixties was the era of free love and all that, and then it occurred to me that I don't really know what our era was all about. I feel like we were a sort of in-between generation. We weren't quite the internet generation and in any case, who wants to be known for looking at a lot of porn and pictures of cats? But I don't feel like we were defined by a particular set of ideals either. So I was wondering what our zeitgeist was supposed to be.' She picked at the remains of Allegra's birthday cake, which had started the day as a glitter-covered figure nine but had now been reduced to a pile of crumbs and smears of sticky red icing.

'Nihilism?' suggested Lucien, who'd got into Nietzsche in the prison library some years earlier.

'No, that's not true, we did care,' interjected Sylvie, turning her face to the breeze to blow thick strands of copper hair from her eyes. 'We cared about all sorts of things. Global warming. Iraq. GMOs.'

'Well, yeah, just not enough to actually do anything about them,' said Lucien.

'Really? Is that all we can say for ourselves?' Eva sighed and rearranged herself slightly to catch the sun. '"We cared, but not enough." That was the ethos of our era? Instead of standing up and fighting for something we believed in, we just stepped away and each tended to our own corner of the world?' She pondered this for a moment, and reached a conclusion. 'It's awful, but in many ways that does seem about right when I look back on my life.'

'Not just you,' said Sylvie. 'It took us all a while to work out what life was supposed to be about. Benedict was the only one of us who had his priorities straight from the start, and in the nicest possible way, he is a bit of a freak of nature.'

'True,' agreed Eva. 'He's always had this unswerving sense of purpose. I've often envied it, actually. When I was making plans I mostly thought about what I wanted to get away from, not what I actually wanted to achieve.'

'So you made out like a bandit in the City till the economy broke,' teased Lucien.

'Hey.' She punched him lightly on the shoulder. 'That's not fair. I was a tiny cog in a huge machine at a time when nobody was really seeing the big picture.'

'Hmm. Didn't you get sacked for insider trading?'

'No I bloody didn't! I left by mutual agreement, and it was market manipulation, not insider trading.' Eva paused and then continued more slowly. 'But with hindsight I realize that I may have done some . . . questionable things.' She lowered her voice. 'I've seen things you people wouldn't believe. Markets moving fifty basis points in milliseconds, billion-dollar fortunes made and lost. Attack ships on fire off the shoulder of Orion.'

Lucien grinned. 'Yeah, yeah, all right, Deckard.'

Eva grinned back, but quickly returned to looking serious. 'The thing is, at the time, everything we did felt like it happened in isolation from the rest of the world. It's only when you get older you really understand how everything's connected: money, power, politics, markets, people's actual lives.'

The song on the radio changed abruptly, replacing the Beatles with the angry staccato of the latest Rihanna hit, and all three of them looked towards the shore, where Allegra was busy trying to put a bucket on Will's head.

'This new generation, though,' continued Eva, waving a hand in the direction of the radio, 'they seem worse than we ever were. To read the news you'd think it was all meow-meow and donkey punching. We thought we were pretty wild, but this new crop, it's like they're dead inside. Or does every generation think that about the next one? I dunno, maybe it's just that I'm getting old.' Eva reached up unthinkingly and smoothed away the lines by her eyes that seemed to grow deeper every morning in the bathroom mirror. She had realized just the other day that she was now older than her own mother had been when she died.

Sylvie laughed. 'I think we're all fundamentally the same. Us, them, every other generation. We all think we're unique snowflakes, but we're not really. Do you remember how we thought we were so different when we were young, like we were on the fringes of society because we dyed our hair and did drugs at parties? Christ, we'd have loathed it then if we knew how like everyone else we are, how people are just the same the world over. Funny, because it feels rather comforting now, I feel sort of grounded by it.'

The children had quietened down now and were collecting pieces of shell washed up on the shore, and the teenagers had packed up and taken the radio with them so that the only sound was the sloshing of the water and the occasional call of a seagull. The air was warm and the glare bounced off the water with dazzling intensity, making them squint and transporting them to other places of shimmering light. For a moment Sylvie was far away in a valley in the Languedoc, and Eva was haring along a road in Corfu, Benedict beside her.

'Nothing really turned out how we expected, did it?' said Eva.

'Nope.' Sylvie shook her head. 'I didn't realize how much things would change and how little we would be able to control.'

'It felt like we were invincible,' said Lucien. 'Back in the day, I mean. We weren't stupid, I knew life didn't stay the same forever, but I didn't really *know* it, y'know?'

Sylvie took up the theme. 'And there was always going to be a way out. You'd go over a cliff in a Ferrari, or overdose in a squat in a tragic-yet-glamorous act of artistic excess. I never really thought about having people relying on me. Let alone trying to raise a child on my own.'

A mischievous look crept over Eva's face. 'By the way, Sylvie, Big Paul happened to let slip the other day that he'd been over to your place last week. Called it an "investor update" when he cottoned on to the fact you hadn't mentioned it to me. But of course, you two wouldn't be conducting investor meetings without your CEO there, would you now?'

'Oh, jog on. He just comes by for a coffee and a walk on the Heath with me and Allegra every now and again. He gets a bit moony-eyed sometimes but I don't really think there's anything in it. Believe it or not, men aren't queuing around the block to take on a single mother with a disabled child. Anyway, I'm not even sure I'd want one. I haven't done too badly on my own, have I?'

'You've been brilliant,' Lucien told her. 'I'd never have dreamt of having kids, what with how messed up our own childhood was. You know how that shit runs in families. So double pat on the back to you.'

'Oh, Lucien, I know we're going to still be having this argument when we're eighty, but having Allegra has made me sympathize with Mum more. I mean, it's really tough, being a parent. She asked how you were doing when she phoned the other day, you know. And I think she's drinking a bit less now.'

'Whatever.' He held his hand up in the air, last two fingers looking pinker and shinier than usual in contrast with the tanned skin of the rest of his hand, and turned it around slowly in front of his face. 'I know who my real family are. They're right here on this beach.'

'Speaking of which, Sylvie, you do know you're not really on your own, don't you?' said Eva. 'Even if you got hit by a bus tomorrow, there'd still be me and Benedict and Lucien to look after Allegra. And when we're gone, Will and Josh will be here to make sure she's all right, she's virtually a sister to them. If there's one thing that I've realized since Keith died, it's that friendship and love are pretty much all we've got that's worth anything. Everything else is noise.' She reached out and took her friend's hand, and they all fell quiet.

'Talking of love,' said Lucien eventually without opening his eyes, 'did you know that Eva used to be in love with me?'

'Yep,' answered Sylvie casually, and then at Eva's squeak of horror, added, 'You could hardly miss the way you used to hang on to his every word. I used to wish he'd just put you out of your misery.'

'Bloody hell! Put me out of my misery? It wasn't all un-requited pining, I'll have you know.' Eva glanced towards the shore to make sure Benedict was out of earshot. 'Do you know what he did? He slept with me. Back in Bristol, in our first year. And then acted like it never happened, the complete bastard.'

Sylvie looked up and arched an eyebrow first at Lucien and then at Eva.

'Really? You actually shagged her? And *you* didn't tell me?' This last directed at Eva.

'Yeah. Sorry. I didn't know how you'd take it. I figure you can't bollock me for it now, seeing as it happened a good couple of decades ago.'

'Christ. You could have ended up my sister-in-law.'

'Not exactly,' said Lucien. 'I wasn't really looking for the white picket fence experience back then, and she was way out of my league by the time I realized what she was worth.' He tugged her towards him so that his arm was around her neck, half embrace and half headlock.

Eva laughed and inhaled deeply, her face in his neck. 'You still smell the same,' she told him quietly.

Sylvie made a gagging noise. 'I heard that, you know. Now you're really grossing me out.'

They all laughed and settled back down against the blanket. Eva stared out at the luminescent water and thought back to the day when she had scattered Keith's ashes into the sea. She wriggled out of Lucien's embrace and peeled off her dress to the bikini underneath, then walked down to join Benedict and the children at the water's edge.

'Find any sea monsters?'

'No, but we did find some seaweed and a dead starfish to decorate our sandcastle.' Benedict waved towards the elaborately moated and turreted fortress that the boys had built, which was now being demolished under the onslaught of Allegra's enthusiastic embellishment.

Eva smiled weakly but didn't say anything, so he took her hand and led her into the water, close enough to keep an eye on the kids but far enough away to talk.

'What's up?'

She looked down at her feet. 'I got my period this morning.'

'Ah.' Benedict rubbed his eyes. 'Eva, I'm sorry.'

'Me too.'

'So that's it, then.'

'Yes.'

'Unless you want to keep going.'

'I don't think so. Do you? It's not like the odds aren't stacked against us, what with my age and four failed IVF cycles under our belt.'

'No,' he said slowly. 'I don't want to keep going. I'd do it for you, but I don't want it for myself. I don't want to live under the shadow of it anymore, I feel like it's suffocating us and sucking all the joy out of the other things in our lives. And there *are* lots of good things in our lives.'

'There are, aren't there? Maybe it's time to start focusing on them again. Look at what we've got: each other, Allegra, Josh, Will, our friends, my business, your research. That's a lot, right? More than most people have. Shouldn't this be enough?'

Benedict slid his arms around her waist and pulled her body close to his. 'I'm not sure there's any "should" about these things. But I know it's enough for me.' He paused. 'Eva, do you think it can be enough for you? Really? Because I have everything I need so long as you're happy.'

'It's not perfect, but then, what is? I'll get used to it. To be honest, I think I already have. I think I stopped daring to really hope for it quite a long time ago.' She tightened her arms around him and rested her head against his shoulder, savouring the warmth and the salty smell of his skin. They stood leaning against each other up to their knees in the water, watching the children and swaying slightly with the waves.

After a while she said, 'Yes.'

'"Yes?"'

'I can be happy with this, with what I've got. I'm happy right now, in fact.' Eva turned her face up to his and smiled. 'Now, you get back to your sandcastle. I'm going for a swim.'

Benedict looked at her like she was crazy. 'You do realize the water's freezing further out?'

But Eva was already heading away from him, out along the shore.

⋆

Faster and faster she runs, feet flying across sand and hair streaming behind her, until finally certain that the children won't notice and try to follow her, Eva plunges into the sea. The cold paralyses her momentarily, pressing the breath from her chest so that she comes up kicking and gasping, but soon she has swum far enough out that her body is beginning to acclimatize. She loves the elemental feeling of the ocean, its vastness. The way a human is a mere speck within it, the way its sheer force and indifference is both frightening and compelling at the same time. Something washes past her leg and she shivers, because you never know whether it's a skein of seaweed or a giant squid, and to quell that thought she swims further out, feeling her muscles straining pleasurably at the effort.

After a while she stops and bobs about on the surface, tossed and buffeted by the waves. Eva tries to look back at the others on the beach but they are tiny figures now, and her eyes are dazzled by the light. She spreads out onto her back and drifts, savouring the sensation of weightlessness. These days she has a knee that aches in winter and her back makes her groan whenever she tries to lift Allegra, but here in the sea all of that slips away. The waves wash against her and for a moment it feels as if Keith is there with her, and not just Keith but something that feels like maybe a mother would too, all around her in the water. She feels light and clean, like the past is sliding away from her. Just for a moment, it feels like coming home.

Acknowledgements

I am indebted to a number of people for their help in bringing *Invincible Summer* to publication: my early readers, Katie O'Rourke and Elspeth Leadbetter, for their enthusiasm and encouragement; my wonderful literary agents, Kerry Glencorse, Susanna Lea and Mark Kessler, for loving and believing in the book; and my brilliant editors, Francesca Main, Judy Clain and Amanda Brower, who let me get away with nothing and as a result made *Invincible Summer* twice as good as it would otherwise be. More generally, this book is dedicated to David, Mark, Diane, Catherine, Jessica, Adrian, Anabelle, Anne, Eden, Elspeth, Lila, Rachel and Zlatina.

About the Author

Alice Adams is half Australian but has lived in England for most of her life, growing up in a house without a TV and as a result becoming a voracious reader. Careerwise, she's done everything from waitressing to investment banking, and in addition to a BA in philosophy she has a multitude of geeky math, finance, and computer qualifications. She lives in North London but escapes into the wilderness as often as possible. *Invincible Summer* is her first novel and she's hard at work on a second.